ROYAL SPY INSTITUTE

1

THE CROWN HEIST

Flutterbye Trail Press
797 Sam Bass Road #2541
Round Rock, TX 78681

First edition

Editing by Red Loop Editing
Cover Design by Black Bird Book Covers
Chapter Art by Etheric Tales
Printed Interior Design by Enchanting Covers
Published by Flutterbye Trail Press

ISBN: 978-1-954582-20-0 (E-book)
ISBN: 978-1-954582-21-7 (Paperback)
ISBN: 978-1-954582-27-9 (Hardback)

Feedback: Encounter a problem with this book? Let us know at
elisehennessyauthor@gmail.com

BOOKS BY ELISE HENNESSY

Books in the Altare World

GRYPHON RIDER ACADEMY
Second Chance
Chosen
Storm Front
Wild Flight
Gryphon Rider Academy Omnibus 1: Books 1-4

ROYAL SPY INSTITUTE
The Crown Heist
Five & Chance

Also by Elise Hennessy

BLOOD LEGACY SERIES
Dream Walker
The Winter Key
Queen's Return
Court of Illusions

Shadow Dance
Rule the Night
Dhampir's Wish
Blood Curse
Blood Legacy: The Complete Series

ROYAL SPY INSTITUTE 1
THE CROWN HEIST

ELISE HENNESSY

CHAPTER 1

A YULE HEIST

I KNEW this heist was a bad idea. It was the perfect setup for a routine theft, but some little wiggly feeling in my belly told me not to go into the Gladbeck mansion. Uncle Jace was always telling me to make a "gut decision" when presented with a choice, but I only learned what that meant when I realized the discomfort came from that direction of my body.

I turned to the man crouching next to me. We were mostly protected from a chill evening breeze behind the swaying limbs of a shrub that'd bronzed with the coming of winter.

"Y'sure this is a good idea?" I whispered. The distant chimes of the city bells suggested we'd been waiting here for an hour.

Cartier tightened his expression. He had a mean face, like a starving weasel's, all greasy, overlong hair, beady black eyes, and too-generous lips I knew he'd flipped up with a sneer behind his threadbare scarf. "Shut yer gob, Mouse," he hissed, pinching my arm.

I flinched away from him and rubbed the sting away. I should've expected that kind of response, considering the clorets on the line this evening. When Uncle Jace had heard the sum, he'd practically shoved me into Cartier's arms despite it being Yule night. Most everyone in Kaiamear was still out celebrating in one way or another, and the Gladbeck family was no exception.

My belly rumbled unhappily. Maybe my gut just wanted to be with the rest of my gang family, as Jace always took us to the free feast and bonfire that was hosted in the palace. My mouth watered. It was a holiday tradition for us to eat everything in sight and rest like sated hunting dogs by the fire afterward, and I very much wanted to be doing some basking rather than waiting in the cold with Cartier for a signal from within the mansion.

"Y'think, maybe," I ventured timidly, preparing myself for another pinch. I could practically feel Cartier's stink eye, daring me to finish my request. "After this, we could go t'the feast?"

"Listen here, you little—"

He cut himself off, and we both froze. Someone was passing by the bushes, whistling a Yuletide tune. My eyelid flickered with anxiety. It was time.

Cartier lifted to his feet with a groan, and his knees popped. I slipped into his shadow, averting my gaze when he caught the arm of the guard walking by and lowered his scarf to kiss her. *Ugh. Yuck.*

"We're in," whispered his wife, Rozma, once they were done wasting time.

She confirmed that the coast was clear and that the south entrance now had two guards taking a forced nap. Rozma was burly for a woman, with the kind of no-nonsense resting face few wanted to mess with. She'd easily convinced the Gladbeck family to hire her, and it must've been for a while, as she told us the direct path to follow to avoid any more attention.

I checked myself over with my fingertips and wiggled my

toes. I wore my quietest slippers and favorite pair of gloves, so well-loved the stitching had come undone on one. My sister, Jackie, had tried to mend it for me, resulting in a small pull on my third and fourth fingers from her uneven needle-work. My belt was still securely loaded with lock picks, a coil of rope, a screwdriver, a pouch with matches, and…

I sucked in a soft gasp when my fingertips met an empty loop. As much as I obsessively checked and rechecked my belt, I'd never lost a tool until now.

"What's the matter?" Rozma asked.

She wasn't quite as unpleasant as her husband, but that didn't mean they both wouldn't beat me senseless for losing the pouch that should still be on my belt. It was the most important tool for stealing from someone rich enough to feasibly hire a Tulari mage's services for protecting their valuables.

"I, uh," I murmured. "My powder."

Cartier scoffed and went back to the shrub, rustling around it.

"I have some. You're going to need it. They recently had a Tulari around recasting stronger spells," Rozma said quietly, drawing my attention back to her. She stood confidently with her legs spread, not a care in the world. I recognized that stance. She thought she'd done her part of the job and was free to relax.

Lots of adults were like that, I'd noticed. Jace tended to lend me out to jobs big and small, as long as they were hosted by the group these two were from, Springfield's gang. It had no other name, as Springfield was the kind of demanding man who said either you belong to him and obey him, or you don't. The two bosses were good friends, which meant Jace's kids became Springfield's adults. It was just the way of things.

Cartier and Rozma were no exception, and it gave them this attitude, like they'd already earned their places and could do the bare minimum, while it was up to the kids on each job to go into danger. My eyelid flickered again. Losing my desda mushroom powder was a guarantee that I'd fall into any magic trap set up to catch would-be thieves.

"There it is. Be more careful, Mouse." Cartier's whisper had me breathing out a bit of tension. He shoved a worn velvet pouch into my hand, and I bounced the slightness of the powder within with a nod. My fingertips shook as I secured it back into its spot.

Crushed desda mushrooms could nullify just about any spell. They were a brilliant scarlet color out in nature, only discovered by accident when ordinary, magic-less humans could eat them just fine, just for magic-wielding Tulari to keel over dead even at the taste of one. I remembered that every time I sprinkled some of this red powder around, cautious not to use too much.

"I'm always careful," I mumbled, ashamed I'd nearly lost the pouch. I followed Rozma as she led us to the right entranceway.

She turned and offered a different pouch to Cartier as soon as I slid the door open without as much as a creak. "You have ten minutes or so," she whispered as a bit of parting wisdom.

Turned out, her part in this heist *was* done. Cartier blew some dust in her face, and her eyes rolled up. He caught her and laid her splayed out in the middle of the hall. She'd be able to deny that she had anything to do with the theft tonight.

I nodded to myself, starting to count down from sixty in my head. I knew what I had to do—go ahead of Cartier and disable any traps along the way. The first floor was occupied by only a couple guards and well-lit by the eternal glow of magelights. It was the second floor that we wanted, which had the Lady Gladbeck's rooms and our target this evening, an opal necklace.

An *enchanted* opal necklace, if it was truly worth over a hundred thousand clorets.

I took Rozma's suggested path through the kitchen at the back of the mansion and waited against the wall as an older woman went walking past the doorway on her rounds. With the two wars going on, it was getting harder to find men for jobs like home security. I wondered how Cartier had weaseled his way out of the draft to distract from my belly cramping hard with hunger at the lingering food smells drifting from the kitchen.

Two minutes down. I was thirty-seven seconds into the third minute when I felt it safe to proceed to the servant's stair and open my powder pouch. I dropped a couple grains on each step, locating and stepping over the telltale deep blue etchings of a spell while the desda powder ate and nullified it. Just a basic rooting trap, the kind a scullery maid could set up before leaving for the evening.

Bigger spells weren't quite so invisible. My gaze roved over every inch of space as soon as I reached the top step. The carpet under my slippers was worn from the hurried steps of many people, trampled flat and a little dingy under the eye of a dim magelight.

Uncle Jace had walked me through a book of Tulari spells when I'd first shown promise as a thief. The words had been too big for me, but I'd copied and recopied every feasible sigil, rune, and squiggly until I could see them behind my eyelids. Were the magelight much brighter, I would've missed that it had the concentric circles of an alarm spell etched into its glasslike surface, but it was a fairly common hiding place for one.

If I'd just opened the door to the second-floor hallway, the spell would've been triggered to screech out an alert. This kind of magelight could easily be posted around the mansion; that explained why there were only guards on the first floor, per Rozma's information.

I flicked scarlet powder up at the magelight, making sure to hit the alarm spell first. The orb started melting immediately, turning into a sizzling chunk of floating glass until, with a *pop*, it stopped emitting light and fell.

I caught it even though I didn't want to. *Musty devils*, it was hot. Placing it on the carpet to melt, I flicked my hands to release some of the heat. It'd cool fast once the magic in it died fully, and I added a sprinkle more powder over it to speed up the process.

Four minutes, twenty-one seconds down, and the easy part done. I checked the door for any signs of magic and stood in the darkness of the hall, waiting for my eyes to adjust. The magelights on the rest of this level were already off. I'd need to be extra careful not to make a sound. Even a short *clap clap* to turn the magelights back on could trigger a more complicated enchantment attuned to the slightest noise.

I smiled to myself. This was the kind of challenge I lived for, the reason Jace had given me the title Mouse when I'd turned ten and passed all his homemade tests for the skills that made a master thief. Since then, there'd been no trap or trick that could catch me, no safe I couldn't crack, and no valuable secure once I was on the job.

The recently started war with the Rathi Islands had tightened everyone's belt. It resulted in rich folk like the Gladbecks investing in better, cleverer spells to ward off thieves like me. Now that I'd been a Mouse for three years, I had the skills to appreciate the challenge of locating and disabling the four extra traps and alarms along the way to the wing that Rozma had said was Lady Gladbeck's quarters.

Seven minutes, three seconds. Rozma and the other unconscious guards could be discovered at any moment.

I practically heard Cartier's creaky knees on the servant's stairway behind me. There was a reason he wasn't a sneak anymore—but he was nearby with the knockout dust and his fists should this heist go off like the uneasy nerves that still lingered in my gut.

I had to find the necklace fast. All we knew was that it was in these rooms somewhere, but Lady Gladbeck was not one to parade around with an enchanted necklace, so it was likely in a hidden safe. I lit a match and snuck under the sleeping globe of a magelight, its glass surface glittering from the touch of moonlight drifting through the windows.

I didn't let myself get distracted by any of the finery around me. It was a mistake to become wowed by the wealth of the people I was robbing when I really needed to be checking for spells and safes. I did a cursory search and found neither, feeling my heart speed up as precious seconds passed.

I didn't have time to knock on every floorboard. Doing so ran the risk of activating the magelight in here, too, and destroying it was a risky option. There was a chance I could flick powder on the wrong side of it, so the alarm spell was eaten last and given time to release its noise. Even a few seconds of that would draw the attention of the guards downstairs.

In my gut, I knew it wouldn't be below my feet anyway. If the Gladbecks had the money for advanced home security spells, then they could've easily paid to have a former sneak tell them that the most common places to hide valuables was under the bed or floorboards. I nodded to myself and turned toward the far wall, flicking out the stub of my first match and lighting a new one to inspect the frame of a broad painting.

There. I huffed softly in relief. A series of tiny runes was etched into the frame. I pulled my match backward to illuminate more of the painted canvas and identified more runes lightly imprinted into the pits and valleys of the paint. If I didn't know what to look for, I'd never have noticed them. It was a magical seal—the first one I'd seen in person—which meant the painting wasn't going to budge unless the magic on it was dealt with.

I knew I'd found the safe, hidden underneath this painting, but I was well on my way to eight minutes into this job, and this was a major complication. Magical seals were made of two identical sets of runes or markings on one object—to deactivate it, I had to touch the matching symbols at the same time. They would be in one order on the frame and another on the painting itself, and no doubt would set off an alert if I made a mistake in the dark or used desda powder and missed even a single rune on the big painting, which was more than likely.

My eyelid flickered as I stowed the charred remains of the used matches I'd been holding into an otherwise empty pouch. I had one chance at this, and the markings of the spell were tiny, but I could only trust Cartier to beat me black and blue for needing help instead of getting him to hold a match. So, I grabbed two new ones, stripped off my gloves, and set the powder-dusted fabric aside for a moment.

I took a deep breath and fixed my face into the most confident one I could muster. I imagined how impressed Uncle Jace would be when I told him about this part of the job. But I was eight minutes, forty-five seconds in and had to do this in a minute or less, so I set to the task.

First, I placed the lit matches between my fourth and fifth fingers, holding my indexes extended. I didn't think about how it took only one mistake to be caught, instead forcing my whole focus to the task and shifting my weight to inspect the first symbol on the frame, which resembled a box. I found the same symbol on the painting amidst a cluster of them hidden in the white foam of a wave breaking on a beach.

I touched both box symbols at the same time and watched them light up with faint but familiar blue light.

Circle, circle, I pressed both.

Curved line with curved line.

Triangle with triangle.

The matches were about burned out, so I snuffed them and replaced them fast, taking another, shallower breath as my nerves threatened to close off my air. If I kept doing this right, the worst that would happen with a pause was that the spell would reset and I'd have to start over.

In total, I found eleven symbols and was on the twelfth and last when I couldn't find it anywhere in the painting. Not in the waves, not on the beach, not even in the tiny eyes of the seabirds pecking along the sand. My left hand moved erratically over the length of it, searching desperately for one last etching that looked like a pair of crookedly crossed lines.

I was in danger of burning my skin when my gaze caught sight of it right in the center of the design, hidden in a stretch of blue ocean the same color of Tulari magic. With a relieved breath, I touched the last two symbols at the same time and stepped back as glowing magic outlined the whole frame. I snuffled the stubs of my latest matches and placed my gloves back on, tensing to bolt if I'd done this wrong after all.

With a *whoosh* of released air, the frame dimmed. Part of the wall swung open on an invisible hinge, and by match light, I beheld the Gladbeck's massive safe. I rubbed my hands together, eager for one of my favorite tasks. Withdrawing my picks, I dipped them into my pouch of desda powder and worked on the lock with full focus and my tongue caught between my front teeth.

Ten minutes, two seconds had passed when the lock clicked and the front-facing hatch swung open. Unpleasant tingles walked down my back; I was out of time. I inspected the contents, revealing loose papers and lumpy sacks along the bottom. The second shelf was occupied by a fine wooden box with a gold latch. That had to be it! I withdrew the box and blew out my most recent match, stowing it away.

I placed the box on Lady Gladbeck's bed, weighed down by fine Endoline silk sheets. I'd seen enough to know that if I flipped that latch without one last sprinkling of desda powder along the lid, I'd set off a trap. But I couldn't touch an enchanted necklace with that red residue on my gloves if I didn't want to destroy it. Chances were the powder would eat through the lid once I applied it and drip down on the valuable inside.

That was why I didn't wait for the series of sigils along the lid to completely melt off before stripping off my right glove with my teeth. I unlatched the box with my clean fingers and pulled the necklace out once I confirmed there wasn't a second spell inside with one last match.

The opal pendant was truly stunning. It was cut into many sparking facets that filled its milky surface with fiery specks of color. It'd been set in a disc of gold, with fancy filigree holding it in place on a thick gold chain that'd be quite bold for a woman to wear.

I was caught admiring it when the lid of the box flashed with dark blue light before brightening, throwing eerie shadows off the posts of Lady Gladbeck's bed. *Musty devils*, I cursed as I felt a tingle over the exposed skin of my hand.

That feeling swiftly sent paralysis through my limbs, leaving me with a glove dangling between my teeth and a lit match charring the other one as it burnt down. I cursed myself further as I struggled to breathe past the bitter taste of the desda powder that touched the tip of my tongue.

I must've been too sloppy in my haste to remove the necklace and missed part of the magic carved into the wood. After all this, how could I have been so careless? The opal pendant glinted like a taunting eye as it dangled from my frozen fist.

"Great job, Mouse," whispered Cartier as he crept into the room and crossed to my side. His damp fingertips snuffed the match before it could set me on fire. "Got caught in a fancy trap, hmm?"

My eyelid wanted to twitch when the next thing he started doing was prying my fingers off the necklace, but my whole face was uncomfortably numb and locked in place. I couldn't see his expression, even with the trap spell glowing.

"Do you know what this is?" He spoke low enough that I had to strain to hear him. "Of course not. But let me tell you, s'interesting."

My muscles started to burn as I struggled to move, to make a noise, to do anything at all while he started yanking the necklace out of my hold with enough force to leave bruises on my fingers.

"It's called the Eye of Acuity, and it's far too valuable to sell. You just tell it what y'wanna see and look inside it to see that thing. Works on people and places. Imagine, Mouse." His tone held a giddy grin. "Imagine what me 'n' Rozma can steal with it. We won't need Springfield anymore. We won't need nobody."

Panic started to simmer under my skin as he finally ripped the gold chain free and tucked it away. His plans notably didn't include me. He wasn't just going to *leave* me here, was he? He might've been mean, but he was raised by the same man I was. Uncle Jace had always said, "You never betray your crew. They know far too much about you."

Cartier patted my face. "Goodbye, Mouse. Thank ya kindly for doin' all this work for me 'n' Rozma. We gave ya the weak powder just in case you got to a special new spell like this one." He gestured to the glowing box while I fumed silently and tried to glare at him. He must've knocked my original pouch of desda powder loose while we waited for the signal earlier. I *knew* I'd never lose something like that. "I hear them nobles been paying to have thieves removed, if y'know what I mean. Protects their valuables in times like this. Means we get to keep the Eye, though."

Gods, he was going to abandon me. Betrayal simmered low in my belly alongside that sour gut feeling, a reminder that I'd sensed something off about this heist. Cartier and Rozma had been planning against me all along.

With a chuckle, he left me there. I watched him bump around until he found a window and flicked its latch, sliding it up. Cold wind howled into the room. If him leaving me behind weren't insult enough, he turned to look back at me with a smirk lined in moonlight. He clapped twice to activate the magelight before he slipped into the night.

The glass orb flared up and emitted a deafening squeal.

CHAPTER 2

THE ONLY CHOICE

The peacekeepers moved me when the paralysis spell was partially worn off so they weren't lifting and carrying me like a statute. I shuffled toward my doom one slow, painful step at a time.

They put me in a cell by myself, a tiny stone rectangle with a bucket in one corner and a cot infested with bugs along the other wall. I'd pushed it forward just enough to hide behind it. Curled into a shivering ball, I was small enough to be out of sight, and that's where I cowered for the rest of the night, alone and terrified.

Maybe the peacekeepers would forget about me. I could only listen to the voices that drifted toward my cell, as I was wide awake throughout the rest of the night. The lingering spell made it extra hard to nod off and just added more pain to my misery. It had my muscles jumping randomly, jerking my elbow into the metal side of the cot or jolting my head back into the wall so hard I saw stars.

The peacekeepers on duty sounded tired and grouchy, complaining about being posted here on Yule night. "There are always some troublemakers. Like that kid they just turned in," an older woman's voice said once. My lower eyelid twitched as I reminded myself she could be talking about any kid who'd caused trouble on Yule night.

"Wonder what she stole," came the reply from a different woman.

Never mind. They were definitely talking about me.

Becoming a dried-up, forgotten husk in this musty place would've been a better fate than what waited for me tomorrow. I trembled in my corner thinking about what I could possibly say or do to walk out of here alive. The Eye of Acuity was long gone, and the Gladbeck family would want it back once they recovered from their Yule party.

My belly grumbled unhappily at the thought of the feasting and merriment Lord and Lady Gladbeck may still be enjoying as I waited here for judgment. The hollow, cramping feeling worsened with nothing to distract from my painfully empty belly and didn't help my nerves, either.

The minimum punishment I could hope to experience was to lose my dominant hand. I'd be useless to anyone after that, even Jace. When had I ever heard of a one-handed sneak? Never. I would also lose any opportunity for honest work, since folk would recognize the disfigurement for what it was. I held my right hand cupped in my left over my chest. Not to mention, I was attached to it. The idea of losing it and looking down at a stump for the rest of my life was horrifying.

But I'd only receive the minimum *if* I squealed to the first peacekeeper to question me. The retribution that'd follow would pale in comparison to a missing hand, because there was nothing I could say that wouldn't send the law to Boss Springfield's club. His men would hunt me down like a prized buck and skin me alive, kid or not.

You never betray your crew, but you also *never* spoke to the peacekeepers, not if you valued meeting the Gatekeeper with your dignity—and hide—intact.

Musty devils. The walls seemed to creep closer in this darkened cell, squeezing the air out and leaving me trapped in this airless cage. I rocked myself through the shredding panic of the situation, trying to envision what the future would be like if I got out of this cell with my life *and* self intact instead.

There was a chance Cartier and Rozma wouldn't return to their boss. They had what they wanted, and all they had to do was leave me behind. It sounded like Cartier was eager to abandon the whole cycle, to be his own boss. I was their sacrifice for a new life.

Well, Gatekeeper take them. If I survived this, I'd pay them back double: one comeuppance for Cartier and another for Rozma. I'd make sure they were stuck in an airless box just like they'd done to me. Imagining the sight of both of them behind bars was the only thing that brought even a glimmer of hope throughout the night.

Like many of Springfield's adult recruits, they didn't talk about what their titles had been in Jace's Menagerie, so I gave them the titles that seemed most appropriate. Cartier a Weasel, and Rozma...

Big, solid Rozma. I hadn't worked with her as closely, since we had wildly different parts to play in the jobs we'd done together. No one would overlook Rozma like they did me; therefore, she was a predator to me, a Mouse, prey.

I felt a new pang as I thought of the raggedy book in my corner back home. I was the keeper of *Animals of the World* and had read it cover to cover, noticing with fascination how people could reflect the traits and symbolism of various creatures so well. When a kid turned ten in the gang, as the latest keeper of the book, I'd been the one to consult about what their title should be. And Rozma's new title was Mongoose, I decided with a shaky nod. A similar enough animal to a weasel, fierce and toothy.

A yawn split my numb face. I stirred from my tight ball at last; it was sometime around dawn, with light finally filtering toward my cell. This place was so much worse now that I could see the cockroaches crawling up the wall, alarmingly close to my head.

My glove lay nearby. I'd tossed it aside since its pair was probably still lying on Lady Gladbeck's fine bed, waiting for a maid to discard it like soiled garbage. Reaching forward, I snagged it between my fingers and inspected it with a sigh, tracing the uneven stitches at its cuff.

Jackie had been so proud to "mend" this glove. I wondered if she'd noticed I was gone yet, or if she was sleeping off her overfull belly with the rest of our gang family. The day after Yule was a joyous time for us, when we were sated and warm and happy for once.

Of everyone, Jackie would notice I was missing first. We'd come from the same mother, the last Mouse, whose face I could hardly remember, just the blur of her desperate words as she handed me a bloody newborn Jackie. I'd barely been four when she was a cold body in the ground and my sister a too-heavy weight in my hands.

Jace and the older kids ended up raising Jackie, who'd turned out quite differently from me, even if we had shades of the same looks and build. She was bright, talkative, lovely. She'd be ten soon, and I had a handful of titles that would work for her. She was a fluffy Junfly alighting on a spring blossom, or a cheery Retriever that folk loved and trusted. With a little more training, she could also be a second Mouse if there could be two kids alive with the same title.

That was the thought that finally broke me. I sobbed smudgy tracks down my cheeks and into my knobby knees as I imagined her becoming the next Mouse...because I was gone. Gods, I was going to die. I was going to lose my life because of what Cartier and Rozma had done. I pictured Jackie's face when I told her I was going on a job Yule night, the surprise and ever-present fear that glimmered in her amber eyes when I left her. She feared...this. The day I was caught and placed between the peacekeepers and the gang, destined to lose no matter what I chose.

Kids disappeared from Jace's Menagerie all the time. Jackie and I shared the same pallet with Wildcat, who I figured would be happy to see me gone permanently, as she was the second sneak to get hired from our gang when I was too busy. Now she'd be the one with an excuse to drop out of fundamental school to pick up more jobs to keep the gang fed.

I imagined how the other kids would react when I didn't return home as I tried to get the tears to stop. Some, like Bear and Dexis, would probably miss me. Others would simply move on with a shrug, like we all had to in the end. There was always some new recruit or squalling infant showing up on Jace's doorstep, needing a place off the streets. I was replaceable.

I was still wiping my face dry when a peacekeeper, one of the ones who'd been complaining about being here earlier this morning, said, "Right this way, sir."

Stiffening, I curled my legs in as footsteps echoed toward my cell. The presence of a "sir" was bad news for me. A sir had authority and thus a reason to avoid the draft. Either he was hired on short notice by the Gladbecks to get their necklace back, or he was a high-ranking peacekeeper who'd reluctantly donned his uniform to question a troublemaking thief the morning after Yule.

"Are you sure you have anyone in here?" a man's humor-filled voice said as the footsteps stopped and a key was turned in a metal latch with the satisfying *click* I usually lived for when a lock popped open. The door to my cell screeched open, and I winced.

"Yes, sir. Good luck," she replied. With a second screech and *click*, he was locked in here with me.

There was a new sound, something wooden clacking

against the stone floor. A chair, maybe. "Won't you come say hello?" the man asked as he sat with a puff of air.

I didn't say anything, too afraid to do anything but eye his leather shoes. They must've been recently polished, to be so shiny in the half-light of this cell. He'd placed them flat on the ground, legs spread with the world-owning confidence of a sir.

He chuckled. "I know I'm not talking to an empty cell. Why don't you come out? I have food to share." Paper wrapping rustled as he spoke. I didn't know if he was exaggerating the noise or if I was just that hungry.

Trembling, I leaned forward to peek at what he'd brought with one eye, which was a mistake. He turned toward me immediately. "There you are," he said.

I had the impression of white teeth when he leaned forward and offered me the sphere of a perfectly peeled boiled egg in the palm of a broad hand.

In a blink, I had the egg snatched up and in my mouth. I chewed and made an effort not to swallow the whole thing too fast. My belly hurt with the sudden introduction of food.

I scooted forward a few inches and inspected him with distrust while I ate. He wore nice clothes to go with the leather shoes, a pair of sturdy gray pants and a shirt with all its little metal buttons intact. He was in his fifties, maybe; sirs aged more gracefully than some of the other adults I knew. His hair was more brown than gray, growing patchy in places, though he tried to hide it by scraping what remained over the bald spots. A hint of a softer life rounded his belly and cheeks, and the fair skin on his arms and face was free of scars.

The sir treated me to the same scrutiny. I knew what he saw—a twig of a street kid with a pointy little hook for a nose and brown eyes too big for my face. They would be round and haunted, holding the look of trapped prey under his inspection. My natural skin tone was tanned, with plenty of blemishes across my cheeks and forehead. I had windblown tangles in my chestnut-colored hair.

Though he had smile lines around his eyes and his mouth turned up within the thicket of his beard, I recognized that he was a predator. But an intelligent one, like a bird of prey zeroing in on a mouse hiding amidst the grasses of an open field.

"Martina's Eatery was open at regular time today. I could hardly believe it, but they were doing good business for all the people going about like normal," he said in a conversational tone, reaching into the bag of brown paper he held and withdrawing a round of bread with its top still shiny with butter. I practically salivated at how tasty it looked and watched it like he watched me as his fingers closed around its middle, tearing it into two uneven pieces, like a forty-sixty split.

He glanced down. One of those halves had to be for him. He withdrew a few thin slices of bright yellow cheese and handed me the bigger half with some of the slices piled on top. The cheese was soft, already melting into the warmth of the fluffy bread. I paced myself a little better as I consumed every crumb and accepted the other half with a brief, surprised look at him before I ate it too.

"Why don't you come up here so we can talk?" he offered, patting the threadbare blanket over the cot.

I shook my head, mumbling, "Bugs."

"You can have the stool, then." He stood and gestured to it with his free hand. The other still held that paper bag that had the promising curve of more food.

I lifted myself from the chill of the stone corner slowly and crept toward the seat with a leery eye fixed on the sir. He moved back, keeping a leg of space between us when I finally sank onto the stool's wooden disc. Still, it was hard not to notice that he was a good head and shoulders taller than me and twice as broad, plus the pinch of his lips that was there and gone as he took me in again.

He knelt so we were close to eye level, no doubt staining the knees of his nice pants. "Please tell me your name," he said while flattening the paper bag. In his hand was the last piece of food that'd been within it, a whole pomea fruit.

I took it and bit into it before he could change his mind about feeding me his breakfast. It was an older fruit, incredibly sweet and mushy, but I didn't care a whit. Juice dribbled down my chin, and the seeds within the sweet mouthful crunched obnoxiously between my teeth. I swiped my face and said, "Heather. M'name's Heather."

"Just Heather?" he asked.

I nodded with the fruit pressed to my lips. I didn't hear my real name much anymore, now that I was a Mouse. Most of the adults in Springfield's gang wouldn't say it right anyway, calling me 'Eather.

"Nice to meet you, Heather." He pressed his broad hand to his chest. "I'm Arthur Radcliffe, and I'm here to make a deal with you."

My eyelid flickered, a sign of the sudden spike of nerves within me. I froze. The pomea's taste turned sickly sweet and hit my belly with a hefty weight, feeling like it wanted to come right back out the way it came.

He put his palms up. "You might recognize my last name. I'm the Headmaster of the Radcliffe-Stone Institute for Troubled Youth, but you may know it as..."

"RSI." He and I said it at the same time.

I shivered with a sudden spray of goosebumps up my arms. Everyone knew about RSI, especially kids like me. It was the kingdom's answer to problem children. The young dregs of society went in, and somehow, most emerged as productive members of society. Their methods were whispered about in the dark of Jace's place, how they'd beat misbehavior out of kids and lock up nonconformists in solitary rooms with no food or water for days. How it was one step away from being a prison for teenagers.

It was one step up from where I was now. "Heather, I want to make you an offer," he said.

I folded my sticky hands in my lap, taking a grounding breath and not quite making eye contact with him. It was hard to look anyone in the eye, even folk I'd known all my life. My dark brown eyes held too many emotions, and others read them easily if given the chance. I didn't want him to see the truth; I was still shaking like a terrified mouse on the inside, even if he was kind enough to feed me before we got to the unpleasant conversation ahead.

"I heard what you did last night. You stole the Eye of Acuity from Lord Gladbeck's mansion, but not before you knocked out three of his guards, snuck past the rest, and disabled some of the best anti-theft magic clorets can buy, including a magical seal. It seems you were only caught because you didn't recognize the double-release spell on the jewelry box itself."

I nodded slowly, feeling a tremble of disgrace. I should've been more careful; Cartier and Rozma wouldn't have been able to get rid of me so easily if I'd realized they slipped me weaker desda powder. Then I wouldn't be here at all.

"Heather, that's amazing," he said, shaking his head slowly. "I know full-grown men who would've been stopped by the root trap on the servant's stair."

My eyebrows rose, and I met his gaze for a moment. A mistake. He probably saw the flicker of pride I took in my work from the compliment he'd paid me.

"It'd be a shame to leave you here to be questioned by Lord Gladbeck or a senior peacekeeper. You still committed a serious crime, and the Eye of Acuity hasn't been seen since you picked it up."

"Ain't gonna squeal," I muttered, realizing where this was going.

"I know. Trust me, I know how this works," he replied.

"So…wait. How d'you know so much about—"

"As you should also understand the choice you have," he said over me. "And what my offer is. I want to take you to RSI to become a student. When was the last time you were in school?"

I answered with a shrug. I'd been out of fundamental school more than I'd been in, with my uncle always withdrawing me for one job or another even before I became his Mouse.

His voice softened. "How old are you, Heather?"

"Thirteen."

Headmaster Radcliffe nodded, though he had the kind of frown that said he didn't quite believe me. "A perfect age to return to school, then. But the Eye of Acuity is a very valuable piece of jewelry, and I cannot fully remove you from the reach of the law. You will have to stay at RSI as a student until you can provide the information to retrieve it or return it to the Gladbeck family yourself."

"What happens if I can't find it?" I asked, frowning too. Chances were good that Cartier and Rozma were gone. *Long,* long gone.

"Valuables do have a habit of disappearing," he said agreeably. "However, we educate past fundamental school age. By the time you are eighteen, we can revisit this discussion if this particular valuable does not make a reappearance."

It wouldn't. I was sure of it. Yet something about Headmaster Radcliffe told me he had full faith it would resurface.

"If you refuse this offer, then you will be questioned traditionally by the peacekeepers shortly. I imagine Lord Gladbeck would pay to have some truth serum involved," he continued.

My eyes widened. Truth serum hadn't even come up in my worries, but it was the guaranteed way to get me to squeal. No boss cared if you were forced to squeal or not; the punishment was the same if you caused them a loss or brought the peacekeepers sniffing around their place of business.

"But you don't have to answer any questions or speak to a peacekeeper at all if you come with me to RSI," he said, offering me his hand, palm up. "Don't lose your hand, Heather. Make the right choice."

As I eyed his palm, I saw the wisdom in the offer he made, where I would choose to go to a school known for crushing nonconformity out of its students. The one that was akin to a prison…yet the offer to go there was like a hand extended to lift me from the certain death that awaited me otherwise.

"I'll go," I blurted. "I'll go to RSI." It was the right choice, the only one, in this situation.

CHAPTER 3

THE TOUR

Headmaster Radcliffe walked me to RSI personally. He pulled a bracelet out of his pocket and offered it to me. "To identify you as a future RSI student," he explained.

I put it on and admired it as we left. It was a string of wooden beads painted black and etched with tiny yellow shields and keys. I had no jewelry of my own, so I wanted to keep it even if it was marking me as property of RSI.

He brought me past the scarred table where the peacekeepers had their contraband and picked up the envelope of cloth that held my lock picks while leaving the rest behind. I crept behind him as soon as we emerged into the sun and picked my tools out of his pocket. Out of respect, I didn't touch the pouch of clorets further up his belt, too satisfied to have part of my toolkit back.

The biggest shame was the desda powder, which would be destroyed. It was classified as an illegal substance since it was so deadly to mages. The only way to get more would be through back alley means.

But as soon as I was comfortably three paces behind the headmaster, I turned and bolted, dashing the length of a shadow before I just…halted. It was like the paralysis spell all over again, my limbs stuck swinging, and yet my body wasn't moving.

I felt my soles sliding, though, and glanced down to realize I was scooting backward. The headmaster chuckled. "That didn't take long," he commented.

When he stopped walking, I stopped getting nudged along with him. I realized I was still able to move and turned around and ambled closer to him with a sheepish expression. He held up his wrist, where he now wore a matching bracelet to mine. "Come along now, Heather."

I walked a step behind him, tugging at the band of beads I wore and scowling at them in betrayal when it was obvious they weren't going to budge. I was coming along with this sir whether I liked it or not.

Unconcerned by all this, the headmaster explained a few basic things on the way to the school, and I listened in sullen silence. Since it was the holidays, there were no classes, just open times to take advantage of the "fun" areas before my time was occupied with assignments and grades.

"I think you will like it, once you have your tour," he promised.

I didn't bother scrubbing the doubt from my face. What he didn't realize was he was about to toss me to the wolves— other kids. I'd dropped out of fundamental school without a second thought partially because it meant I didn't have to endure the bullies forced into the same rooms with me for months on end.

RSI was distinctive in the impoverished section of Kaiamear, built like a palace with its spacious grounds and four pointed towers, one at each sharp corner of the building. Its aging gray stone was draped with creeping ivy gone brown with the changing of the seasons. Even though it loomed large over us with two stories and a vaulted roof, my palms grew clammy as we climbed the staircase to the faded entranceway.

As big as it was, this place was about to be my prison. The headmaster paused to show me the other bracelet he wore, a silvery one secured on his other wrist, and explained it was for the school's security. When he placed his left hand flat on the door leading into RSI, the locks clicked open because the magic in them recognized the magic in his bracelet.

Until the staff here could trust me, the headmaster shared, the bracelet they were about to fasten to my wrist would do the opposite. Most of the doors here would lock in my presence, all windows sealing closed.

You chose this, I reminded myself, rubbing the skin below my eye to ward off another uncomfortable flutter.

We crossed a short foyer, sparsely decorated. Nothing about it was designed to impress, with dull, craggy floors and worn carpeting down the center. Sunlight streamed down in a solid block from angled windows set just out of reach.

A dark-haired woman looked up from a letter she was scratching out from behind a prominent desk, straightening with a smile. "You got her," she said to the headmaster.

He nudged me ahead of him gently. "Easily. Heather, this is RSI's secretary, Sasha. You may address her as Miss Barrios."

I opened my mouth and closed it again with barely a squeak. Miss Barrios flicked the sheet of her hair over one shoulder and smiled, stretching the warm brown skin on her cheek and the circular mark branded there. She was a Tulari mage, a real one, touched by the god Orion shortly after birth. The blue of her magical rune meant she specialized in wizardry and had access to a wide range of spells.

"And this is Heather, our newest resident. We discussed her this morning," he continued, and she nodded.

I swallowed my nerves. I hadn't expected to meet a mage

today, even if she seemed nice. Wizards set the kind of magical traps I'd disabled last night, but they had many useful tricks—most of which I'd never been taught. There was a measure of hand waving when it came to Tulari, especially for common folk like me. No one quite knew what they were capable of.

"I'll take care of the paperwork, if you wouldn't mind getting Heather here settled," the headmaster said.

"Of course." She stood, dusting off the pleats of her dress. She was tall for a woman and moved like a prowling feline, her feet barely seeming to touch the ground. I was reminded distinctly of my gang sister, Wildcat, who wielded the same sort of grace to her advantage in freeing valuables from the grasp of the well-off.

Headmaster Radcliffe tapped my shoulder, startling me. "This whole corridor is Aldridge Hall," he explained, motioning to the hallway that stretched to our left and right. "All instructors and administrators have their offices down this way." Now he indicated the right. "Here is where we part ways, for now. I look forward to seeing your progress, Heather."

"Yessir," I answered in a murmur.

He snagged the bracelet he'd given me by one bead, sliding it off like it'd never been stuck to me. I rubbed away the tingling feeling at my wrist. With a nod at me, he patted his pouch of clorets and walked away, leaving me with Miss Barrios. I swallowed thickly, sure he was about to realize I'd lifted my lock picks from him, but he hadn't seemed to notice yet.

Feeling overheated, I followed Miss Barrios to a room that was set behind her desk. It was full of junk and boxes, less an office and more a storage space. "First things first," she said, retrieving a length of coppery metal a knuckle thick and a thin, pointed rod of wood. "Hold out your hand, palm up."

I did as she instructed, flinching when the cold metal touched my wrist. She left it balanced there and motioned for me to keep still before flicking the piece of wood. I realized it was a wand when she used it to write glowing blue lines midair to form a spell. When she was satisfied, she put the tip of the wand through the magic and tapped the piece of metal.

In a blink, the flat length of it snapped into a seamless bracelet that rested above the knob of my wrist. It was an unmarked copper band and didn't budge more than a couple wiggles up or down. My eyelid flickered to know that I was truly trapped here with this on.

"Oh, honey. You'll be okay," Miss Barrios said in a gentle tone. She started to reach for me, and I edged away. "Many kiddos get to come and go from the institute after a few months. You just have to earn our trust."

The breath I took came out ragged. The band wasn't etched with "Property of RSI," but I knew the next step would be to don a uniform with the institute's shield stitched into the shoulder. RSI kids were easy to identify, only allowed to wear distinctive uniforms around the city.

"Heather. Are you with me?" Miss Barrios passed her hand in front of my face. I blinked and met her gaze, recognizing the kindness in her dark brown eyes.

Mine narrowed back in distrust. No adult looked at me that way unless they wanted something in return.

She spoke in a pitch meant to soothe. "Everyone at this school has been through this moment. Headmaster Radcliffe, the instructors, even me." Raising her hand, she flicked her wrist to spin a gray metal bracelet studded with small gems. Hers was more of a cuff, like the headmaster's, not designed to trap her. "Someday, yours may look like this."

"You were a student here?" I asked.

As far as I could tell, her smile was genuine. She lit up at the question; I imagined she was picturing her time as a student and liking what she remembered. "I was. That's how

I got my job here. Come along. Let me give you a tour of the grounds, and I'll share some of my favorite memories with you," she promised.

She coaxed me into the hall and explained how the institute ran as she showed me the most important places. Aldridge Hall's first floor was attached to a massive cafeteria that held the lingering smells of baking bread and savory food. My belly grumbled despite its recent meal.

I glanced down and then over at Miss Barrios, tentatively hopeful the smiling adult would get me a second breakfast. She didn't hesitate, leaving me standing at the front of the cafeteria as she went into the kitchen. Alone for a few minutes, I wandered, skimming my fingertips over the back of chairs and the battered surface of ink- and food-stained tables.

Every table, big and small, was shaped with curves, ovals, or circles and sat four to twenty people. The chairs were facing each other; this space was designed for conversation and community. There were few places for a Mouse like me to sit with my back to a wall or alone with my thoughts.

I scurried to return to where Miss Barrios had left me, standing still with my hands folded politely when she came out of the kitchen holding a pastry. She apologized for it being old as she continued showing me around, taking me through the cafeteria and out one of the only doors that wouldn't seal in the presence of my bracelet. It was locked more traditionally after dark.

The center of RSI was a grassy yard called the Square, free for students to roam as long as the weather permitted. I nibbled the pastry and took time to savor its spiced jam center as she showed me how deep the yard went, with enough space for a few ancient shade trees and a garden plot I could help tend if I joined a club for it.

She spoke of student-run clubs, and I arranged my face to one of vague interest. I had to join exactly one club—it was mandatory—but I could pick one once I got a better understanding of how things worked here.

Meanwhile, I eyed the walls of the institute and its steeply angled roof. There was no ivy here, but I could climb a tree. I noted it as a possible escape route until I also spotted the waves of a spell in how the roofing tiles were arranged. A slipping trap, simple but effective in keeping would-be thieves off roofs. *Musty devils.*

"This way now," Miss Barrios said.

We went along the corridor of Aldridge Hall back the way we'd come, passing the offices of several more teachers than I expected. The hall closest to the cafeteria was Irving Hall, where the boys lived on the first floor. Running parallel to it was Hawthorne Hall, for the girls, closest to the staff offices.

"Are the halls named after folk?" I asked, finally speaking up again.

"Of a sort," she said vaguely.

Our next stop was a supply closet, where she loaded up my arms with a tower of various folded clothing items and a pair of sturdy boots. She carried some extra items in a sack with the basic tools I'd need for learning.

"How old did you say you were, Heather?"

"Thirteen."

"Right." She raised a brow before leading me further into Hawthorne Hall. "Thirteen... We do have a couple beds open for you to room with your peers."

"I'm good with littler kids, too," I ventured tentatively. I'd stayed with Jackie and our younger gang siblings without an issue since I'd never wanted to be away from my little sister. Uncle Jace had always called me "small size" anyway.

She waved her free hand. "Oh, there's no need for that. Let's see..." She poked her head into a room halfway down the hall before motioning me in. It wasn't much more than a box with eight sets of the same basic furniture. Cots in an orderly line against one wall, with chests for belongings at their feet. The opposite wall had eight matching desks and chairs.

There was a smattering of art pinned to the wall, and a couple of the cots were dressed up with colored sheets. One had clothes and cosmetics bottles scattered over it. It was pretty obvious there were two open spots for me to choose from.

I couldn't help but compare it to what I knew. Back at Jace's, I had a corner and a wall to put my back to. There was never privacy, though, and even rarer a moment of peace, as the room sometimes had double the number of kids stuffed into it than this one did.

Here, at least, it was quiet with just Miss Barrios and me. She pointed out the wooden name plates hung above each cot. I could have either the third or the fifth bed in from the left side, but either way, I wouldn't have a wall unless someone wanted to trade. I picked the third bed, between "Carmen" and "Harper," and dropped my clothes onto the plain gray sheets to be sorted later.

We went to see the last hall so this tour could be finished, passing a wave of humidity from the girls' bath set toward the end of the corridor. I longed to go inside and scrub the musty funk of the jail cell off me before finding a quiet corner to sleep.

"All of our classrooms are on the top floor," Miss Barrios explained as we walked. "But this will be your favorite hall. Most of our special interests are here."

The first place we stopped at was a library spanning both stories and the peak of one tower. My eyes widened to twin rounds as I craned my neck. The center of this area was open air, showing how the stacks stretched to the far ceiling. I'd never seen so many books in one place, fitting into orderly lines and tracks and rows.

"I spent so much time here when I was your age," she said, leading me to a few study areas hidden behind the stacks or purposefully shaded with sheer curtains.

I could tell I would be doing the same. This was the perfect place to hide from others.

"I like reading," I murmured. It wasn't that I was good at it, but folk left a reader alone. Maybe there was a reading club for me to join, so I could hide behind the covers of an open book.

Miss Barrios lit up again. "Oh! Tell me about the last book you read," she invited.

"Um." Well, this kicked back at me. Back at Jace's, I only had the one book. "'Twas about animals."

She took me from the library with a nod. "We have a robust nonfiction section for you to enjoy."

I nodded too, biting my lip. What did robust mean? It sounded like she meant it as a good thing.

She showed me the next few rooms, which had a few other kids inside from very small to older than me. This was the section for art, for "fun," like making paintings or pottery.

We skipped over the gym, where a training session of some sort was taking place. Miss Barrios didn't want me to go inside and see what was going on, so I didn't do more than glance over my shoulder at the closed door. The tour ended with us on a stage spotlit by a single extra bright magelight. I picked up the shadowed forms of a hundred seats or more, plus a second tier of seating high above.

Miss Barrios twirled, spinning her skirt and beaming. She struck a smooth pose with one arm up, the other extended toward me. "Finally, my favorite place, the theater. I was in drama club and had the lead role in *Bane of the Nameless* before I graduated.

"It's the one place we allow visitors. RSI is known all through Kaiamear for having productions throughout the year. Theater is a requirement for most of our students for the many practical skills they can learn," she said. The look she flashed me was apologetic. "The headmaster hasn't finalized your schedule yet, but I'm sure he'll be eager to see how you do on stage."

My eyelid twitched in reply. *No, no. No no no.* She thought that *I* could perform out loud for an audience?

Musty devils. I couldn't get out of this place fast enough.

CHAPTER 4
"FRIENDS"

Once Miss Barrios left me alone back at my new room, I retrieved a change of clothes and put the rest in the chest at the base of my new cot. There'd been a key at the bottom of the chest, which locked my new belongings inside along with my old slippers and single glove.

I bathed, changed, and returned to the library to curl up in a quiet nook to sleep. Nothing woke me except for the distant chimes of the city bells marking the morning hour. I counted the rings and realized I'd slept through nearly a whole day and night.

With a yawn, I scrubbed the film from my eyes and returned to wakefulness slowly. The leisure of it was a luxury. Uncle Jace and the other kids never let me sleep this long, between jobs and the chatter and the younger ones' constant needs.

My fingertips landed on something furry, and I blinked, patting the soft side of a calico cat with big blotches of color on her fur. The first smile broke over my face since I'd arrived at RSI and been given an "old" pastry. She must've found my still, sleeping form as the perfect spot to curl up against, and my stirring had woken her to a slow blinking state.

"Hi there," I murmured, petting her when she started to purr.

My gang siblings and I were always bringing in strays to stay with us. We were a group of misfits named for animals, so there was always a kinship if we could find the real thing. Mice wanted nothing to do with me, but cats and dogs were good companions until Uncle Jace eventually got fed up with their presence and turned them out.

None of our temporary pets had been as well-groomed and plump as this one. She was either a skilled mouser or made inept by a steady diet as someone's pet. A fabric collar around her neck snagged my fingertips, and I checked the tag hanging from it, blinking twice to see the symbol of RSI etched into a circle of copper about as large as my thumbnail. I remembered where I was and why I smelled like fancy soap, like I'd rolled around in a flowering field.

The heist, the jail, the reform school; an unreal dream, except I was wearing the black uniform with a stitching on the shoulder, the iconic yellow RSI shield with a pair of crossed keys underneath. I'd laid the cloak over myself like a blanket. It was dyed a purple-tinged gray, and the back had a yellow ribbon stitched into the fabric to form the same shield-and-keys symbol. There was no avoiding the fact that I was owned by this reform school, just like the cat. I minded...of course I minded, but the clothes were good quality, soft instead of scratchy. I'd wear them until I figured out how to get out of here and back to Jackie and the others.

I missed my sister fiercely. I could use her cheerful presence and childish advice right now. As comfortable as my wakeup was, I knew I couldn't stay here. The Gladbeck family would want their necklace back, and I wasn't sure even a sir with the importance of Headmaster Radcliffe could keep me safe and away from them inside of RSI.

Someone had to protect the other kids from Jace's anger

when he learned what'd happened. What would he think when I didn't return?

What would *Boss Springfield* think? It depended on whether my two least favorite adults, Cartier and Rozma, came creeping back to his side. If all three of us were presumed dead, then it would be brushed off by all parties...

I sat up slowly and groaned at the thought of confronting whatever unknown this day had in store. After fastening the cloak around my neck, I picked up the cat and snuggled her vibrating body under my chin for comfort as I took a walk around the quiet library. "What would a Weasel and a Mongoose do next?" I asked her, as if she had the answers I didn't. She mrrowed and patted my chin with a soft paw.

My eyelid twitched. There was nothing I could do about those two from here, not even for revenge. The idea of plunging them into some kind of trouble for what they'd done to me was the most distant of goals. The only thing I could do right now was scope out the four walls of my new prison to see if there were any details I missed on the tour with Miss Barrios.

But first, I found the librarian by accident, an older, stout woman wheeling around a cart of loose books. She took the cat from me before I could walk off with her. I learned her name was Patches, an appropriately literal one, while the librarian was Miss Wilkes. "We kept it down for you," she said.

Heat tinged my cheeks. Of course the adult who ran this place knew I'd passed out here. "Yesmum," I answered.

Her watery blue eyes drifted for a moment as a crease appeared between her brows. "Yes, ma'am," she corrected.

I grew more embarrassed and fidgety by the moment. "Yes...ma'am," I repeated slowly.

"Run along now. They're still serving breakfast in the cafeteria." She flicked a wrinkled white hand toward the door, and off I scurried.

I peered around the corner of Hawthorne Hall, hearing feminine voices and the tinkle of laughter. A trio of girls headed in my direction, while another was pressing her bracelet to the door out of the institute at the far end of the hall, offering a tantalizing glimpse of sunshine before it was shut out behind her.

The other girls had already seen me, and we offered a tentative round of hellos as we crossed paths. All the while, I felt their gazes looking me up and down, noting the wrinkles in my new uniform and cloak and the tousle of my dark hair. Nothing like school to make me hyperaware of my flaws and the giggles of people behind me as they walked away.

They're probably not laughing at you, I told myself, using Jackie's voice in my head. Other kids had, too often in the past. I'd shown up to fundamental school ready to be bullied, with too-big castoff clothes from the older kids and some-times without an adult around to insist I comb my hair and wash my face before showing up.

The worst part was the smell, though. My shoulders curled in self-consciously as I passed another girl and flashed a shy smile in response to her curious glance. My gang's home had a lingering musty stink that got into everything—clothes, hair, skin. It invaded every room and pallet, no matter how we tried to clean up after ourselves. I was used to it, but I'd learned the hard way that it was an easy flaw to pick at.

I was always afraid that smell clung to me, even freshly bathed. I scrubbed myself and my clothes before jobs, leaving my skin scoured pink and sensitive. Sometimes, like now, I could smell it even though I knew it wasn't here.

I walked into the cafeteria, reassuring myself that I smelled like flowery soap by sniffing my arm, and nearly collided with someone. Strong hands caught my shoulders. "What are you doing?" another girl demanded.

Flinching away from the physical contact, I started

blushing again. "'Scuse me," I muttered, ducking my head as I tried to walk past her.

She stepped in front of me, hands on hips, forcing me to halt. "My eyes are up here. Are you Heather?"

"How'd you know?" I blurted.

I looked up at her and nearly regretted it. She was probably my age but was a head taller than me and looked annoyed by the slant of her brows. Her features were sharp, a pointed chin and defined cheekbones to go with the twin daggers of her coppery eyes. "Finally. We're supposed to be *friends*," she said.

She sounded like she'd rather kiss a needlecoat's rear. "We are?" I asked.

Rather than continue to make eye contact with her intimidating stare, my gaze drifted to her hairline. This girl had the shortest hair I'd seen, outside of the freshly shorn heads of the men who'd gone off to war or the shiny heads of those who couldn't grow any. It wasn't a feminine cut or even all that well done, her black hair unevenly chopped to be one to two knuckle lengths long.

"Miss Barrios asked me to look after you since we're roommates." She rolled her eyes. "Just come sit with me, okay?"

"Okay," I echoed uncertainly.

I must've stood there a second too long, as she gestured impatiently for me to go get food. A pair of women were refreshing piles of rolls, pastries, and a small variety of cheeses and small, bruised fruit. It was apparently open to take as much as I wanted, so I took too much, trotting over to a table with an edible hill on a tray.

"The food here's not *that* good." The tall girl left the chair next to me empty, sitting one away with her arms crossed.

I begged to differ. The bread and cheese melted on my tongue as I took the first bite, but I didn't start gobbling it all down like I otherwise would with her sitting there waiting to judge me.

"On second thought, you're kind of a pipsqueak. Maybe you should eat more," she said.

"Ain't we supposed to be 'friends'?" I asked once I swallowed.

She set her face, lips turning to one side. The expression was so deeply unhappy that I took back some of my meaner thoughts about her rudeness. She huffed a sigh. "Let's try this again. I'm Carmen Montes, the last new girl before you came along. There's some kind of buddy system we're supposed to have here, but the last person I was paired with ran off to another school."

My next swallow was awkwardly loud. I didn't have the option to be shipped off to a different school, so we were likely stuck together.

"I don't want to be here," she added bitterly.

"Me neither," I said without hesitation.

She reached over and punched my shoulder. With an extra chair length between us, it was at the end of her reach and just a tap, but I hid a small wince all the same. "Would you look at that, pipsqueak; we have something in common, after all."

I took another closer look at her, hoping I'd found someone with the same goals as me. If it took help to leave this place, I could see her being the muscle. She'd rolled the cuffs of her uniform shirt up to better show the defined curves of her arms. Carmen looked strong for a girl, but it made her slimmer rather than bulky like a tough boy would be.

I considered giving her a bit of my trust, just to bait out whether she'd be willing to partner with me to escape RSI together. Her sharp edges reminded me of an earlier time, when I'd been small enough to be cute and trusted in shops with little stealable knickknacks. My favorite shop had "real

Lithosian desert sand" in tiny glass bottles, and I'd coveted them.

Jace wouldn't give me the clorets to buy a bottle, even if I could tip it back and forth for hours, fascinated by the way the grains rolled together so smoothly. Their golden color matched the uneven tan I had from hours baking in the sun, helping some of Springfield's adults run the Lost Child con in wealthy areas.

The first thing I ever stole was one of those bottles of sand when I tipped one once and found a sliver of gemstone inside, smooth and shiny and a pretty brown. When I showed Jace my tiny bounty, he told me it was a carnelian and smashed the bottle on the ground to take it and sell it.

It was a bittersweet memory, because I'd never showed him my personal treasures again unless prompted. But Carmen's complexion was like that carnelian lying amongst the shattered glass, smooth amidst the edges of her pointed features. Perhaps she was an unexpected gem too.

"Have you tried to leave?" I lowered my voice, finally turning my attention toward the copper bracelet she wore, a twin to my own.

She did the same, flicking her hand to shift the tight band. "It's impossible. Pretty much everyone who works here *attended* this school. They know all the ways we could escape better than we do."

"Musty devils," I muttered.

"What's that supposed to mean?" Even the quirk of her eyebrow was sharp.

"Uh." I could just tell her the truth—that I would get beat if I said adult curses where I came from, so I made up my own. "You know how there are devils in the three hells? I just...I imagine they smell."

She stared, making a little "mmm" noise before huffing what I think was a laugh, a *heh*.

"I think I won't mind you. Want to spar after this?" she asked.

"Spar?" I echoed.

"Repeating everything I say is annoying, though. Yes, spar! Do you fight?"

I shook my head rapidly in response.

"Never mind," she sighed. "I should've known better."

"We should take another walk around. Miss Barrios will see us, uh, being friends, and…" I drifted off, not wanting to give breath to the kind of thought that might be overheard.

"We're not going to find a way out. Especially not with these bracelets," she said loudly.

Well, Carmen wasn't one for stealth and secrets. That was usually my job.

CHAPTER 5
COINCIDENCES

Carmen was a long, pessimistic shadow that followed me through RSI. She turned down every little sprouting idea I had when I thought we'd found secret passages or a window that didn't seem to lock in our presence.

"They've thought of everything, trust me," she said over and over. Her presence started to chafe, and I longed to be alone.

Considering how little we had in common, she and I parted ways without complaint as the noon bells were ringing and my second circuit around RSI was finished. She went to the gym, and I crept into one of the art rooms, settling in a quiet corner with charcoal pencils and a few pieces of paper.

I enjoyed drawing, but I'd rarely had the time and supplies to do much of it. Now that I was presented with both things, I tapped the blank page, wishing for references, but I was too shy to ask anything of the older students and teacher occupied with painting and arranging something for an upcoming theater production.

I did my best on my own, but the weasel looked more like some diseased snake with fur, and nothing else turned out how I liked it. I left behind my work in defeat when it was dinnertime, slipping unnoticed out of the art room.

The school had acquired a peacekeeper, not much more than a pimple-faced teen with the kind of long and lanky body that made the white-and-yellow uniform hang off him like a scarecrow. He wore the crested peacekeeper helm crookedly, thrown on like an afterthought.

There were more kids in the cafeteria this time around, and I suspected even more would be filtering in as Yule ended and classes began…soon. I didn't know when they started up and didn't want to draw attention to the fact that I didn't have a schedule. Yet again, I was relying on the "maybe they'll forget about me" hope so I could hide in the library and cafeteria like a real mouse with no responsibilities except to scavenge, survive, and inevitably escape.

I should've known that wouldn't happen, but it took returning to the same art room the next day for it to sink in. The front chalkboard had one of my sketches clipped to it, with "Who made this?" written underneath in chalk.

I turned to the art teacher, a harried young woman with cinnamon-colored curls sticking out around her head and obscuring the lenses of her glasses. Her apron was stained with multiple hues of paint, more added on than she had yesterday.

"It was you, wasn't it?" she asked, pointing to the drawing.

"Uh. No," I mumbled.

"I don't know you yet. I'm Miss Hawthorne." She spoke over me and stuck out her hand to shake. She grasped my limp fingers and shook like she was in a hurry. "Are you going to be taking art?"

"I don't think—"

"Well, you are now!"

"But," I protested quickly and realized she'd paused to listen. "But that's all I know how to draw."

I'd developed it over time, a sketch of a mouse peeking from a couple stalks of heather. Uncle Jace had told me that good thieves didn't leave behind tokens like a tiny drawing, only if they wanted to be caught or if they had a *huge* ego and the skills to back it up. "Remember what happened to Foxglove," he'd say.

Foxglove was the name of an infamous thief from before my time. She would leave a single foxglove flower at the scene of her crimes, placed where a valuable used to be. Thus the name and all. Uncle Jace was jealous when he talked about Foxglove; actually, he'd known enough about her to guess that she was a kid when she'd eventually been caught.

A Tulari mage traced her poisonous gift back to her location and had her arrested. That was the end of her tale; no one had returned to the streets with foxglove flowers to pass out. If she was still alive, she'd learned her lesson. She now existed as a warning to all young thieves to show how easily leaving something behind could be dangerous.

"Nonsense. That's why you would take art," she said, waving away my concerns and bringing me out of my realization. "Listen, you don't strike me as the actress type. *They* rely on *us* to bring productions to life."

She circled her hand in a motion to follow her to what she and those other students were working on. "RSI puts on a show every fortnight, and you're looking at the most valuable team for making it happen," she said.

A few of the older kids looked up from their project to wave. "Backstage crew only has to appear in one play a year," one young man added.

I was swayed, except I didn't know how exactly I'd help. They explained the prop to me and handed me a paintbrush, apparently too excited to have another set of hands to assist. This weekend, the oldest age group at RSI, the eighteen-year-olds, would perform *Burn the Night,* and the art department was responsible for making props and a backdrop that actually looked like a city aflame.

This prop was one of the final touches, but they were struggling to get it right. It was a canvas propped up on a solid wooden frame that would be sitting in the background throughout the show. It was already painted to look like a cityscape, but they needed help creating realistic-looking fire to attach to the frame with bendable wire. There was a lively debate about colored paper, scraps of painted canvas, and who would stand behind the prop and shake the wires to make the effect more real.

While I wasn't much help, I had fun doing as Miss Hawthorne and the other students directed and let the time melt by. I squeezed in a question toward the evening bells which started the dinner hour, asking the one young man here, "Is Hawthorne Hall named after Miss Hawthorne?" I glanced toward the art teacher in question, who fussed with strips of foiling in the supply closet across the room.

He blinked at me for a moment. "What?"

I realized I'd mumbled the question and repeated it more loudly. I didn't miss how he glanced down at my wrist and made a *tisk* noise before replying, "Just a coincidence, I think."

My eyes narrowed. That was a mighty strange coincidence. I thought of Headmaster Radcliffe, whose name I'd accepted without further questions. It made sense that the sir leading the school would be related to one of the founders, the Radcliffe of Radcliffe-Stone Institute.

I left the group to their work as I slipped out to head to the cafeteria, lost in thought. There were four halls on the first floor, all with names: Hawthorne Hall, for the girls; Irving Hall, for the boys; Stryker Hall, for special interests; and Aldridge Hall, with its offices for staff and the cafeteria. On my way past the offices, I decided I'd take a closer look at the names, to see if it was just an odd coincidence.

As I went down the girls' hall, I nearly walked into a young woman standing with her arms crossed. "Watch it," she snapped.

I sprang away from her, shocked out of my thoughts and looking around with wide eyes. She scoffed my way and turned her attention back toward a janitor. A man, no less, with more pepper than salt in his thinning hair and unblemished, toffee-toned skin.

He appeared to be deep in conversation with a different girl, idly sweeping the hall. He wasn't much to look at, with a long, wrinkled face and brown overalls, yet I found myself taken aback for an awkward moment. What was a man doing here? He didn't look like he was above the age to be drafted.

Ultimately, I decided it wasn't my business and moved myself along, more motivated by food than names and strange occurrences anyway. The cafeteria was more packed than ever, with no seats available where I would be eating on my own. More and more, my surroundings seemed like a sea of people in the same uniform as me, all of us blending together. With a resigned sigh, I picked one of the smaller tables and plopped down across from a stranger…who immediately smiled like I'd made his day.

He waved. "Hello."

"Uh, hi," I replied, my shoulders raising on reflex.

"Are you new here?" he asked. I hadn't realized it until he spoke more, but he had an accent, and it was rather noticeable in the way his words bounced to their own cadence.

I'd heard his accent overblown and mocked before, considering we'd been at war with the desert kingdom of Lithos for years and our differences were now considered something undesirable. But this boy seemed nice, giving off the same sort of prey energy as some of my favorite gang siblings.

"Yeah. I'm Heather," I mumbled.

His teeth were bright against his deep bronze complexion,

black hair short and neatly combed to one side. "I'm Fariq Irfan. A pleasure to meet you." He spoke slow and careful. "I been here less than one year. My Altarian is not great."

"Sounds like you're doing fine t'me," I said, wondering if his face would get stuck beaming in such a way. I started eating, and he did the same, saving us both from needing to talk.

"What club will you be in?" he eventually asked.

"Dunno. I don't even have a schedule."

With a hum, even this boy was eyeing my hand—my wrist, and the bracelet fixed upon it. "You should do language club. With me." He tapped his chest.

I raised a skeptical brow. I had enough trouble with Altarian, and I'd already been invited to join the art club with Miss Hawthorne.

"Learn better with friends," he said, flashing his big smile.

"I'll think about it," I replied. He bobbed his head with the same kind of energy I'd use if someone said they agreed.

When we parted ways for the evening, he waved farewell like he'd miss me. I thought of Fariq as I drifted past the teachers' offices, skimming the name plates next to their doors. They only had last names past Headmaster Radcliffe's door: Brown, Gery, Tran, Maxin…and then Stone. I paused, tracing the tarnished metal with the familiar name. As I kept looking at the name plates on the other offices, I eventually identified the six names I expected to be present, from the founders Radcliffe and Stone to the names of the halls, Hawthorne, Stryker, Irving, and Aldridge.

That couldn't simply be a *coincidence*. I just didn't know what to do with this information.

I woke up the next morning in the library nook I was starting to think of as mine, with Patches sitting a foot away staring at me. There was a piece of paper tucked into her collar. She got to her paws with a chirp when she realized that I was awake and reaching for her.

After giving her cheeks and neck a good scratch, I plucked the paper out from under her collar and squinted at it since the first sheet was a letter addressed to me. I read it but only understood about half of it.

Miss Heather,

I'm pleased to inform you that your schedule has been set and classes begin in a few short days. I hope you enjoy the experiences RSI has to offer its students.

This will be the last day you are permitted to sleep in the library. You won't find it a very restful place once late-night study sessions are happening all around you. I'm sure Patches would still appreciate you visiting her during daylight hours.

If you have any questions about the attached schedule or just want to talk, I am often in my office. I look forward to hearing what you think of RSI and its quirks.

Sincerely,

Headmaster Arthur Radcliffe

I scowled at all the unfamiliar words on the page and flipped it over my shoulder in a huff. The schedule was equally concerning, considering it spanned all the time between breakfast and dinner in a solid block of learning. My eyelid twitched, and I had to set the paper aside, breathing raggedly.

The school hadn't forgotten about me. I was going to "learn" alongside dozens of other kids, just like fundamental school. They'd notice me too, observe my weaknesses, eat me alive. A Mouse wasn't supposed to be seen.

Soft fur pushed into my fingers. Patches chirped again, climbing into my lap and turning to make a snuggly ball. I curled my arms around her and held her until my heart stopped fluttering in my chest like an agitated bird.

She blinked slowly at me, patting my arm with a paw. If she were a person, it'd be a soothing gesture, but I knew not to attribute a person's actions to a pet. "I know you belong to Miss Wilkes, but I wish you could come with me. I could use a friend like you," I murmured.

Her paw flexed on my skin, and she meowed back, tilting her head. If she *were* a person, I'd say she was thoughtful in that moment.

I gave her one last scratch down her spine and stood with the letter in hand, wandering the library until I found the librarian, Miss Wilkes, shelving books. "Uh. 'Scuse me, mum," I mumbled.

She looked up after a moment too long and startled when she saw me standing there looking at her. "Gods, do announce yourself." She placed a hand on her chest.

I fidgeted uncomfortably; I thought I had. "Sorry, never mind," I said, starting to duck away.

"No, no. Did you need help?" she offered.

Cheeks stained with embarrassment, I tentatively held out the letter to her and murmured back. She took it, and a furrow appeared between her brows. "Speak up, sweetheart. I'm old," she said.

I cleared my throat and lowered my shoulders from where they threatened to creep up around my ears. "Could ya read this to me?" I repeated.

"Will you read this to me," she corrected before brightening. "Of course. Come along, let's have a seat." We sat side by side at a nearby table, and she took me one painstaking word at a time through the headmaster's letter until I understood everything it said.

I gulped a nervous swallow. The library was where I felt safest, and Miss Wilkes was one of the only adults I trusted even a small whit. Being thrown into a regular set of classes and then a room to sleep in with six other girls was terrifying.

CHAPTER 6

TYPES OF INTELLIGENCE

I MET MOST of my roommates right before bed and exchanged few words outside of names and hellos. They weren't all that interested in me, which I preferred. Three of the girls had assembled their own group already, and they sat on the floor in a circle and gossiped about their holiday break.

Their leader was one I'd need to watch carefully. She'd purposefully ignored me, inspecting her nails while Carmen attempted to make introductions. Mahogany-haired Sybella Creedmoor, with her perfectly tailored uniform and a shrewd glimmer in her eyes, had a lot of predator energy, seeming like the kind of girl who'd eat a Mouse alive to get ahead. Her friends, Nessa and Harper, followed her cue and turned their backs to me.

I wasn't staying here for too long anyway, still sure I'd figure out how to escape RSI. Admittedly, though, the cot was more comfortable than sleeping on the floor in the library, but I woke up missing Patches and the warm feeling of rousing on my own time when a hand jostled my shoulder roughly.

It was Carmen, looming over me with a knife in her other hand. I glimpsed it and yelped, scurrying away and falling off the side of my cot with a *thump*.

"Gods above," grumbled the girl who'd been sleeping on that side, Harper.

"She's got a knife!" I squeaked.

"Relax. It's dull," Carmen sighed. I sat up and realized the few girls still trying to rest were all up and in various states of grumpy dishevelment, their ire pointed at me. My eyelid flickered, and my cheeks heated.

I disentangled myself from the sheet and arranged it back on my cot. Carmen didn't hold the blade like a weapon, instead keeping it dangling between her thumb and first finger. "I just wanted some help with my hair," she said with a scowl.

My gaze flashed from her knife to her roughly cut hair. "With a dull knife, though?" I asked.

She shrugged, motioning for me to come along. "It's all they let me have."

I followed her into the hall, mirroring her shrug as I tested the sharpness of the blade she handed to me. The dinner knives here weren't much keener.

"They let you keep something contraband too, right?" she asked.

My eyes widened. The set of lock picks in my pocket seemed to weigh double with the question. "What d'you mean?"

"Every student here has something that's not otherwise allowed. Usually, it's to remind us of home or help us maintain some sense of self." She gestured to the little knife I held, and I nodded. Her unusually short hair must mean a lot to her, to go to such lengths to maintain it. "So…what's yours?"

I patted my pocket before I could lie to her. She raised her brow pointedly. "They didn't really give them to me, but I have lock picks," I admitted.

Headmaster Radcliffe had set me up to get them back from him, and I hadn't even questioned it. They did represent a "sense of self" for me, even though they weren't very useful for the locks I needed to pick. The magically sealed locks to the outside would snap my precious tools.

They were about as useful right now as a dull knife, I figured. When we reached the girls' bath, we settled before a mirror. She dragged up a stool, and I inspected her hair with a sigh. What a mess.

She held her finger and thumb less than two knuckle lengths apart for how long she wanted it. I got to work, wincing with her as I hacked at a lock of her hair. "Confidence, pipsqueak. Cut right through it," she said.

"Back home, we had shears for this," I muttered.

I'd cut plenty of hair for my gang siblings, helping the younger ones maintain their manes. Sometimes it felt like I was the only one around who cared enough to keep them clean and groomed, to the point I that became the older kid the younger ones would turn to when they needed help.

Carmen had no way of knowing I was something of a barber, even though my claim to that hinged on being able to cut long hair in a straight line. I'd gotten help learning how to braid and style textured hair like my younger gang sibling Bear had. He and I spent hours keeping his braided in rows like he liked.

I pictured Jackie sitting on the stool instead of Carmen and rubbed away a stab of wistfulness. This wasn't much different, except the knife needed more force to use effectively than a pair of shears. "Surely the boys' barber would do a better job?"

"He refuses to cut a girl's hair so short," she replied.

"Why d'you want it so short anyway?"

"Better in a fight."

"Are you expecting a fight?"

She huffed and rolled her eyes. "All the time."

I focused on the task of evening out her hair with a furrow between my brows. No one I'd met at RSI had seemed like the type to pick fights...except for Carmen herself.

"It's what I'm good at, all right?" Musty devils, now she was getting defensive. "My father taught me, like his father taught him. My great-grandfather learned how to use his body as a weapon from an Endolian master, and the secrets of his teachings stuck with my family all this time. We call the style *Tosh Zorena*."

"What does that name mean?" I asked.

"That's what the master named it, for my great-grandfather's take on his combat teachings and the city they founded together, Zoreen. My family has taught Tosh Zorena for generations so we stay strong, united, and protected despite being so close to Lithos." For perhaps the first time, Carmen's ever-present moodiness seemed to lift, a glimmer of pride in her eyes.

I smiled shyly. "That's amazing."

We made eye contact in the mirror, and I suppressed an expression of dismay when she shut away that sparkle of happiness in an instant. Her scowl returned stronger than ever. "Yeah, well..." she started to snap before taking a deep breath. "You almost done?"

I could've done more to even everything out, but she stood abruptly and inspected herself in the mirror, combing her fingers through the fluff that remained atop her head. "Not bad, kid," she said, soon charging out of the bath.

"You're welcome," I sighed at her back.

I CHECKED my schedule again as I flowed with a uniformed tide up the stairs to the many classrooms that lined the four upstairs halls. Other teenagers pushed me out of the way, striding with purpose toward their learning or to their friend groups. Nearly everyone traveled with someone, raising the noise level in the halls with the chatter of many voices.

I hadn't been on the second floor much. Most of the rooms were locked until now, with all the teachers present and ready to resume classes. I caught glimpses of them as I searched for classroom A203, seeing women with smiling faces for the most part. The *A* ended up being for Aldridge Hall. I was one of the last students filtering into their assigned room when I finally found A203 and my first teacher.

Except she was already in conversation with Miss Barrios as they stood in a recessed nook back from the main hall. "… Just be gentle with her, all right, Mei? She's going to be one of my Littles one day."

I froze a step away, somehow sensing she was talking about me. "You should know by now not to assign me some junfly puff. I'm not here to baby the candidates," answered an unfamiliar woman. "If she's soft and meek, just send her away like the last one and be done with it."

"Arthur's sure she's already figured out—"

I tensed as another voice sounded behind me. "Did you already get lost, pipsqueak? This is my first class." Carmen practically announced me, and the two adults hushed. Resigned, I stepped forward as Carmen shouldered past me, heading into the classroom.

The door shut behind her, and I stayed still under the scrutiny of the women who stood on either side of it. Miss Barrios said, "Heather, this is your language teacher, Miss Liang."

"We were just discussing you," Miss Liang said. While not unfriendly, she seemed unimpressed as soon as her dark eyes had taken my measure. She was petite and professional, with a tight bun, and dressed in a crisp black pair of pants and a buttoned-up white shirt unmarred by even the hint of dust. Her features were classically Endolian, from her rounded eyelids and flared nostrils to the olive tone to her skin.

"Oh?" I asked faintly, my eyelid flickering under the intensity of her gaze.

"You'll be coming with me for a few days," Miss Barrios said, drawing my attention to her. She put on a cheerful smile for me, stretching the Tulari mark on her cheek. "It's pretty standard. Before you're dropped into all your classes, we want to make sure you're ready for them."

My eyes narrowed. I'd been here for over a week, plenty of time to "make sure I was ready."

"Come along, Heather," Miss Barrios said, walking away without a second glance to see if I followed.

I turned to Miss Liang, hoping to say something that'd impress her and make her think I wasn't just some *junfly puff*. But the words wouldn't come, and she merely raised a brow at me, waiting with thinning lips.

"I'll be back," I eventually said. I didn't even know why I was promising this, not when I still intended to escape at the first opportunity.

"See to it that you are," she answered with a dip of her chin before heading into her classroom.

I followed Miss Barrios into what I thought was another classroom at the end of the hall, but inside was a series of smaller rooms for tutoring. We sat across from each other in the first one, a pile of books on the desk between us.

"Now that you're acclimated to RSI, the headmaster wanted me to assess your capabilities in certain areas before you join your peers. Judging by how difficult it was to retrieve your academic records, he's thinking you may have some…gaps in your fundamental knowledge," she said.

She picked up a book and began to flip through it while I inspected the desk's wood grain. That was definitely nice adult speak, and what she really meant was the headmaster suspected I was stupid. Now I was about to prove him right.

"Don't worry, though. We'll meet you where you're at and work up to the same level as your peers," she said before placing the open book before me and gesturing to the pages. "Read this aloud for me."

I picked it up and skimmed over what it said, more than aware that I'd lied and told her I liked reading. With my cheeks burning, I did my best. "King Altare co...con... conorred..."

"Conquered," she supplied.

"Conquered," I repeated, "the lands that would b'come Altare through a bloody...what's this word?"

Miss Barrios leaned over and read it upside down. "Campaign." She took the book back when I struggled with "spanned" and "peninsula," mumbling about finding an easier passage.

"I can tell y'what happened. He fought a war to make our country what it is today. And when the common folk got mad about him telling them what to do, he slayed the three great dragons and established the gryphon riders so no more dragons came along," I said, hoping to save some face. "He made Altare safe and prosperous."

"He was a conqueror, though," she said idly, still skimming before giving up and starting with a different book. "That means he started a war to take what wasn't his to become a king. You learn the cleaned-up version in fundamental school."

"Are you sayin' we learn the truth here?" I asked.

She chuckled and waved the thought away. "Nothing so pompous." She happened to catch my squint at the unfamiliar word. "I mean, we don't think *that* highly of ourselves."

With a sigh, she placed the second book aside and folded her hands on the table. "Let me tell you what RSI does believe in, since I see how nervous this process is making you. Everyone is smart in their own way. Nobody knows that more than a graduate of this school. Most of the kids that come to us are either straight from the streets, from the scene of a crime, or turned in by their parents for being 'difficult.' For all involved, getting an education is a low priority. Hells, back when I came through RSI, there wasn't fundamental school at all."

"Which one were you?" I asked quietly.

"Hmm?"

I repeated the question. "Of those three, I mean."

"Oh." There was a little blue sparkle in her eyes, the same color as her Tulari magic. "I came here from the scene of a crime. But that's a story for another time. What I'm trying to say is everyone has a different type of intelligence. I bet you I know where you'd excel." She stood and went out of the tutoring room, coming back with a wooden sphere the size of my head.

It shattered into hundreds of little pieces when she dropped it on the table. I flinched backward at the sudden clatter before realizing it was designed to do that, since it was a detailed puzzle with irregularly shaped pieces that locked together. I looked up at her for permission, and she gestured invitingly before picking up a third book, this one stamped with arithmetic symbols.

I answered her questions while putting the puzzle back together, sometimes counting out answers with the pieces before slotting them back to where they belonged. It helped to have something to do with my hands and a nonthreatening place to put my focus while Miss Barrios judged my progress.

Soon, the city bells were chiming the hour, and a single bell in one of RSI's towers added a ring in a higher pitch to signal the change of classes. Miss Barrios put her hand on the side of the puzzle. "Heather, before we continue, I want you to go take a walk and listen to the conversations out in the halls. Come back with anything odd you hear."

CHAPTER 7
RST'S QUIRKS

I SLOGGED through the chaos of the halls in full class shift. Some groups going downstairs, some going up, but full of chatter in all directions. There had to be a reason why Miss Barrios sent me out to listen. Yet I was jostled around and disoriented by all the noise around me and came back with mere scraps of overheard conversation.

She wasn't too impressed and sent me out again with the next class change. This time, I nearly ran into the Lithosian boy, Fariq, whose face lit up when he saw me. "Hi, Heather. Where are you going? Are you lost?" he asked.

"Uh, no." I didn't know how to explain the task I was given, so I just shrugged. "I'll follow you to your next class."

"Okay," he said, leading me through the maze of other students also heading in their own directions. "How do you like RSI?"

I struggled to focus on his question and also listen in on the pair of girls just ahead of us. They were talking about a project they had to do for a class called Innovation, which I thought was odd enough to deserve getting reported to Miss Barrios.

"It's a school," I sighed.

There was concern on his face. "Is fun, right?" He nudged me with his elbow.

"No?" I answered, puzzled. "You's at a reform school, Fariq. It's not meant to be fun."

He seemed just as confused as I felt for a moment before raising a finger like he was about to make a point. "Other students," he said, "are not great. But learning, I like."

We turned down Aldridge Hall, and he slowed his steps. We must've been nearing his destination. I considered this cheery young man with narrowed eyes, wondering what gave him such pep. "How'd you get sent here?" I asked.

He considered for a moment, like he hadn't understood the question. "How did I...oh! I ask to come and learn from the best, Miss Liang."

Startled, I realized he'd led me back to her class. He nodded to me and turned to the woman standing before her classroom door. Placing his hand flat over his heart, he bowed to her at the waist, inclining his upper half a few inches. He said something in Lithosian in a polite tone, which Miss Liang echoed, down to the hand over her heart, though she didn't bow.

I returned to the tutoring room and told Miss Barrios about that short conversation and the Innovation class. She nodded and just said that I'd done better before consulting a folded sheet of paper. "You'll be going to your elective at the end of the day. It looks like Hawthorne got a hold of you for her backstage team, hmm?"

"She said I didn't need to be as involved in theater if I'm making set pieces. I didn't want to take theater," I mumbled, remembering her talk about how much she loved her time as an actress.

"Everyone takes theater, but we'll ease you into it. One step at a time. You don't just get dropped on the stage. First, you have to practice." She tilted her head thoughtfully. "Just like you don't get pushed into classes."

I nodded, saying, "First, you need tutoring."

She shook her head no. "First, there's something to figure out, like a puzzle." She gestured to the loose wooden pieces in front of me, and I got back to work on placing them in the original puzzle, chewing on my tongue as I considered her response.

"There does seem to be something I'm missing," I said quietly.

"What makes you say that?"

I wiggled another piece into place. It was looking like half a sphere now, with a few pieces poking out from the center, waiting to meet in the middle with their matches. The answer was just out of reach, but it had something to do with the names of the halls, the classes, and students themselves.

"I'm not sure yet." My response did seem to truly disappoint her. Her shoulders lowered. "But...I'll figure it out."

She nodded. "I believe in you. Now, take a look at this book. I think you'll find it easier to read. You like animals, right?" She placed a cheap, spiral-bound book before me, but I lifted it like it was embossed with gold.

It was called *Altare's Native Animal Species*, and I showed her that I could read and understand it.

UNCLE JACE HAD ENROLLED me in five different fundamental schools over my brief academic career, hoping to find a place where the bullying wasn't so bad. I remembered the false hope at each one, as there was no meanness for a week or two. But inevitably, I slipped up and did something weird, or another kid realized I was the one coming to class with that lingering musty smell on my clothes, and the cycle started anew.

For a week, I waited with my fingers clenched for

Carmen's gruff manner to become shoving and demands for me to finish her homework or hand her the clorets I'd managed to pickpocket from some of the older students.

I waited for pretty Sybella Creedmoor to notice me when we turned in for the night and point out that I didn't know how to use cosmetics. Or maybe she'd question why she caught me bathing twice in one day more than once, when I thought I'd caught a hint of mustiness on my skin.

Or at least for some group of kids to pick at Fariq and me as we sat together at most meals, exchanging shy half-conversations between my street slang and his basic grasp of Altarian. Ironically, he'd started correcting some of my pronunciation, and if anyone was bullied, it was him. He kept smiling even with a pair of older boys mocking his accent or when someone "accidentally" bumped into him while his hands were full with books or a tray of food.

Musty devils, I didn't like it here. I'd take Fariq out of this school with me if he didn't keep saying he enjoyed the classes and learning.

No one commented on how I kept circling RSI after classes were over, looking for a door to the outside that wouldn't lock in my presence or a window I could open. I inspected the walls of my cage like any Mouse and didn't stop searching for a way to return to Jackie and the rest of my gang siblings, even though my hope for an easy exit waned with every day that passed.

My first week of classes at RSI came and went without any bullying, just the hints of contempt from a few people, like Sybella and her two close friends. I didn't dare put my guard down, because deep inside, I knew I was too weird for the other kids here not to notice and pick at.

"Okay, Patches, we're going to figure this out," I said in one of the library's study nooks on the second floor. It was very early on a Tuesday morning, after yet another day I seemed to let down Miss Barrios. She kept hinting there was something about the school I was missing, between the classes and the bracelets everyone seemed to wear, but she wouldn't tell me what it was, leaving me to assemble the bits and pieces of hints myself.

The nook I'd first slept in was taken by a few boys finishing a project at the last minute, so I relocated with the chubby cat, spreading out a map of evidence—my schedule and scraps of paper I'd used to write down every individual hint and overheard conversation in my childish handwriting.

When she'd first seen me write, Miss Hawthorne had *tisked* and made me practice with a charcoal pencil held properly, rather than help with painting and assembling the next production's props. Her class was the only one I'd attended, otherwise spending the rest of the time with Miss Barrios in the tutorial room. That was one of the hints I'd written out: different schedule from the other kids.

Patches whisked her fluffy tail, patting my arm for attention. I was sure she liked me special, as she came to see me every time I visited the library, tolerating my squishes and hugs more than the old gang pets I'd had in passing. "Focus, girl. We're almost on to something," I said, squinting at my evidence like it would make the puzzle come together.

Spread around the nook, my hints read:

"Miss Barrios: one of her Littles?" I hadn't overhead anything else about Little or Big anything, but she'd said it with such emphasis to Miss Liang that I knew it was important and capitalized.

"Strange classes." Now this, I had picked up by being in the hallways during class change. The other kids talked about assignments from Innovation, Alchemy, and various foreign languages. None of that was taught in fundamental school.

Nor was "Counter Intelligence," which I'd done my best to write out. I had no idea what that was, though.

"No fights?" This was supposed to be a reform school for some of the worst of the worst, yet I hadn't seen a single punch get thrown. The fact that we had a few peacekeepers patrolling during daylight hours meant little, as fights should've happened anyway. Many of the other kids seemed to *want* to be here, like Fariq, who even insisted he was having fun.

"Names of instructors." The first thing I'd figured out, that the headmaster and five of the instructors had surnames associated with the names in the school and the halls.

"Different bracelets." Most of the ones I'd seen on my peers were copper, but the older kids wore ones with different markings and materials. Fariq and Carmen, the two kids I talked to most, wore copper bands too, but both of theirs had an engraved pattern of wavy lines through the center, while mine was blank metal.

White, gray, and silvery bracelets opened the locks to the school. The instructors and staff members wore those, as well as the older kids with apprenticeships in the city. But everyone had one, and there were variations I hadn't figured out. No one was willing to answer a question about them directly, which led to my last clue.

"No direct answers." If I pointed any of this out, no one would tell me why it was significant.

With a sigh, I turned my attention to rubbing Patches's ears. "I feel like I'm so close to *something*," I told her in frustration.

She meowed and stood, tail straight up as she circled the nook and invited more scratches and rubs. She nudged and nuzzled my hints before taking a bite of my schedule. It was already battered when I pulled it from her mouth, having survived a whole week at the bottom of my sack of school supplies.

It slid in my grasp, reminding me that it'd been folded with another sheet of paper. The letter from the headmaster, which I skimmed, trying to remember the small lesson I'd had with Miss Wilkes over what it said. And then I sat down heavily, squashing one of my paper hints as I read one line a second and then a third time.

"If you have any questions about the attached schedule or just want to talk, I am often in my office. I look forward to hearing what you think of RSI and its quirks."

Here was the headmaster acknowledging that there was something going on here. As I sat there thinking, I realized I had eavesdropped on the kids but not the adults at this institute, except for one conversation by complete accident. Closing my eyes, I focused on trying to remember…

That's right, Miss Liang had said "I'm not here to baby the candidates," and I'd overlooked it because I'd been overwhelmed by everything else.

Candidates for what, though? That small snippet of conversation had brought about two of my clues, so if anyone could tell me what was going on, it was the adults. "You's just helped me. Thank you," I said to Patches, fluffing her up in gratitude. She meowed back and turned to lick her flank.

It was early enough that the teachers were probably upstairs preparing for the classes ahead. They had their own prep rooms that I'd seen but never been in, and that's where I headed once I secured all my written hints into the sack that bounced on my back with each step.

The upstairs entrance closest to the library was guarded by an unfamiliar teacher, who told me it was too early to go to class and sent me back downstairs to eat breakfast. Sighing, I walked along the hallway toward the boys' side of the building and took their staircase up, ditching my sack in the stairwell for now. I'd noticed there wasn't a second teacher here and knelt down, peering out at the one on duty from below eye level and waiting until she was occupied in a conversation with another student.

Once she was distracted, I crept the length of the hallway and put my back to the corner, where I'd be out of her sight. This was the upstairs Irving Hall, with unmarked classrooms and unfamiliar teachers who usually occupied them, there for the upper-level students. I'd seen teachers coming and going from a work room at the end of this hall, so once I caught my breath, I went that way and pressed my ear to the door.

There was a feminine murmur of a few voices within, but I had to twist the knob carefully to open the door as sound-lessly as possible to eavesdrop on what the teachers were actually saying.

They were…complaining, loudly, about a couple of the students. I muffled a snicker as I picked up what'd happened. A "team" of boys had submitted a cheeky project to an unfa-miliar teacher, and she hated how they never took her "sce-narios" seriously.

"You should see some of the newest candidates they've brought us," said Miss Liang's more familiar voice, and I froze. There she was, saying *candidate* instead of *student* again.

"The first year's the hardest," that unfamiliar teacher answered. "You've got to pay your dues like the rest of us before you get the specialists."

"I'm here to teach espionage, not basic language skills," Miss Liang grumbled.

"Of course," came the answer in a tone that was sympathetic but held a note of weariness, like she'd heard this dozens of times already. There was an approaching sound of heels clomping on the carpet, and I glanced around for a place to hide, panicking when I saw that there was nothing to duck behind in the hall.

The door opened all the way, and in the threshold stood a well-dressed woman who stopped short when she saw me. "Um," I said, hunching in immediately. "What is…espionage?" I did my best to pronounce it, but it came out more like "es-pin-oge."

Her painted lips parted, and she barked a laugh, turning toward the room. "Mei, is this student one of yours?" she asked.

I tensed to bolt as Miss Liang came up beside the first woman. She looked surprised to see me before a smile threatened her serious features. "Were you listening in on us?" she asked.

I nodded sheepishly. "Sorry," I murmured.

"She wants to know what espionage is," the other teacher said. "Good eavesdropping skills already. I think she's going to be one of Sasha's."

Miss Liang nodded. "Sasha claimed her day one." She turned to me. "Heather, I think you deserve an answer, so let's go see the headmaster."

"Well done, young lady," the other woman said with a wink.

Miss Liang swept from the room as I flashed a tentative smile before bolting after her. She held a steaming mug and walked much faster than my usual scurry. "Not that we made that particularly hard," she was muttering to herself.

"Miss Barrios claimed me for *what*?" I asked once I fell into step with her. If anything, I was just more confused than ever.

Her lips quirked, but she gave me the most honest answer I think I'd heard until that point. "I cannot tell you. Actually, there are only two people at this school that can, but one of them will now that you've snuck your way into hearing that particular bit of conversation."

"Did I do...something good?" I asked, getting the feeling that both of these women were casually proud of me, even if they had caught me.

"Let's just say you're coming back to my class, just as you

promised," she answered, taking the stairs down at a light jog.

The school was starting to stir with movement as kids prepared to go to their classes and drifted in that direction. We dodged clusters of young women in Hawthorne Hall and turned the corner past the open door to Aldridge Hall, where Miss Liang flagged the headmaster standing out in the hall. He jerked his chin and sent off a student he'd been talking to.

"Good morning, headmaster," she said. "This student has a question. She was eavesdropping and heard a little bit too much."

Both of them turned to me expectantly, and I felt my face redden. I had to say that difficult word again. "Um, what is espionage?" I asked. This time, it was more like "es-pin-age."

"Espionage," she interjected.

He wet his bottom lip and nodded to Miss Liang, who left me with him. He gestured behind me. "Well, I can spare some time for a question like that. Let's go into my office." As I turned around, he also signaled to Miss Barrios, who sat behind the front desk, watching this whole exchange.

He unlocked the door to his office and gestured me inside, clapping twice to awaken the magelight sitting under a shade in a corner. The office was impressive for how much was stuffed in it. The back wall was a personal library, stacked with spines and a few bristling pieces of paper.

Headmaster Radcliffe's desk, overburdened with piles of documents and knickknacks, sat off center, making room for a curio cabinet that I drifted to on instinct. There was only one thing in it, a platinum crown studded with precious gems that sat on a velvet cushion. They glittered up at me, safe behind the etching atop the layer of glass set into the cabinet doors.

My fingertips faltered a knuckle length over the glass. I recognized the spell with a chill. One never forgets what does them in, and even though I'd only caught a glimpse of the double-release spell on Lady Gladbeck's jewelry box, its twin was clearly protecting this valuable with its intricate loops and swirls.

"Come have a seat," the headmaster said. I flinched away from the cabinet, drawing back one of the seats across from his desk and sinking into it. He smiled when Miss Barrios entered and sat next to me. "She's in."

"Finally," she breathed, patting my shoulder.

I glanced between the two of them, uncertain and stiff, not sure what I'd done to merit a private meeting with both of them. Yet Miss Liang had just said only two people could tell me… "What did you claim me for?" I asked Miss Barrios directly.

She blinked once in surprise. "Oh. From the moment we heard about your heist at the Gladbeck mansion, I knew I would be teaching you one day."

I bit my lip to keep in the first thought that I wanted to blurt out. *She's a secretary and a Tulari, what would she teach me?*

"Heather, I want to tell you a few things I've learned about you in the past couple weeks," the headmaster said, drawing my attention back to him.

My eyelid twitched as he sat straight, serious-faced like he was about to strip me down to all my flaws.

"You've spent significant time trying to find a way to leave RSI, despite knowing the function of the magical bracelet you wear. There's something, or someone, on the other side of these walls you feel a need to return to. You have no academic records, which means you were enrolled under a fake name—or fake names—each time you went to a different school in Kaiamear." He ticked each point off on his fingers. "You used to belong to the gang Jace's Menagerie, living outside the Crown's laws."

I broke into a cold sweat the more he spoke. How did he know all this? Had he spoken with Uncle Jace? My nerves warred with a brief kernel of hope—that Jace had come here trying to get me back.

"At age ten, you were given the title of a small, stealthy animal, so amongst your gang family, you were known as Heather the Mouse. You've been involved in quite the lengthy list of crimes the last three years, tallying several thousands of clorets lost from various families and businesses across our fair city. Most have no evidence the Mouse had come and gone, except for a residue of desda powder over where their valuables used to be." He watched me squirm and sink further in my chair, finally granting mercy. "Need I go on?"

"N-no, sir," I said shakily.

"Ask the only question that matters," Miss Barrios urged.

For once, I knew exactly what she was talking about. "How do you know all this about me?" I asked in a small voice.

"Because I'm a spy, Miss Mouse. I am very invested in the practice of *espionage*, otherwise known as the practice of obtaining secret information. It is, of course, also my business to know everything about my students," he said. I was just glad I was sitting down, because I knew my knees couldn't handle the shock that hit me. I merely stared at him, my eyes twice their usual size. "Miss Barrios is also a spy, as are all the instructors here."

I turned in her direction, and she smiled at me. "Let me be the first to tell you that RSI is actually the *Royal Spy Institute*," she said.

CHAPTER 8

PURPOSE

"Everything you've experienced thus far has been a test. From giving you extra time to explore the school, to locking you within its four walls, to dropping you hints to see how long it takes for you to realize something's off about RSI," Headmaster Radcliffe said. "My name isn't actually Arthur Radcliffe. Most of your instructors have fake names as well, otherwise known as aliases."

He shuffled some of the papers on his desk. "You have a choice ahead of you, now that you've reached this point. Everything about RSI is a front designed for us to find young talent to mold into the next generation of spies and informants in service to the Crown. But you don't have to join us if you don't want to.

"We will teach you everything you need to know to be successful at your placement, whatever it may be. We will take your talent as a sneak and teach you ways to be more effective, techniques you would've never dreamed of. But at the same time, you will be magically bound to keep the secrets of RSI and the Crown should you choose to remain here. If you stay, first you will learn acting and self-defense and be tutored privately in your reading and arithmetic skills.

When the time comes, we will place you in an apprenticeship that suits you with one of the guilds in Kaiamear that we're partnered with, where you can learn a trade and earn guild membership and honest clorets. A far cry from the life you used to have."

"But my gang family…" I murmured.

"They've moved on without you," he said, which was like a knife to the chest. I choked on a sudden rush of emotion, threatening to flow like a torrent of tears.

I hadn't returned to my old home or shown up in one of the jails. My gang family thought I'd died to protect their secrets. *Jackie* thought she was alone.

I bowed my head, sobbing. Miss Barrios—if that was her real name—reached over and rubbed my back in soothing circles as I gave in to the grief of my "death." For once, I let her try to comfort me, since I didn't have anyone else. No one from Jace's Menagerie was waiting for me to come home, not even my sister.

"You have a family here now, if you want it. There's no group tighter than the king's spies," she said.

I tensed, pulling away from her touch. She folded her hands back in her lap, and the headmaster cleared his throat. "I know this is a lot to take in," he said. "But now that you know the truth about RSI, you will need to decide tonight about whether you're staying or not. Stay, and Miss Barrios will bind you to the oath. But if you're leaving, she can erase this conversation from your mind since it's fresh. We will find you a placement at a true reform school."

Unexpectedly, I remembered a snippet of conversation with Carmen. *"There's some kind of buddy system we're supposed to have here, but the last person I was paired with ran off to another school."*

That girl had said no when given the same choice. If I did the same thing, I would have a much easier time leaving the next school and returning to Jace and my old place as his

Mouse. I could come back from the dead. But there was a good chance Springfield would then demand the Eye of Acuity from me and I'd be punished just as harshly as I feared before coming to RSI.

"Consider this, Miss Mouse," the headmaster said, interrupting my thoughts on my potential untimely death. "All those skills you've developed to become a skilled thief translate directly to the art of spy craft. Instead of stealing for your gang, you would learn how to acquire assets for the Crown. We need talent like yours for rescuing hostages and tightening weak spots in security. Take it from a professional—you have a gift. Don't waste it by leaving RSI and trying to get back to what you left behind."

You have a gift. I could count on my fingers the times an adult had said something so kind to me.

"My gang won't miss me," I said in a small voice. They'd be okay, because they still had the older kids to look after them and Uncle Jace when he visited.

"But?" the headmaster prompted.

"My sister, Jackie. She's only nine," I burst out. "I promised I'd always care for her, but I can't from here."

Selfishness wasn't an option when I lived with my gang. The only way we survived was by working together and doing our part to beg, borrow, and steal enough for us all to go another day. The choice they presented me was unnatural, because in the end, if I stayed, I would be doing it for myself alone.

But again, it was the only choice. I was protected from Springfield and the Gladbecks here. All I had to do was accept that the gang didn't need me. I could do that, but I couldn't let Jackie down.

The two adults exchanged a glance. "You'll likely have the clearance to come and go from the school in a few months. I'll permit you to invite her here at that time if you put forth your best effort to learn from us," the headmaster said.

Why not now? I fiddled with the copper bracelet, feeling its edges dig into my wrist as I chewed on the corner of my lower lip.

"That's the best compromise I can offer you. Any more information to explain this decision is classified, but rest assured that there *is* a reason why." He spread his hands like it was out of his control.

Something told me I would be encountering "it's classified" as an excuse often. I knew it wasn't his job to reassure me, but in that moment, I just didn't want to feel so selfish and alone for leaning toward staying.

But the other adult here *had* made me feel better in the past, so I turned back to her. "What is a Little?" I asked.

She sought approval with a glance at the headmaster before saying, "What you overheard was a reference to our mentor system. Instructors and staff are assigned teams of junior spy candidates to mentor. I requested to be the Big Sister of your team."

"Why?" I didn't mean to sound so vulnerable, but she struck the thread of emotion most wounded within me.

"When I look at you, I see a young version of myself. Small, hungry...*afraid,* but so talented in the most unlikely of ways. I want to help you exceed your potential." Her smile cut through some of the tension I felt, a beacon of positivity to keep in sight.

"You think I could do it?" I whispered.

"Anyone can be an inf—"

"Headmaster," she interrupted, then cleared her throat. "I think you would make an excellent spy, Heather, and I promise to help you get there."

"It won't be easy," he added.

She nodded in agreement. "It will require hard work and your very best effort. Nothing in this life worth a lick comes easily… I'm sure you know that as well as I do."

I bowed my head, mustering myself to say the words, to

choose myself. "I…I would like to stay," I managed in a small voice.

She sighed with relief and stood, beckoning for me to do the same as she said, "I'm so happy that's your decision. You're going to learn so much from us."

The headmaster rifled through the drawers of his desk and retrieved a blank book bound in black leather while Miss Barrios pulled her wand from the inside of her sleeve. "This is our registry of graduates," he told me, opening it to show rows of names signed on the yellowing paper. "One day, you will have the chance to add your chosen name to it, but until then, your oath to the Crown will be made upon the names of those who came before you."

I swallowed thickly as he passed the book to Miss Barrios, who held it and her wand, which she used to write a detailed spell midair. The headmaster had me place one hand on the registry, raising the other as a mirror to him. Magic created a static charge in the air, lifting the little hairs on my nape as I repeated the oath after him.

"I, state your name, do—"

"No, you're supposed to say your name there!" he cut in with a laugh.

"Oh, right," I mumbled, slowly regaining my confidence after that stumble. "I, Heather the Mouse, do solemnly swear this oath and accept that it is magically binding. I will not repeat the real name or purpose of the Royal Spy Institute to anyone who has not sworn this selfsame oath. Nor will I reveal that I am a spy candidate to anyone who has not sworn this selfsame oath. I will use what I am taught to protect Altare and its people to the best of my abilities, for I am the Crown's agent, one key of many that unlocks each door and ensures no secret goes unheard and no danger goes unnoticed."

I felt a tingling within, and it wasn't just the magic as Miss Barrios put the tip of her wand through the spell she'd made and tapped it on my bracelet. "Welcome, officially, to the Royal Spy Institute," she said.

The copper around my wrist was now marked with the same waves Fariq and Carmen had on their bracelets.

"Now that that's out of the way, there's a secret I want to show you," she added brightly.

"And I should be heading out to walk the halls," the head-master said, extending his broad hand for me to shake. "Con-gratulations, Heather. I look forward to seeing your progress."

"Thank you, sir."

I followed him and Miss Barrios from the room, which he locked behind him. He went one way, and she took me the other, up a flight of stairs and toward the back of the school. Stryker Hall had a row of classrooms on one side, while the other had access to the second-story seating for the theater and the catwalks over the audience and stage.

Down this hall, I'd seen had a single door marked "Deten-tion Rooms," but that wasn't where Miss Barrios took me. She pressed her palm on a different door at the other end, which should've led to the library. The door unlocked for her, and she ushered me inside.

"This room is only open at certain times a day," she told me, clapping to wake two magelights on either side of the space. It was long and narrow, with a lot of blank wall space that'd been decorated unusually. Hundreds—no, thousands—of copper clorets had been nailed to the wall, and many gleamed under the shine of the magelights.

There was no furniture, other than the magelights and a set of three pegboards. The other door out, which I was sure would lead to the library, was nearly concealed under a coating of coins. "Look a little closer," Miss Barrios invited, gesturing to the wall.

I edged toward the clorets with the hesitancy of a thief in

the light of day. Even though they were the cheapest, smallest coins in circulation, this many clorets could buy…

Nothing, I realized, because all of them were ruined. I got a nose full of a sharply metallic scent as I leaned in, inspecting the different things engraved on their faces. "This is our Wall of Achievement, and what you're looking at are individual tokens that represent a great deed."

"There are no names," I said. Only symbols, like animals, or flowers, or even crudely formed faces. No words.

"Each means something to the spy candidate who placed it there, but in the end, it shows you that our work is anonymous. If you stand back, you see a tapestry of deeds completed for the good of the Crown," she explained. I did as she suggested, admiring the shine of the coins. In some places, they overlapped like lizard scales, but the students of RSI hadn't yet covered every inch of wall and—I checked—the floor and ceiling, though a few cheeky individuals had managed to place their tokens in either place.

"What do you need to do to get a token for the wall?" I asked quietly.

"When you go above and beyond, you earn one. Perhaps you will accomplish a few deeds in your time here to add to the wall." She beckoned for me to come to the pegboards, which were covered in strips of parchment. They were labeled across the top. One board for Advanced, one for Intermediate, and the last for Beginners. The Beginner board had three rows of nearly pegged stripes, half of which had writing on them. The other two boards had two rows, but each had some kind of name on them.

"Finally, rankings. These strips are fastened in place by magic, so don't go thinking you can move your team up without earning it," she said with a chuckle. "Your team will be added once it's assembled and named. As you can see, we're still forming teams for our most junior candidates. We can discuss who's available for you to partner with tomorrow."

She faced me. "Heather, listen carefully. Most of the kids we recruit are here for a reason, but raw talent or good grades isn't enough to get you a good rank on their own. RSI's curriculum is designed to be completed in groups because at the end of the day, the best spies live and die by their team."

I nodded slowly. It wasn't too dissimilar to the crews I'd been placed in. Not many adults could be a sneak like me, but I had to rely on bigger, meaner personalities like Cartier and Rozma to do their parts too for jobs to be completed successfully. The most legendary thefts and cons that I knew of were all done with skilled crews of professionals, with Foxglove's deeds being the one exception.

"Your team's ranking affects what jobs the Spymaster will ask of you once you graduate. The majority of our students become informants, comfortably positioned in careers they started from apprenticeships they were placed in through RSI. They never gain clearance to act in a way that endangers them, only authorized to pass along information to the spy network.

"Then you have sleeper agents, who are given clearance to watch for threats to the Crown and act accordingly. They may be waiting twenty years, but they are positioned to intercept dangerous individuals and situations. Usually, they are effective once," she told me. "Many of the teachers here were sleeper agents. Once they blow their cover, they can't go back."

"Which were you?" I asked.

She seemed too young to be here, in her late twenties at most. But I hadn't noticed too many Tulari amongst the other kids here. Maybe her skills were needed for bracelet management or something.

"That's not the most polite question to ask."

"Sorry," I said meekly. "Never mi—"

"Only because no matter what label and role you're given when you leave RSI, you're still a part of the spy network and working toward the same greater good. I was a sleeper placed at the Tulari Academy, but I can tell you about that at another time." She sighed, running her finger down the center of her magical rune. "For me, I wasn't *only* a sleeper, but I wasn't cut out for full-time spy work. Only the best teams get asked to put their identities aside and engage in the truly dangerous aspects of espionage. And the competition to get the Spymaster to notice your team for that honor is fierce. But I believe you can get there, Little, if that's what you want."

I considered her and the boards full of ranked teams, fiddling with the bracelet fit tightly over my wrist all the while. As I traced the new etched lines, I knew I was on the cusp of a great change. "I'm just glad to be here," I said.

Informant, sleeper, or spy, it didn't matter right now, because I was someone with potential to use my talents for a reason. She'd given me a gift I couldn't put into words but felt to my marrow, an injection of confidence and determination that I would later give the label it deserved: *purpose*.

CHAPTER 9

CHALLENGING BY DESIGN

I HAD one more day of tutoring apart from the rest of the students. The next morning during breakfast, I received a new copy of my schedule when Miss Barrios sat in the chair between Fariq and me. We had our little four-seat table toward the back of the cafeteria, which meant there was one more spot for Carmen to take.

"You kept me waiting for *so long*," Carmen grumbled.

"You mean to say, congratulations," Fariq put in.

I was still trying to read all the changes to the schedule when Carmen launched into what she came over here to say. "C'mon, it's obvious this place is hiding things, right? Anyway, I've been waiting a lot longer than everyone else for a partner."

"A partner," I repeated quietly. "Oh. Instead of *friend*."

"Spy teams start as groups of two," Miss Barrios said, gesturing between us. "Since you two are the newest students, you're now partnered."

Carmen twisted her lips, looking about as thrilled as I felt. They couldn't have pushed two more different people together.

Partnership was vital on the streets. This meant that

Carmen was crew, and after my last crew betrayed me, I didn't know if I was ready to accept someone else in that way. But maybe we'd surprise each other and end up making each other better.

"Where's your partner?" I asked Fariq.

He shrugged with a sigh. "I don't know yet. He is different person every day."

I opened my mouth to question that further when Miss Barrios said, "Anyway, teams are assembled over time and shuffled infrequently if there is a conflict. The purpose is for you all to learn to work together, even with personalities that are wildly different from yours. A good spy is nothing without a rock-solid team behind her. Heather, Carmen, you two have almost all of your classes together by design. You're expected to make a joint effort at all challenges, academic and otherwise."

"Yeah, yeah," Carmen muttered.

I went back to reading my schedule. All that'd really changed was that the classes were named properly. "Reading" with Miss Liang was now "Rhetoric and Persuasion," and I would be taking Innovation, Self-Defense, Beginning Lithosian, Alchemy, and my elective, which Miss Barrios had written as "Theater/Art," which wasn't comforting. There was also a space midday for tutoring.

"Where's the spy classes?" I blurted.

Miss Barrios raised a brow. "Hmm?"

"Like…espionage." That word again. I did my best to pronounce it right this time.

She pointed toward my bracelet. "You don't have the clearance to learn anything like that yet. We don't want to teach you everything and have you run away with it, but over time, you'll have opportunities to upgrade your bracelet and thus your clearance. It doesn't stop with you getting the clearance to come and go from the school."

I hesitated before nodding. That did make sense, and it

explained why it seemed like no two bracelets were the same amongst the older students.

I flipped to the back of my new schedule, where she'd written three extra lines. "Oh, those are extra credit for beginners," Miss Barrios explained. "We encourage all teams to attempt three challenges each year."

"What kind of extra credit?" I asked. The challenges read:

1. Deliver a properly coded message to Altare's Spymaster.

2. Make the detention minder's day.

3. Steal Stone's Crown without being caught.

My gaze rested on that last challenge, and I pictured the curio cabinet in the headmaster's office, with the glittering crown on display. I could make that disappear...if I knew how the double-release spell actually worked.

"Improved marks and quicker bracelet upgrades, but that's not all. We won't break up a team that completes even one of the challenges. About half of our teams each year finish only one challenge, but those that get two or even all three done move up in our rankings," Miss Barrios explained. "Once you're older and your team reaches the advanced tier, extra-credit challenges are the type that gain the Spymaster's attention."

My head hurt, but I thought I understood her enough for now. No matter what, I'd be put with a team and, later, an apprenticeship. Along the way, I'd upgrade my bracelet so I could be taught more spy-focused stuff. The labels from there didn't matter as much to me. Street kids had no hope to be placed with a guild, let alone a chance to spy for the Crown, so I was humbled by my luck.

To think in a few short months, I'd have Jackie sitting at this table too. I'd asked Miss Barrios, and she'd told me that RSI accepted kids as young as eight and placed them in fundamental-school-like classes until they understood they were at an institute for spies. It usually took them much longer to figure it out.

Jackie would need tutoring too, but I think she'd take to the school and its unique classes easily, especially theater. She was a favorite back in Jace's Menagerie for a reason, able to strike up a conversation with anyone and bring a smile to their face. But in thinking of her, I pictured the other gang siblings I'd had to leave behind, and my mood fell.

I shook myself from my imaginings. First, I had to do well in the classes and get along with my team, else I wouldn't stay here long. Miss Barrios hadn't said what the consequences were for failure or poor behavior, but I could easily picture the headmaster plucking away the shining future I saw for myself and my sister should I displease him.

The bells chimed for us to head to our first classes. "Well, I'll see you later for tutoring, Heather," Miss Barrios said.

"Okay," I said, and then more faintly, "Um, thank you."

She waved with her fingertips while I turned to realize Carmen was going charging off alone. "Wait for me!" I called, scurrying in her wake.

"Right," Carmen sighed, slowing once I caught up to her. "Well, partner, get ready. Our first two classes are really hard."

I assumed that was her ever-present pessimism and...I was wrong.

Miss Liang greeted me at the door with a nod. "Welcome back," she said.

"Thank you," I murmured. She gestured to the open class-room, and I went inside for the first time, well aware that a dozen of my peers turned to watch me.

"Look who's finally joining us," someone muttered. I located the owner of the whisper as Nessa, who sat in the same row with Sybella and Harper. They all whispered behind their hands together, so I guessed those three room-mates had to be partners.

I recognized other groups of two and three who sat together with desks angled toward each other. The desks were lightweight, slabs of thin wood on four legs, designed to be moved around, and right now, they were in lazy rows at the whim of the students. Each had a textbook and just enough space for a journal to take notes.

Carmen led me to the back of the room and gestured to one of the only desks left, right next to a window still fogged over with frost crystals. I shivered from the draft coming off it, but at least I was next to her if I had questions.

We studied the inauguration speech of the current reigning king, Alonso Cortes, with the other students taking turns reading his words aloud and Miss Liang waiting to correct any pronunciation.

"What's *inauguration* mean?" I whispered to Carmen.

"Shh," she hissed.

Well, maybe she wasn't that much help, but I figured it out from all the promises he was making folk to maintain Altare's greatness, plus the references to his father's rule. It was the speech right before the crown was placed on his head.

The class was mostly lecture on the persuasive elements King Cortes used, and my eyelids grew heavy as the seconds trickled into minutes far slowly than they should've. When class was dismissed at the bell, Miss Liang called my name. "I'll write you a pass to your next class," she said.

I watched Carmen walk out the door to our next class, Innovation, before turning back to the teacher nervously. She handed me a copy of our textbook. "I want you to read a couple sentences aloud since you didn't get an opportunity today in class," she said, pointing out where to start.

It was from a story rather than the speech we'd been studying. I read it over a couple times before working up the nerve to do as she asked. "The butter on the floor caused him to slip and bump his head on the cabinet—"

"Okay, stop, stop." She waved her hands. "This is what

you sound like..." She mimicked me back with my street slang, exaggerating it even further. She sounded like some of Springfield's adults as she said, "The butta on the floor caused 'im to slip and bump 'is 'ead on the cabinet."

"It's not that bad," I said defensively. I know I didn't hear myself as everyone else heard me, but I really tried to speak up as little as possible and, when I had to, measure out the words and really try to say my Hs so I didn't sound like a lazy adult saying my name like 'Eather.

"Heather," she sighed. "We're going to get that pronunciation out of you, all right? That's what I'm here to help you with. Do you realize you sound like you came straight from the streets?"

I shifted uncomfortably and ducked my head. "Well, I did," I answered faintly.

There was a pause, made more awkward since my response caught her off guard. "Oh, I'm...sorry. I just want to help," she said, shuffling around the things on her podium. She quickly wrote me a pass to class, which I handed to my Innovation teacher when I finally found the class in session.

It was impossible to hide my lack of arithmetic skills or how the teacher put me in the back with a workbook for me to play catch-up while the other students spent the time building catapults from scrap timber. This was day two of a week-long project. Carmen grumbled but worked on the project on her own, while Fariq dragged a desk over to mine and plopped down.

"I'll help?" he offered, reaching for my workbook.

"Don't you want to do all this?" I asked, pointing to the open area where our peers were measuring lengths of wood and drawing diagrams. The teacher circulated and observed them, paying Fariq and me little mind.

"Eh." He shrugged both shoulders and rewrote a few equations in neater script for me.

As we worked together through the hour, I realized Miss

Barrios was right. Everyone had a different kind of intelligence. Fariq seemed to have just as much fun teaching me basic arithmetic as the other kids did with their catapults, and he had the patience to get me to understand a couple difficult concepts. For a few unguarded moments, I smiled over at him, happy to see him in his element and grateful that included helping me.

I was thankful to return to Miss Barrios and the tutorial room afterward to give my mind a break. She scratched out some letters while I worked on reassembling the sphere puzzle for a third time, this time trying to finish it as quickly as possible. I left in on my seat, completed, when the bell sounded for class change.

As I'd been warned, Self-Defense required a trip through the girls' hall to change into a short-sleeved, lightweight version of our uniform. The class was for physical education as much as learning self-defense, which I figured out when we were asked to run laps around the gym to warm up.

I lapped Carmen once, which seemed to irritate her. "Just wait until we go to the mats, pipsqueak!" she called after me.

That wasn't exactly comforting to hear from a partner.

The gym was mostly padded, with mats laid out in the center of its broad rectangular surface and more fixed to the walls. We ran around the perimeter, with two teachers watching. I was surprised one of them was a man. Big, muscular Mister Stryker must've been hiding when the peacekeepers made their rounds for the draft. The other kids called him Coach.

The teacher beside him was his wife, and the kids called her Coach as well. Names weren't all that serious or permanent for spies, I was learning. She was small and lean next to her husband. If I had to learn to fight, I hoped I did so from her.

We were partnered from there and given one rectangular length of mat for each pair. I swallowed nervously as I faced

Carmen, only a little ready for her to show me Tosh Zorena up close and personal.

The female Coach came over and spoke with Carmen briefly, causing her to heave a sigh. "All right, come here," the grumpy girl said. "Before you learn to fight, let's go over some basic stretches and exercises."

I breathed out in relief as we sat on the mat together and she led me through loosening up my muscles. "Don't expect me to teach you my family's fighting style. I'm not allowed to use it in class," she muttered. "It's much different from what you'll learn here anyway."

"Got it," I said.

Carmen was the one who dictated what I did in that class. She quickly figured out that, while I was small and fast, I had the upper body strength of…well, a mouse. I practiced on free weights while the other kids spent time with the coaches or sparring with each other.

Sure to be sore tomorrow morning, I was grateful when one coach blew a whistle and sent us out of the gym before the next bell. We had enough time for a quick trip to the bath and to change back into our uniforms before it was time for the next class.

I checked my schedule, recognizing the classroom it was in even with Carmen by my side. We passed by Miss Liang on our way back into her room for Beginning Lithosian, and I stopped short when I spotted a familiar face sitting in the front. "Fariq? Don't you know Lithosian?" I asked.

He smiled and motioned enthusiastically for me to sit beside him. "Of course. Miss Liang calls it *social learning*. I help teach you Lithosian; you help teach me Altarian. Learn better with friends!"

I sat in the open seat next to him, with Carmen hesitating before she took the spot behind me. "That's smart," I said.

"That's why you should join language club. Like class but better," he said. "Oh! My partner, Vance."

Behind Fariq sat a boy with hair so dark it was like ink. His hair was really black, and for some reason, I found it odd, like it didn't match the slight tan of his skin tone. And his teeth, they were far too shiny white when he spread his lips with a charming smile.

He had the kind of jawline that would be defined once he lost a bit of stubborn baby fat and a pair of vivid green eyes shaded by a solid brow. "Hey," he said, fixing his bright smile on Carmen, who actually made a halfway pleasant expression back.

"Hey," she replied, her tone a little higher than her normal.

Fariq had planted a hand under the ridge of his nose, shaking his head incrementally as the two of them struck up a conversation. I'd have to ask him about his partner later. As soon as Miss Liang started class by speaking fluent Lithosian and having short conversations with students she chose at random, I knew this would be a hard class too. I turned to Fariq, who was happy to help me start on a workbook of basic vocabulary words.

It was that class period that solidified my desire to be on the same team as Fariq. He was my lifeline, already proving himself more worthy of being crew than anyone else I'd met so far. Carmen and Vance, I could do without, but they were part of the deal if we couldn't just…choose to partner.

I barely dragged myself through Alchemy, another hands-on class, and practiced my penmanship under Miss Hawthorne's absentminded eye at the end of the day. I fell asleep with the alphabet half-written for the fourth time and woke to the dinner bell.

Musty devils, what a day. I dragged myself to the cafeteria, seriously worried I didn't have what it took to make it here after all. If everything was meant to be challenging by design, I would be a failure because of my lack of basic academic skills and Carmen's refusal to do anything with me unless it involved the gym.

But I wasn't going to give up on day one. I just needed to work up the nerve to have a heart to heart with Carmen, which sounded about as pleasant as a mouse negotiating with a hungry, looming predator.

CHAPTER 10

TOSH ZORENA

It took me a week, but I asked the question. "Will you come study with me in the library? Please?"

"I guess," Carmen sighed.

I packed up all the materials we needed to study for a test in Alchemy and picked out a nook for us to settle in. Her unhappiness was palpable sitting this close to her, and she scowled at the journal pages covered in untidy sprawl that I spread between us.

Since Carmen had pet her too roughly, Patches settled in a purring ball in the middle of my crossed legs, slowly kneading on my thigh. I took comfort from her, as getting Carmen here was only step one of my plan.

The classes were only going to get harder the more I caught a grasp on the basics. If Fariq wasn't in a class with me, like Alchemy, I was destined for failure. So was Carmen, actually, who either did everything alone or just…didn't. Her marks had to be really bad. I didn't have much faith I'd change her mind, but I wanted to pass and get a bigger team, so I was forced to try to talk to her.

But after ten minutes or so of halfhearted quizzing, she made to stand. "I think I got it," she said.

"We didn't even cover half of my notes," I protested. She stood and turned away, so I blurted at her back, "Don't you want to pass this class?"

She glared over her shoulder. "It doesn't matter if I do or not."

"But it matters...if I do..." I protested, which faded to a murmur as her stance went rigid.

Wordlessly, she sat back down and seemed to stare until past the point it got uncomfortable. I ducked my head, focusing on the cat slow blinking up at me. "Look, I guess I never told you..." Carmen crossed her arms and leaned back against the wall. "I'm not going to be at RSI for very long."

"You're not?" I asked. "How long have you actually been here?"

She shrugged. "A couple months. At first, it sounded like a good deal, that I could serve Altare with my fighting skills and become a spy. Headmaster Radcliffe even told me that he admired Tosh Zorena and wanted to learn. Then I had time to think about it, see what changed when I became a spy candidate. I figured out that the school just wants me to teach what I know to the other kids."

"And you don't want to do that," I murmured.

She heaved one of her heavy sighs. "No, pipsqueak, I *can't*. I'm not a master, and I haven't earned the right. One of the core tenants of the art is 'the apprentice shall not misguide the beginner,' and that's what the headmaster and the coaches have asked me to do. And since I said no, they're punishing me by making me learn their style of self-defense in class instead."

I listened to the way a lump got lodged in her throat. Something about this was far more emotional for her than teaching others what she knew. I could've said something, but I just waited, giving her space to vent.

"My father and uncle are fighting on the Storm Front right now," she added, a note of vulnerability in her tone. "We have no other family than my uncle's wife and their three little kids, so I moved in with them for a while. My aunt… couldn't handle me, I guess."

Carmen shrugged like it didn't matter to her, but it obviously did. "So, she sent me here, and I have to stay so my father can find me. When the war with the Rathi is over, he's going to come back and take me to our gym in Zoreen.

"Because of that, I just can't bring myself to care about all the tests and projects and such. They didn't mean it when they said I could be a spy, because if they were serious, they'd have put me on a team already." After gesturing to me and seeing the way my face fell, she pulled her hand back with a visible cringe. "No offense. No one else has been able to keep up with me, either. I should've just pretended I was of age so I could've gone to the Storm Front too."

I didn't take her bitterness personally, but she'd revealed a problem much deeper than I imagined. It was pretty obvious there wasn't another kid at this school that could "keep up" with her when it came to her passion, the art of Tosh Zorena.

"Have you considered that you giving up might be why you haven't been placed with a team yet?" I ventured.

"Sure. But I don't see why it matters when I'm not staying."

"Wars can last for years," I pointed out. Our first war with the Lithosians had been ongoing since before I was a Mouse, some five or six years.

"Yeah, I guess," she muttered, her expression shuttering. I bit my lip, seeing the same tensing in her body language before she exited situations and conversations abruptly.

"Is there… Can I help?" I asked, earning a sharp look. I put up my palms. "I don't wanna make you teach me Tosh Zorena. Look at me, I'm not a fighter." I knew my role as a sneak, to be small and unobtrusive. Fighting wasn't a part of that.

Her brows rose. "You could be."

"What?" I practically squeaked.

"I mean…there is something you can do, if you can find a drum," she said in answer to my earlier question. She made her soft bark of a laugh, a *heh*, at that thought. "They can't keep me from practicing on my own."

I tilted my head and squinted thoughtfully. "Actually…"

THE THEATER SUPPLY room had a few drums and no supervision, so I stole a little potbellied one and rejoined Carmen in the gym. Since it was a weekend, the space was watched by an older student, and there were a few kids on the mats paired up for extra practice. The middle-aged janitor was cleaning the unused mats and the exercise equipment while talking to a pair of eager-looking boys in hushed tones.

Carmen had changed into the lightweight version of our uniform and was stretching as I trotted up to her with a tentative smile and the drum in hand. "You know how to play that thing, pipsqueak?" she asked while bent sideways at the waist.

"Uh…no."

"All right. It's not that hard," she said, kneeling on the other side of it where I'd set it down and sat with it cross-legged. "You play with your fingers and palm in beats of four." She tapped the belly of the drum with her hand flat and alternated with her fingers closer to the side, counting to four. "Now you try."

I did, and my first attempt made little noise. "Hit it! You won't break it," she encouraged. Soon I was playing it properly, chanting beats with Carmen. One-two-three-four. One-two-three-four.

"Okay stop, stop." She waved my hands away from the instrument. "I wish you could just *experience* a training session at my gym. If you're not sparring, you're setting the beat for those who are. It gets your heart pumping."

"I could visit," I said, my voice sounding so much smaller in echo to the drum.

She clapped me on the shoulder so fast I barely had time to flinch before she was hopping to her feet. "You'd better now. Take a couple lessons while you're there with a master. Now—you're going to set a beat for me. The faster you go, the faster I go, and vice versa. Try to shake it up a little bit."

"Okay."

"Start slow, with a second between each beat," she said, launching back into her stretches.

"Got it," I murmured.

I furrowed my brow in concentration to keep my playing consistent for her as her warmup transitioned from stretches to fighting with an invisible enemy. One, two, she leaned back and balanced her weight. Three, a kick that lifted her leg near horizontal to her hip. And four, she hooked that leg back in a sharp motion and threw a punch.

She practiced a few more moves, her movements seeming a little jerky to match the beat I played. When she told me to pause, she was breathing a little heavier and nodding to herself. She stepped back on one leg and lifted her forearm, leaning forward. "All right, I'm ready. Go faster and have fun with it, pipsqueak. I'll match whatever pace you set."

We took identical deep breaths before I worked up to playing a faster pace, and off she went. Carmen flared her wrists and kept both of her arms up, ready to protect her head or middle, while flowing into something that looked more like a dance than a fight. She spun, and there it was, a kick with her heel up toward shoulder height.

She shuffled side to side before bending and lifting her whole weight onto one hand, twisting to kick out with both legs before her feet found the ground again. I played faster, fascinated that her fighting dance shifted to match the beat just as she'd promised.

All the while, her face was split into the biggest grin. She'd forgotten her reluctance and shed the ever-present pessimism in the process of practicing her art, free as a zephyr that twists and spins its way through Zoreen's famously fertile lands.

I recognized in those moments what animal she reminded me of, the kheneas birds that roam the parched lands bordering the deserts of Lithos. I didn't know how I hadn't seen it sooner. They were tall birds, with stilt-like legs and rounded bodies draped in long feathers with even longer necks but, more appropriately for Carmen, known for having poor tempers and a tendency to kick out at any threats with force and deadly claws.

A kheneas wasn't meant to be out on its own as a middle link on the food chain. Their numbers were the only defense against rozash, as even the dumb single-headed serpents knew not to risk the wrath of multiple adult kheneas birds if they didn't want their skulls dented.

Carmen was away from her flock…her family, gym, and the friends she must've made through practicing Tosh Zorena. I couldn't help much with that, but I could make this drum walk back to our room and give her this chance to connect with her past again. Maybe it would help us forge as unlikely a friendship as one between a real Mouse and Kheneas.

"Slow it down," she said, winded. With a slower beat, she practiced blocks and punches until finally coming to a stop, breathing hard with her hands on her hips.

Applause broke out around us. My hands paused atop the drum, and I was surprised to see we had an audience of the other kids on the sparring mats, plus the janitor, cheering on Carmen's practice like it was a performance.

"That's right," Carmen said. Instead of scowling, she lifted her chin with pride.

CHAPTER II

DAVIT'S DAY

I passed my Alchemy test, but the projects and challenges didn't stop there. At least when I whispered to Carmen questions like "What's *converse* mean?" in Innovation class, she'd grumble the answer.

When Miss Liang finally made her way around the class in Rhetoric and Persuasion and asked me to read part of a speech out loud, I sat there nearly frozen and trembling, aware that every eye in the room turned my way. "I...uh... it..." I stammered out.

With an annoyed huff, Carmen loudly started reading instead. The teacher hadn't told her to stop, only jotting something down on a journal she kept on her podium.

In return, I never said no when she asked if I'd help her practice. It became a daily ritual: first dinner, then studying together until she couldn't stand it anymore. Then she'd change and practice her art while I played the little drum for all I was worth, and we both went to bed tired but fulfilled.

The snow flurries outside were transitioning to full howling gales as winter reached the peak of its fury when my carefully balanced routine was shaken up. One evening, an older boy deliberately slapped Fariq's dinner onto the ground and said, "Outta my way, geek."

I trembled while my friend knelt down, starting to clean up the mess. "Hey," I said louder than usual. "He didn't deserve that and you…" I faltered when the bully turned an angry stare my way.

"Don't, Heather," Fariq murmured.

"Oh, you *do* talk?" The boy looked me over with a sneer, then jerked his chin toward Fariq. "How do you know he's not here to spy on us for Lithos?"

"He's not," I answered without hesitation.

"Yet he looks like a desert rat here to take advantage of our innovation lab until someone calls the exterminator," he said, smirking.

It must've been clear by my expression that I thought he'd gone too far with that comment. "My mistake. You two are dating, huh. The desert rat and the street rat, what a match," he mocked.

I reddened in surprise and hurt, for as often as I sat with Fariq, it was because he was safe and nonjudgmental, not because either of us were fostering any kind of feelings. "No. I just know a bully when I see one."

He actually rolled his eyes. "Why don't you forget about all this and come sit with my team? We're Davit's Day. Remember the name. You'll find us on top of the Intermediate chart."

I raised a brow. With the prideful way he said the team's name, he had to be its leader. "And you must be Davit?"

He flashed crooked teeth. "That's right."

"Leave Fariq alone, Davit." My eyelid flickered with my nerves. "You just look like a…a stupid jerk."

He *tisked* and walked away while I bent to help Fariq pick up what should've been his dinner. "Thanks," he sighed. "But now they go after you, too."

Unfortunately, he was right. All my careful wariness of

identifying bullies—sure Sybella would be the first to turn her words into knives against me after I found some peace with Carmen—I'd drawn attention not because of my own weirdness, but because I spoke back to Davit.

And my comeback hadn't even been *good*. I should've called him a musty devil, because he was, with all the energy of a playground tyrant. I identified each of his teammates as the other boys who'd been going out of their way to torment Fariq. Now they whispered snide things in exaggerated street slang toward me in the halls or made sure I bumped into walls none-too-gently.

They were the size of an average team, having five members, and to my dismay, Davit's Day really was at the top of the Intermediate group when I went to look.

Still, it took two days of being a new target for Davit's Day before I started striking back in the only way I knew how. Davit's coin purse disappeared off his belt first, which yielded a disappointing twenty-four single copper clorets. The buddy of his that liked to barrel into me and call me a rat lover had a much more respectable palm full of giant gold clorets, which I was excited for until I figured out that they were painted… fake decoys.

I supposed a respected team in RSI would be smart enough to know my strengths, but I felt a sinking dread as I inspected the wood under the shining paint. "He's not even a Rat," I muttered. If anyone were to be mislabeled as a Rat, it would be me, the street rat, not Fariq.

Up until now, I'd only seen my friend outside of class occasionally, but I followed him the next evening after dinner to talk about the problem we now shared without them lingering the table over from us in the cafeteria. "I have already reported them to the headmaster. Just like all the others," he said with a sigh.

"What? That don't help," I balked. "Squealing will just make them worse."

"Doesn't, Heather. You mean to say it doesn't help. But what is *squealing*?" he asked, leading me toward the stairwell.

"Telling the authorities what they're doing," I said.

He smiled over at me. "Well, you are right. Sometimes they get worse after. But it doesn't matter, because they can't do much to me." As we emerged from the stairwell, he gestured down the hall, where the Wall of Achievement was behind a locked door. Rumor had it that there was another new kid around, which meant that particular room was off limits until further notice.

Fariq headed the opposite direction. "They lose rank if they do more than be annoying," he concluded. "I just ignore. What will come of arguing with a lack of knowledge?"

"It doesn't bother you, what they're saying about you?" I asked in disbelief.

He walked past our Innovation classroom and produced a key, unlocking the way into the next room over and gesturing for me to head inside first. "They don't know this," he said, patting the space over his heart. "They cannot hurt me or take this workshop away."

I clapped my hands to activate the magelight in the room, revealing a space cramped by supplies. I recognized the assortment of boards we used in Innovation to make various things, but also basic metal components like cogs and bolts. Fariq dropped his book bag beside a workbench and withdrew a journal, thumbing through it to the end.

"Are you here often?" I asked, poking around the odds and ends as he retrieved a half-finished project from a bin on the other end of the room.

"All the time. That's why they give me the key," he laughed.

I felt a little bad. As much as he'd helped me in the last couple weeks, I hadn't known where he spent his spare time or thought to ask.

"We do innovation club in here. I would invite you..." He

drifted off as I picked up a few marble-sized spheres of metal and juggled them like I wanted some extra clorets as a street sideshow.

"I get why you haven't. I'm not good with arithmetic." I shrugged and caught the spheres, putting them away in a spare pouch on my belt. The next things I stole were a handful of metal widgets a couple knuckle lengths long with a hole for a thumb and two sharp sides cut into an arrowhead. I already had a distinct plan for those.

I'd never stopped being a thief through my time at RSI. Once my childish impulses to simply take the things I want were reinforced and encouraged by Uncle Jace, it'd become a bad habit to pocket anything I wanted without a thought for the consequences. Especially if they had use to me.

"No. You haven't come to language club," he said.

I almost shrugged again, but even facing away from him, I got the feeling that he cared that I'd blown off the invitation. I wasn't any good at speaking Lithosian, but I'd only gotten started in the class.

Maybe being talented meant less to him than showing up. "Well, I've gotten my fill of art club," I said tentatively.

Miss Hawthorne had made me put the handwriting work aside to help her frantically repair and repaint a giant set piece that'd gotten damaged during practice. Art club just meant I had extra time after classes last Monday to paint more. After it was done, she promised I'd get some time to listen to the theater teacher and spend some time in the acting club…a fate I preferred to avoid.

I sat down across from him, snagging his journal. My eyes widened as I looked at a complicated diagram of a drawbridge, labeled neatly with angles, measurements, and the components needed to make it. Looking up from it, I saw he was halfway through constructing the real thing in miniature and fiddling with the cogs that would allow a wooden bridge to raise and lower.

With his attention captured by the task, I flipped backward through his work, amazed at what he'd planned out and presumably constructed with his own two hands. "Fariq, this is…"

He leaned over, taking the journal back and consulting his notes on the drawbridge. "I know," he said, sounding a little self-conscious. "I'm a geek."

"You're the smartest person I know," I replied.

He paused, gaze flicking up to me. "Really?"

If only he'd meet my old gang family. We'd had half of a fundamental school education between us. I'd never seen work like this before or met anyone with a brain close to the size of his. "Really," I said. "Don't say geek like it's a bad thing. That's what's in here, innit?" I tapped my chest.

He flashed me a playful look. "No, in here." He mirrored the motion back at me. "You have not shown what's in you yet."

I didn't say it, but that statement sank in far more than he probably intended. I spent the rest of the evening thinking about it while he showed off his various innovations, most of which were diagrams, as the creations themselves been taken apart again after they were done. But he had various pieces here and there that hadn't been repurposed into another thing, and I had to admit, I saw the draw for a smart person to create working innovations from scratch and then take them apart again.

Fariq wasn't a Rat. He was one of the only people I'd spent so much time with yet had no one animal to assign to him. What animal was smart, generous, and possessed such a lack of vengeance? I'd need more time to figure it out, but maybe I'd have a breakthrough like with Carmen the Kheneas.

And as I saw what he'd created, I also witnessed an opportunity unfolding before me to have a new set of tools to replace what I'd lost when I was arrested. I'd already found a set of screwdrivers in this room... The school wouldn't miss one.

Fariq had demonstrated a little grabber by attaching its metal jaws on my finger. "Strong, yes?" he asked. "I make a trigger to open these from a distance, with a lattice to extend and retract."

"Fariq," I said quietly, seeing brilliance in the diagram he'd opened to. It looked fragile, but I wanted one. "Can you make another?"

"For you?" He smiled. "Of course."

Maybe he didn't recognize it yet, but I knew what was still inside me: an opportunist, a sneak, a thief. And I was picturing what kind of things I could steal with those metal jaws.

"Do you have something to tell me?" Carmen asked pointedly as we worked together in Alchemy the next day. I was pouring a second compound into our beaker, and she was supposed to be writing down notes about the reaction.

My eyelid twitched. Did I? Did she miss my drum playing that much yesterday?

She made a gesture behind her. "Some clown keeps barreling into you right before this class. Is it on purpose?"

Oh. Today it'd been another one of Davit's friends, the one who liked to imply I loved rats because I was one. I'd slipped a gift into his pocket for his troubles. I eyed Carmen, a little concerned she'd take Davit's sudden interest in me as a chance to use Tosh Zorena against someone. "No, I think he's just clumsy," I lied.

While I'd found the best way to shut someone up was a good ol' fashioned beating, I had to consider that we were still not part of a complete spy candidate team. I didn't want anything to mess up our chances there.

"Hmph. You know I'd defend you if you needed me to, right?" She looked at me pointedly. "You poured in too much, by the way." The scent of burning hair hit me on a delay as the liquid in our beaker smoked out of control.

We hurried to smother the solution before it could coat the whole room. "That's how you make liquid smoke," I murmured, recognizing that I hadn't poured in too much, but rather too little to make a dramatic billow of smoke to disappear into.

I jotted down the results in my journal too, though I was well aware I was barely passing Alchemy even with Carmen's help. Rumor had it anyone who showed a talent in this class would be sent to the Alchemist Guild so fast they had whiplash, as RSI graduates in general had a constant list of alchemical needs, from health tinctures to liquid smoke vials to poisons of various potencies. I was perfectly happy learning the basics of how the trade worked.

"Are you in theater class next?" I asked.

"Yeah. Why?"

"I have to go for the first time, since Miss Hawthorne finished her emergency project." I'd gotten the note earlier, with her instructions to report to Miss Stone's theater class rather than the art room. It might be more bearable with my partner there. "Anything I should know beforehand?"

"Well…it's one of the only classes with kids a lot younger or older than us. You know, for variety in casting." She shrugged. "We're in the middle of practicing for *Arrow in the Knee*, so you won't have to do all that much."

Having not much to do was more of a curse than a blessing, as the strict Miss Stone had me sit up in the front row of the theater and watch the actors rehearse while she stopped them occasionally to deliver feedback on line delivery or body language. All I could focus on at that moment was how the leading actor was one of Davit's friends, a young man named Wyatt, who was well-liked by most of the kids, even though the times I'd seen how he sneered at Fariq made me simmer with irritation to have to watch him pretend to be someone else for an hour.

Miss Stone sat next to me, so I had to sneak Wyatt a gift in his book bag when she was up on stage, deep into pantomiming how an adventurer would react to having an arrow shot through their knee. By the time she was back in her seat, so was I, my face arranged in studious innocence.

When we were dismissed for dinner, the whole Davit's Day team sat a table away again. Carmen had decided to sit with Fariq and me tonight, already muttering something about training. She seemed unaware of the way I watched the other table to see if Davit and his other two friends noticed what I'd slipped into their pockets or coin purses in the dinner line. I figured it wouldn't take too long.

One of the boys smacked his leg while laughing at a joke from Wyatt and then yelped. He reached into his pocket and withdrew one of the pointed metal bits I'd lifted from the innovation workshop, the one with a thumb grip and two sides sharped to form an arrowhead. It was stained with a bit of his blood.

One by one, they checked themselves for the bits, and I started to snicker. The bits were heavy enough to shred through pocket linings with some time and luck, and one had gone down a boy's pant leg.

Davit looked up and noticed me laughing at his team's expense. He slapped his palms on his table and stood but, in the process, brushed his coin purse against its side, and a bit shredded through the bottom, scattering a couple clorets on the ground. I muffled a harder laugh. For a moment, he looked down with a confused crease between his brows at the clatter of metal before extending a finger at me accusingly. "Think you're funny?" he demanded.

Fariq froze at the angry tone. I suddenly didn't find the situation quite so amusing with Davit charging over with a murderous expression. I stood, palms going up, an excuse on the tip of my tongue when he grabbed my shoulders.

"Hey, let go of her," Carmen barked.

"She's just coming over here…" He grunted as I panicked, trying to squirm out of his hold. He caught a hold of my cloak even when I slipped my shoulders from his grasp, trying to drag me toward his table and his four buddies.

Carmen stood, cracking her knuckles. "Wait, no," I protested, seeing the eagerness glimmer in her eyes before she was in motion.

Instead of going around the table like an average person, she took a couple steps back and then used the wooden surface as a springboard for a cartwheel that ended with her kicking Davit's shoulder. He cursed and released me, putting his fists up when she landed on her feet and twisted to put her weight on her back leg, one forearm raised in her usual ready position.

I scurried away before I could get caught between them. When he punched, she swatted the blow away with a swipe of her hand. He advanced on her, and she smirked, letting him try to punch her again. This time, she twisted out of the way and seized his wrist and arm, using his momentum against him. In a blink, she had him down on the ground, flat on his back, and was in the process of pinning him with her forearm under his chin when a shrill whistle pierced the air.

"You two, knock it off!" It was the pimple-faced peace-keeper, rushing over with his baton gripped white-knuckled in both hands.

Carmen left an embarrassed Davit to get up on his own and brushed off the knees of her uniform. "It's fine, I already won," she said.

CHAPTER 12

DETENTION

The headmaster saw us one by one that evening in his office, and by the time I sat across from him, he was looking rather annoyed as he held one of the sharp metal bits between us. "This came from the innovation workshop," he said. He sniffed and dabbed at his nose with a handkerchief. I'd noticed his nose was redder than usual.

"Yessir," I murmured.

"But this one in particular is one of five found in Wyatt Freeman's book bag. Embedded in his journal, in fact," he stated.

Couldn't happen to a nicer person, I thought sarcastically.

"Young lady…why was this necessary?" He tossed the bit upward in exasperation, and it landed tip-down in a stack of papers. Oops. Hope those weren't important.

Silence stretched between us as I inspected the grain of wood on the side of his desk, my leg shaking with some of my internal agitation. I didn't mean to squeal, but… "They were being mean to Fariq and accusing him of nasty things because he's Lithosian and likes Innovation class a lot," I admitted quietly. "They were running into him on purpose, throwing his food on the ground, just keeping it small to preserve their team rank. And the school wasn't doing anything about it, even though Fariq squealed."

"So, this was your response?" He gestured toward the bit with a raised brow.

"I told them to stop first, and they just called me a rat lover and started doing the same stuff to me," I told him with a helpless shrug.

He pinched his brow. "*So,*" he said with extra emphasis, "you put sharp pieces of metal in their things."

"Yessir." Though usually I was much more creative. I didn't share how I'd tormented some of Springfield's adults in the same way in the past, slipping them unpleasant gifts like live centipedes in their pockets or scooping a mound of ants with their shoes for being mean to my gang siblings. But the stakes were higher then, and I made sure to never get caught.

He mumbled under his breath as he swiped at his nose with the handkerchief again, "Every child is a blessing, and a work in progress." Then, more directly to me, he said, "Heather, if you want someone to learn to change their ways, the discipline has to fit the infraction."

I mouthed the word *infraction* to myself, making a mental note to ask Carmen what it meant later.

"For example, let's say we caught you cheating on a test of your arithmetic. You took the answer key off the teacher's desk," he said.

"Okay," I said with an eyelid twitch. Had they caught me doing that last week, or was this really just an example?

"What do you think would happen if you were caught?"

"You'd be really mad?" I asked meekly.

"No," he sighed. "Discipline-wise."

"I'd fail that test."

"What else?"

"I'd...need to talk to you about it?" When it looked like he was going to encourage me to keep answering, I added on, "And I'd have to take the test again."

"That's about right. It wouldn't be fun, but you'd learn not to do that again. Now, if I, say, randomly put sharp bits of metal in your pocket, coin purse, or book bag, you wouldn't understand I was disciplining you for cheating on an arithmetic test, would you?"

"No, sir," I mumbled.

"In truth, we have already disciplined several students about Fariq's placement at this school. Miss Liang has volunteered to come in this weekend and teach Davit's Day a class in respect for our differences. She is highly effective." His lips turned down. "In the meantime, you, Fariq, and Carmen will be going to the detention rooms tomorrow rather than attending class."

"But he didn't do anything wrong," I protested. "Just punish me and Carmen."

"Then you owe him an apology, don't you?" he replied.

He took a jerky breath and then sneezed into his handkerchief. "Darn winterbog," he said. "Unless you have any questions, you're dismissed, Heather. Stay out of trouble."

"Yessir." I was eager to get out of this room and catch Fariq if I could, pretty sure he was assigned detention because he'd taken me to the innovation workshop in the first place.

Aldridge Hall was empty except for one of the usual evening peacekeepers who patrolled the front of the school. I heard her sniffling too as I turned heel and headed back to my room. If these adults, who were allowed to leave the school when they weren't working, were already starting to get sick, it was only a matter of time before they tracked in the mix of pollen and mold that made the winterbog and I got sick too.

Carmen had already turned in for the evening, asleep with her back to my cot. I got comfy under the covers and went limp, thinking of Jackie. While I was mildly allergic to the winterbog, she was always miserable around this time of year. I hoped someone had made her some tea from the stash of sachets I kept hidden under our pallet.

I went to sleep heartsick.

AND I WOKE up with a stuffy nose. "Musty winterbog," I muttered.

Though I looked for him, I didn't see Fariq at breakfast. Instead, I sat with Carmen, who shifted with restless energy. "Did you see how I took that guy down?" she asked for the third time.

"Yes, you were very impressive and saved me. Thank you," I said dutifully.

"I'd have had him begging for mercy if they didn't break up the fight so fast," she complained.

"What is *detention* anyhow?" I asked her, blatantly trying to change the subject at this point.

She looked at me like I'd sprouted a third eye between my brows. "C'mon, you're joking, right? You should know what detention is." I shook my head no, and she released a little *heh* at my expense. "It's where the bad kids go when they mess up."

"But...*we're* the bad kids." I gestured to our surroundings.

She scoffed. "Where kids in RSI go when they need to be taught a lesson. It's just like in fundamental school. You punch a kid who tried to steal your lunch money, and you go to detention. Then you get more detention when you punch the other kid there for being too mouthy."

I blinked at her for a couple moments. That was far too specific for it not to be something she'd done in the past. "Do you know why they keep referring to detention as 'the detention rooms,' then?" I asked.

"Oh, yeah." She waved a dismissive hand. "You'll see when we get there. I hate that place."

I shrugged to myself and checked my schedule, which had the three extra credit challenges written on the back. *Challenge two: make the detention minder's day.*

I figured I'd know what that meant when we got there too. Carmen and I walked together, and while I was dreading what was to come, she seemed carefree as she shadowboxed her way to the detention rooms.

We entered a smaller space than I expected, just enough room for a desk for the detention minder and a single chair pressed up against the wall. There were two doors on the right side of the room, one marked as the entrance and the other as the exit. Standing there waiting for us was Fariq, his back turned, and Vance, who fixed a perfectly sparking smile at us as we came in. I eyed the latter boy with confusion. Wasn't his hair black? It shone brown with a few golden strands by magelight.

"Why are *you* here?" I asked him.

He shrugged. "Sounded like fun. Did you know you can choose to take on the detention rooms at any time? Besides, this is the first time I think my partner has *ever* gotten in trouble."

Fariq stiffened next to him, shooting over a dirty look. *Musty devils,* he was mad at me. I shrank in on myself and turned as the detention minder cleared her throat. I tried not to stare—she was quite elderly, with a liver-spotted scalp visible through her thinning hair. She was the age where she should be knitting peacefully by a fire, not working at a reform school. In a thin voice, she said, "You kids are in for just one day. If you clear all the rooms, you can leave and get back to class early, else we'll come and get you right before dinner. Good luck."

She gestured toward the entrance with a wrinkled hand.

"Um, excuse me," I said. She didn't seem to hear me, so I repeated it louder. "What could we do to make your day?"

The question seemed to annoy her. With a huff, she gestured behind her. "Set a new record time," she answered. On the wall over her head was a small chalkboard with a list of six names, plus a time of four hours, thirty-six minutes, and twenty-nine seconds. When she lifted a stopwatch, it all came together in my head.

She started the time when we filtered into the first room, a small box of space decorated like a lavish sitting room decorated in shades of brown and gold, complete with drapes over a window that looked into what must've been the next room. There was a couch, side table, and a scattering of odds and ends placed on it.

Vance dropped onto the couch with a smirk. "All right, who's been here before?" he asked.

"Me," Carmen answered. "Doesn't look much different from the last time."

"How many rooms did you get through?"

She lifted a shoulder. "Just three. But I was on my own."

"What's all this?" I finally asked.

"Well, pipsqueak, there are ten rooms, and if we work through the puzzles in all of them, we get to leave early," Carmen explained. She opened the drawer atop the side table and rifled through it, retrieving a slip of parchment and handing it to me.

Clue 1: I tell the truth, but only in reverse. What am I?

"In the meantime, all the teachers know we're here," Fariq said tightly. "Every class we miss is double the work when we return."

My shoulders curled in. "I'm really sorry, Fariq. I don't know why you're being punished with us."

"The first clue's answer is *mirror*," Carmen interrupted, picking up a big, ornate hand mirror with a crack running through its face. She flipped it over and pointed to a screw on the back. "There's a secret compartment in this one. Anyone here have long fingernails?"

Wordlessly, I handed her the screwdriver I'd secured to my belt.

She looked down at it and laughed in disbelief. "You just…have this?"

"Did that come from the innovation workshop too?" Fariq asked, turning to face me at last. "Heather, why? I trust you and take you there, and this is what I get?" He gestured to where we stood.

"Yes," I said. Standing toe to toe him like this was hard, and I couldn't bring myself to meet his gaze, for him to see the truth of me. "Usually I don't get caught." *Or have a partner eager for a fight sitting nearby.*

"That's your answer?" he scoffed.

Meanwhile, Carmen sat beside Vance, the two of them pretending to look at the mirror.

"Well…yeah? I wanted to force Davit's Day to leave you alone." I sniffed and rubbed my nose on my sleeve. Talking only aggravated my stuffiness.

"I told you to ignore them. Now is going to be so much worse…again. Like kicking a sapstinger nest," he grumbled.

I knew of sapstingers from my books. Though they preferred to make their nests of wood pulp in trees, they were a real nuisance in Lithosian villages, where they'd build colonies on the side of rooftops or directly on clay structures.

"Then I'll do worse back," I promised. "I've made grown adults stop messing with my…friends."

He made a frustrated gesture with both hands. "This isn't about getting even! You go against my wishes and get me in trouble!"

"I'm really sorry," I murmured, bowing my head rather than look at him angry.

"If I may," Vance said, drawing a look from both of us.

"I think Carmen had the best approach to this problem. Sometimes you gotta punch a mouthy kid to get him to shut up."

"That's what I'm saying!" Carmen exclaimed, elbowing him none too gently.

He winced and rubbed his arm. "Besides, if we want to get out of here anytime soon, we gotta work together."

Fariq heaved a sigh, seeming to deflate. "What is going on with all this?" He gestured to the room. "I do not understand."

Carmen drew both of us over to the couch to look at the arithmetic problem hidden in the secret compartment in the mirror. "There's a series of clues like the riddle, and problems like this, hidden around this room. We have to work through them all to find the key to the next room, which will have a different theme. Like I said, there are ten rooms, but if we work together, we should be able to get through all of them. I think they change out the problems and clues occasionally, but I should be able to get us through the first three rooms pretty easily."

"See? I told you this was fun," Vance said. "Plus, we don't have to go to class."

Scowling, Fariq grumbled, "Let's get this over with."

I doubted I'd be much use to the group, but I saw a place for myself as Carmen walked us through the whole first room mostly on memory. I felt like I could solve the riddles if she wasn't spoiling the answer within a moment after reading them out loud. We turned the room over, not even the couch cushions going untouched, as the key to the next room was hidden within the fluff of one.

"Interesting. Last time, it was stuck to the bottom of the table," Carmen commented.

Fariq didn't crack a smile as we worked through the second room, this time with less of her help. Since Vance had claimed the stool to the side of this area, which was reminiscent of a healer's office, complete with dulled tools and empty jars, I handed my journal to him.

"What's this for?" he asked.

"Take notes," I said. I recognized that he wouldn't contribute otherwise. "The order the clues are in, what the riddle answers are...where the key is. Just in case we come back trying to set a record."

"Why—oh, you actually care about those silly challenges?" He flashed a grin I'm sure was meant to be charming.

"I need the extra credit," I mumbled. "And I want to learn esp—err, spy stuff."

Besides, I imagined it was frowned upon to pick the locks, which I was sorely tempted to do as we worked together with a stilted lack of conversation. I had no doubt we'd make it through ten rooms of this, but the fun was sucked right out of the air for me by Fariq's silence. It wasn't that he was seething angry, but he did seem defeated in a way I'd never seen before, and such a look didn't suit him.

I'd been a bad friend, and I didn't know if he'd forgive me. But between us, we unlocked the next door and the next with the bells signaling a class change in between. On habit, I kept a rough time in my head, thinking we were about forty minutes into the second hour when Carmen got frustrated by the unfamiliar layout of the fourth room.

"You help, for once," she barked at Vance, taking the journal from his hands and pushing him toward me.

I glanced up at him, not quite meeting his gaze either. "You good at riddles?" I asked.

My eyes were starting to water. We were in a mini florist shop, with well-tended blooms all around and the pollen to go with them. Vance took the current riddle from me and hummed.

The clue read, *I'm the belle of the ball and delicate as a lady's hand. What am I?*

"Not one for plants, huh," he said, walking over to a hanging pot full of creeping vines. The flowers were shaped like little upside-down bells, with pink tongues sticking out toward the sky. I could see the pollen from here.

In answer, I sneezed. "Winterbog," I said with a sniffle.

"Ah. I know of a nice herbal blend for it. Just remind me after dinner," he offered. He pulled the vines aside carefully and withdrew another clue, which he passed to Fariq to solve.

Fariq lifted his chin and seemed ready to say something before thinking better of it with a shake of his head.

"There's a whole alchemy lab of possibilities in this room, actually," Vance commented.

Carmen glanced up from her notes. "Are you good at that class? A certain someone is terrible with her measurements." Her sharp look cut toward me.

"You could say that," he answered. Evasively, I noticed.

"There's hope for us after all, pipsqueak."

I bobbed my head in agreement. "What kind of things could you make from the flowers in here?" I asked him.

Vance toured the room, touching the pots that held various flowers as he named different potions and tonics. The purple tulips could be a part of a sleeping tonic, the white bells a main ingredient for a "poultice for minor abrasions," which I later realized he meant to say *for scrapes*, and by the end of the row, he grinned down at a couple delicate, flat-faced flowers that were brown with bright blue tips. "And a real find, coro de mare, which can be distilled with a healer Tulari's magic to make an invisibility potion."

"Really?" I asked, suddenly eager. "Like, it can turn someone invisible? I didn't even know that was *possible*."

He grinned. "Yeah, you'd be surprised what a talented Tulari alchemist can make."

"Know many of those?" The question came from Fariq, who raised a brow with obvious disapproval over at his partner. Vance's smile faded.

"I used to," he answered.

I glanced between them and made a mental note to ask Fariq what that was about, if he ever trusted me again.

Thankfully, we left the flowers behind, and my nose stopped itching from the direct presence of pollen. We'd figured out our strengths by this point. We kept Carmen on note-taking duties, while I worked with Vance on most of the riddles. He was...clever, actually, more so than I'd originally thought.

Between the four of us, we were able to solve all ten rooms, but my mind was exhausted by the end when we stumbled out of the exit to find the detention minder leaned back in her chair, fast asleep.

"Ma'am?" Vance said, going over and tapping on her desk. "We're done, ma'am."

She woke mid-snore and peered up at him blearily. With a soft "oh," she took up the stopwatch. "Five hours, twenty-seven minutes, and twelve seconds. You kids might as well go get dinner," she said. "Congratulations on finishing the detention rooms. Now, don't come back."

CHAPTER 13

LANGUAGE CLUB

Perhaps to continue my punishment, the next day, I had my tutoring period without Miss Barrios, who worked up front while I struggled with two days' worth of assignments. My teachers had assembled everything I'd missed yesterday in a neat packet, and this felt like the true burden as I spread it across one of the smaller tables in the cafeteria, eyelid twitching as I considered what to tackle first.

I was alone in this big space except for the janitor, who was mopping and cleaning away any crumbs left behind on the tables around me. He wasn't the only janitor at this school, but he was the one I found most memorable, as a man who was of age to be recruited to fight and his usual accompaniment of a student or two who wanted to talk to him.

After cleaning up the area under my feet, he said, "You seem distressed, miss."

I lifted my gaze, head in my hands as I tried to pick a place to start on my schoolwork. I didn't know why I was surprised he'd decided to say something to me; the other kids seemed to like him. My lips quirked upward at an uncertain angle; I wasn't sure if I trusted him yet.

"I missed a lot of work yesterday," I mumbled.

"Ah, out sick?" he asked, a look of sympathy creasing his forehead. Even though Vance had given me some kind of tea for the winterbog, I was still stuffy.

My shoulders lowered a notch. "No, sir. I was in detention." I expected his sympathy to evaporate like morning dew, but he kept looking at me like something was wrong.

He set his mop's handle against the wall and had a seat across from me. "What happened?" he asked.

As soon as I reluctantly started telling him the story, it all fell from my mouth like a flood. How Fariq was getting bullied and the school didn't seem to be doing anything about it. What I'd done to get back at Davit's Day and how it got back at me instead.

"I got one of my only friends in trouble," I told him. "I acted against what he wanted and took advantage of his access to the innovation workshop. He didn't want to talk to me at all yesterday, even though I said sorry." The corners of my eyes stung, and I sniffled, pretending it was the winterbog as I swiped at my nose with a rag.

Sharing all of this with a stranger just made me realize my anxiety wasn't about all this schoolwork in front of me. I was more worried that I'd pushed away one of the nicest people I knew. If Fariq had second thoughts about me, he wouldn't want to be a part of the same team…and I was starting to see my future at RSI as being a team of me, Carmen, him, and Vance. I didn't really know anyone else here.

The janitor rubbed down the path of hair that framed his mouth, pulling the sagging skin of his cheeks tighter. "It sounds like you tried to help your friend in your own way. Have you considered he just needs some time to recover from all this?"

"Well, yes…" But it didn't stop the fear that I'd messed up forever and that there was no coming back from it.

"You just need to give him space for now. Seems you've

got enough to occupy yourself with, hmm?" He gestured to the work I'd laid out on the table between us.

I sniffled again, glancing down with a sigh. "You wouldn't happen to know arithmetic, mister?" It was a long shot to ask a random adult, but I always needed help with arithmetic. It was my weakest subject.

"It's Manny," he offered. He stood and brought his chair around to my side.

I introduced myself a little sheepishly, considering I'd told him my problems before my name. "You won't get in trouble for taking a break?" I asked as he took up the sheets of arithmetic work I was supposed to complete by tomorrow.

He waved dismissively. "I like to help students where I can. Where's your quill? Let's get started."

Fariq was nowhere to be seen during dinner, but I still sat at our usual table next to the Davit's Day team. I was aware of their dirty looks and would've moved to another spot if Carmen hadn't slid into the seat next to mine. She faced them directly and cracked her knuckles one at a time. She didn't blink as she stared them down. "Hey, pipsqueak. Want to help me practice tonight?" she asked.

"Can't," I answered. I took a sip of tea prepared with one of the sachets Vance had given me, breathing a sigh of relief when I practically felt the pressure in my head loosen. "I've got club tonight."

She slanted me an irritated look. "Art club meets at the end of the week."

"Different club," I murmured. Maybe it was a bad idea, but I thought maybe I should finally attend the club that I'd been blowing off since I'd met Fariq. It was another hour in

Miss Liang's room, and I didn't know what to expect other than my friend found it fun.

But he also found Innovation class fun, so maybe he wasn't the best judge when it came to academics I'd enjoy. Still, I finished my food and brought the mug with Vance's tea with me as I scaled the stairs and went into Miss Liang's classroom.

I'd already stepped inside when I saw only two people in the room, eating dinner and chatting in Lithosian. The teacher herself and Fariq, who turned a frown my way as my arrival interrupted whatever they were talking about.

"Um, I'm here for language club," I said, already moving to take a step backward and hooking a thumb over my shoulder. "I could come back later…?"

Fariq's mouth popped open in surprise, while Miss Liang put her hand up. "You're just a little early. Welcome, make yourself comfortable," she said.

I looked over at my usual place at the back of the room when a chair scraped the ground. Fariq dragged one over to join him at the teacher's desk and gestured for me to sit. "You're in for a treat tonight," he told me as I eased into it. His usual smile and enthusiasm was starting to show on his face.

"Yeah?" I murmured.

"Miss Liang is the best codebreaker in Altare. A true master," he said, gesturing toward the teacher now making sure to finish her meal quickly. She waved away his words with a little shake of her head. "She's teaching how to write in code tonight."

I started to perk up too. This was a skill I was supposed to know, judging by the first challenge written on the back of my schedule: *Deliver a properly coded message to Altare's Spymaster.* But it hadn't come up until now, and I wasn't sure which class it applied to.

"Since you're still learning Lithosian vocabulary words, I'll teach you a basic cypher," Miss Liang promised.

"What's *cypher* mean?" I asked automatically.

"You'll see," she said.

Since I was early, I ended up helping Fariq set the desks and chairs up in a circle while other kids filtered in. There were a good thirty people in the room by the time Miss Liang called the club into session. Immediately, everyone was partnering up and chatting in a different language. Fariq turned to me and said, "Usually we practice speaking. I learn a lot of my Altarian here."

"I've learned," Miss Liang corrected from behind him as she made a loop around the room.

"I've learned a lot," he repeated. "When you know more Lithosian, we can practice in language club."

"Yeah." I flashed a shy smile, realizing he was suggesting we'd be talking to each other more in the future. He didn't seem mad at me, here in his element. "That'll be great."

Miss Liang wrote in the Lithosian language on her chalkboard as Fariq explained, "Language is a key part of sending messages in code. Miss Liang is an expert because she knows seven languages and how they apply to the most complex cyphers."

"Wow," I murmured. I had enough trouble with one.

He beamed. "I tell you, she's the best."

"She's why you wanted to study at RSI, right?" I asked.

He glanced away from me with a shrug, something unknown crossing his expression. "Ah, sort of. She was one of many Altarians that came to support my village after it was hit by a rozash attack."

I looked at him with blatant curiosity. Rozash were the monstrous flying snakes that Lithosians tamed and rode to battle against Altare's gryphon riders. But I had always assumed he was Lithosian due to his accent and appearance. Had his village been attacked by their own people?

Before I could ask, Miss Liang called our attention to the board, and I followed everyone else's lead in taking out my journal. What followed was a short lecture that was beyond me, but I still took notes to reference when I knew Lithosian better.

As most of the older kids worked out the coded message she'd written on the board, she drew me over with a few others I recognized from my classes and instructed us on writing a basic cypher. I quickly picked up that we were doing the same thing as the older kids and Fariq but using the Altarian alphabet, unscrambling a second message she'd written below the first from gibberish to something readable by shifting the letters back three in the alphabet.

The message was: *When you can read this, write your own using the same cypher.*

It took me nearly the whole hour to figure it out, and I had two words scrambled when we were done. Since I was disappointed that I didn't get to finish, I decided to practice later. The Spymaster was getting a coded message from me, whether he, or she, liked it or not, because I needed that extra credit and the chance to upgrade my bracelet faster.

I packed my things in a hurry and hustled to join Fariq as he left the room. "That was fun," I said.

"Just like I told you." He slowed his pace so I could catch up with him, but I quickly realized he was heading to the innovation workshop. Maybe he was always in there by evening, being a self-proclaimed geek. A habit that made him a target for folk like Davit's Day.

"Well, good night," I said, passing by him like a shadow when he dug for the key to the workshop. I knew if he let me in again, I'd be tempted to steal more odds and ends that could come in handy later.

He hesitated for a moment before nodding and echoing, "Good night."

That went better than I expected. I just needed to tell Miss

Hawthorne that I was switching clubs and hope she didn't panic from losing my extra help with painting and assembling props once a week.

I fiddled with my empty mug, feeling almost clear of the winterbog ick from the last few days. I'd need to thank Vance when he next decided to reappear, because his tea had worked like magic.

A long meow drew me out of my thoughts, and I blinked down at Patches, who peered around the corner of the stairwell with her mouth hanging open. "What?" I laughed.

She chirped a few more times, darting forward to wind around my legs. When I bent to pet her, she moved away, looking over her shoulder when she was a few paces away. I followed and stooped again, just for her to do the same thing. "Okay, you want me to follow. Got it." It wouldn't hurt to spend some time in the library working before bed, since that was where she led me with her bushy tail straight in the air.

She slid around the curtain to the first-floor nook where I used to sleep. I found her sitting when I slipped in after her, and she patted a paw toward a pile of cushions moved to the side of the small space. It was almost like she was telling me to sit, and once I did, she turned tail and left.

"Odd," I mused. I pulled out my journal and some of my work, sighing when the written words seemed to blur. It felt like I'd worked all day and was still more behind than usual.

A muffled meow had me looking up. Patches returned looking all too proud of herself as she tilted her head and dropped something small and furry onto the open pages of my journal. I thought she was being a typical cat, bringing me a dead prize. I recoiled with a gasp.

The mouse stood on its back paws and mirrored my flinch. "Oh, you're alive." I breathed a sigh of relief and tentatively held out my hand toward it. Its little whickers flickered as it sniffed my fingertips.

Patches purred and snuggled into my side, still looking

smug. "I'm not going to eat it or anything, you little hunter," I told her. She stopped purring immediately, ears flattening. Again, I had that uncanny feeling that she understood me.

I didn't know what to do with the mouse, actually, but giggled as it climbed into the scoop of my hand and licked the salt from my skin. It was a tiny ball of fluff and mostly brown, with a twitchy nose and a white star between its round ears. It reminded me of the field mice that roamed Kaiamear's streets, but they were far too skittish to be held like this.

It lifted its head and met my gaze with its dark, beady eyes, rising to its back paws again as it seemed to inspect my face. "Hi," it squeaked in a small voice.

I yelped and dropped it, flinching away. "Ow!" It rolled to its feet and rubbed its head a few times with a paw.

"You…" I looked over at Patches, who watched this inter-action with her tail flicking. "You talk?"

It scampered back onto my journal, standing up and waving its paws in my direction. I held out my hand again, this time lifting it closer to me when it climbed on. "I talk, yes yes," it squeaked. "Patches say you lonely. Need friend."

The cat stirred and trilled.

"She take long time. Search high and low," it apparently translated. "But find you a friend, me, hi hi." It spoke so quickly my brow bunched up as I tried to follow what it was saying.

"Hi," I echoed before bursting into a huge smile. "You're a talking mouse. Patches, you found this mouse…for me?"

She meowed. "Yes yes," it squeaked. "I'm a carpenter mouse. Live in little box humans make for fairies."

"Really?" I asked, delighted. I'd loved to visit the fairy gardens at the park. Folk with more time and resources than me liked to put out tiny, highly decorated homes outside their own apartments or houses or in specific public places to attract fairies for good luck.

It bobbed, seeming just as excited as I was. "My family

lucky. Other families make houses themselves not as good." Then it extended one of its front paws to me and wiggled what I realized was a thumb, an extra digit past the four mice usually have. It was less a paw and more a hand like I had. "Patches say you not know why we special. She want you take off collar."

I looked over at the cat for confirmation, and she tilted her head to show the back of her neck. I dug into her fur until I felt a little buckle, which came apart easily. Glowing specks of magic surrounded her as she got to her paws and shook herself out, changing all the while.

I watched in astonishment as she doubled in size in what seemed like a blink, her partially unsheathed claws turning into little knives and her teeth becoming sharper and longer. She displayed them in a yawn while she arched her back in a big stretch that showed off the biggest and most shocking change.

Patches had *wings*. Big, feathery calico wings attached to her sides from shoulder to hip.

I pinched my arm but didn't wake up, so this wasn't a surreal dream. "What's happening?" I whispered.

She lowered her head and bunted my arm, purring deep and thunderous as I scratched behind her ear despite her being the size of a wildcat. As she made cat noises, the mouse continued to translate. "She say she fe…feeeeel…feligryph, like I carpenter mouse. We small friends like gryphons big friends. Now I *your* friend." It put its paw on its fuzzy chest.

"This whole time, you've really understood me," I said to her in awe.

"She say she already friend with librarian. She want find friend for you that fit you. She say you sensitive to Link magic like librarian."

"I need to talk to Miss Wilkes," I mumbled while running my fingers through one of Patches's wings. I'd never heard of a feligryph before, but the name suggested *feline* and *gryphon*, which seemed pretty accurate for her. Real gryphons were monstrously large, though, able to carry people in the air on their backs, while by comparison, Patches seemed...

Well, I guess *small friend* was accurate for them both.

"In a minute," I added, too distracted by petting both of them. The little mouse bobbed with each pass of my hand, but I had the sense it enjoyed the affectionate touch. In the meantime, the purring feligryph crawled into my lap, curled up just as she had as a cat, and got comfortable despite her increased bulk, as she was still chubby in her true form.

"Do you have a name?" I asked the mouse.

"Do you?" it countered. "Maybe I name you good carpenter mouse name. I'm Chauncey Balenciaga the Seventh."

I blinked a few times. "I'm sorry, what was that?"

It huffed. "Are all humans this slow?" It then repeated the name more deliberately, Chauncey Balenciaga the Seventh. "I have same name as my dad and my dad's dad and my dad's dad's dad and..."

"I get it," I said as it...he, rather, caught his breath. He did seem to be living life at twice the speed I was, judging by how he talked. "That's too big a name for you, little guy. I'll call you Chance."

"Okay. Shorter name for slow human mouth to say, yes yes," he said.

"Well, Chance, I'm Heather. Back where I'm from, I'm called Mouse for being small and quiet."

Patches made a throaty trill. "She know. I know. That why I come be your friend. A mouse for a Mouse," he said.

CHAPTER 14

GOOD LITTLE MICE

I PUT the collar back around Patches's neck, reluctant to see her extraordinary features tucked away to leave her an ordinary-looking calico cat. She led the way to Miss Wilkes, who lived in a room at the back of the library. Patches disappeared through a flap in the door, and soon the librarian was opening it and beckoning me inside.

"I see Patches found you," she said with a smile.

"Yes, ma'am." I'd made no move to hide the carpenter mouse now riding on my shoulder, constantly observing the world around him with quick twitches of his head back and forth. Chance seemed to relax in Miss Wilkes's presence, though.

Her front room was about as big as the quarters I shared with all my roommates but just as cluttered with extra bookshelves, sharing space with a cabinet full to the brim with what looked like clay figures. She'd added in a couch and settee and a circular center table covered in a lace drape and several half-finished knitting projects in their own individual bowls. The whole place smelled of old parchment, leather, and a hint of the sour tang that clung to the skin of the elderly.

Miss Wilkes was dressed for bed in a fluffy robe with wildflowers knit up the sides and all around the belt tied at her waist. "I don't want to take too much of your time," I said, embarrassed to realize I was invading her space when she was intending to sleep.

"Nonsense, dear. You must have questions?" She went to rummage in the cupboards set into the wall beside the entranceway and retrieved a tin of cookies that she upended onto a plate. Chance and I perked up at the same time as she came over and set them on the table between us. I picked one up and took a modest bite, realizing it was stale when it stuck to the moisture at the roof of my mouth.

"Some for me too?" the mouse asked.

"Careful," I mumbled around the mouthful I tried to pry loose with my tongue. I broke off a bit that he clutched with both front paws and nibbled on.

Patches was back in her feligryph form, purring by Miss Wilkes's side by the time I swallowed what I'd bitten off. "This is Chance," I said, gesturing to him. "He, um, talks."

"He talks to you. You're the only person who can understand him," she said with a smile. My mouth dropped open as I turned to look at the mouse. "Just as I can understand Patches. They're both species of little wonders," she answered.

"Little wonders," I echoed.

"That's what we call animals that can Link but aren't any one of the gods' blessed beasts. There are tons of different species of little wonders, and we tend to lump them together, while they prefer to be referred to by their individual species names."

Patches meowed. Miss Wilkes nodded and added, "Sometimes, they call each other cousins."

"Are they a secret? Is that why I never knew little wonders existed?" I blurted out.

She smiled down at her feligryph, who slow blinked back

up at her. "Of a sort. They are just exceptionally rare, to the point of being myth, and smart enough to either coexist with humans unnoticed or avoid us completely. Most species of little wonders look almost identical to another kind of animal and know how to fit in with them."

"That makes sense," I said thoughtfully. "Wait...didn't you say they Link, like a gryphon does?"

"Correct. Gryphons, as blessed beasts, share emotions and thoughts on a powerful psychic Link with their riders. What you and I have with our little wonders is simpler because they are just one step up from a common animal that can't Link. You'll grow to have a great mutual affection but won't have the same kind of ever-present empathetic bond. What you do have is a friend for life, who will, in fact, live as long as you do. The trade back is that you'll be unable to Link with anything else. You won't be the next Sivana Walker," she said, sounding a little apologetic.

I was only disappointed for a few moments before smiling just as brightly as before. As much as I admired the first female gryphon rider and the hearsay of her exploits, I knew I'd get crushed into powder at the military academy where riders were trained. "That's fine by me. I just didn't realize it was so permanent. Chance made the decision to Link with me really fast, apparently."

"That happens. We have an energy to us that little wonders can sense. If you're compatible, there's no hesitation to initiate a Link," she said. I had a little wiggle in my shoulders, feeling really special to have had it happen to me. "Patches here is rather sensitive to reading what a person needs, and she was sure you were ready for this responsibility. She's been a bit of a matchmaker for decades now. I just have to warn you, having a pet mouse at RSI will be...odd."

"No one else has a pet, do they?" That would make me stick out.

She shook her head. "Not at the school. There are two

other students, that I know of, who have little wonders, but both of them are well into their apprenticeships and soon to graduate. I strongly suggest you keep Chance's little wonder status a secret. You don't want anyone coming around trying to steal him from you because they think he'll talk to them."

I nodded in agreement, gulping a swallow at the thought.

She smiled over at him and said, "He is obviously quite young, too, as he hasn't created any clothes or small tools to carry along with him. The older, more experienced carpenter mice always end up choosing a profession and dressing like their human counterparts. As I understand it, the only other difference between his species and an ordinary mouse is that he has an opposable thumb and is comfortable standing upright."

As if to prove her point, he was on his back paws again, making grabbing motions for the half-eaten cookie I had dangling between my fingers. I gave him another little piece to nibble on.

"So, no having conversations with him in front of others," she instructed.

"Yes, ma'am," I said reluctantly. I already imagined how I'd look, having a seemingly one-way conversation with Chance.

"And, of course, he relies on you for safety. Make sure you don't let him out of your sight, especially with a cat around. They kill birds and mice for fun."

I nodded, checking my belt. I'd already started modifying it to hold extra slots for pouches and tools, so I'd add a comfortable space for Chance too.

I had the sense that Miss Wilkes was rather tired, even with her willingness to stay up and answer my questions. She'd told me plenty for now, though, so I quickly said my goodbyes to her and bent down to kiss Patches on the forehead. "Thank you," I said.

She meowed back. "She say you welcome," Chance translated dutifully. "She happy you like me, yes yes. We be good little mice together."

"We will," I agreed. I took him out of the library, trudging back to my own room. With a quick glance left to right to confirm no one was watching, I drew a folded pouch from my pocket. "Wanna learn how to pick a lock?"

CHANCE DIDN'T UNDERSTAND the concept of picking a lock when he could just go *under* doorways, able to squish himself down to fit through even the narrowest gaps. Maybe it was for the best that I didn't teach him the bad habits I still had from my life before RSI anyway.

I decided not to hide him except for that first night, bundling him under a sheet with me. He ended up curled just under my chin and woke eager to experience the adventure of my classes. One problem, though…the headmaster was roaming the cafeteria at breakfast, telling certain students that their first classes were canceled and to remain behind.

Carmen and I exchanged a glance when he shared this message with our table and skipped over Davit's Day. "Today might be the day," she muttered.

"What day is that?" I asked. I was a little distracted feeding Chance bits of a cracker. He perched comfortably on my forearm and watched Carmen like she was the most eminent threat to his safety after she'd joked that I was babying him too much since he was the library cat's next lunch.

"Look up from that mouse for a minute," she grumbled.

I did, noting the faces of those leaving as the bells rang. All older kids and established teams, the likes of whom would have names on the intermediate and advanced ranking boards. "We're getting a bigger team today," she supplied. "Gods willing."

I tried not to let my hurt feeling show at that statement, especially when I was secretly thinking the same thing. I was eager to feel more like a spy candidate and less like a kid struggling with basic schoolwork. Judging by the clumps of older kids that wandered the halls of this school, whoever I was teamed up with would become my friends and partners in all of RSI's challenges.

Headmaster Radcliffe called us all up to the front of the cafeteria with Miss Barrios and a couple teachers helping herd us toward him. "Good morning, everyone. You must be wondering why I wanted to see all of your smiling faces at the same time today," he said.

I looked around, counting upward of four dozen students milling around or sitting at the big gathering tables closest to the headmaster. Most listened to him intently or whispered to their partner. There was a wider range of ages than I expected here, kids a few years older and younger than me were blended into the crowd.

"The season will change soon, and so too will your teams. Today, we wanted to give you all a chance to separate back into your assigned pairings. If your current teams are not working out, it's time to reform your group with students you feel you get along with," he instructed. The murmuring of a few kids turned into a sea of whispers.

Carmen elbowed me with a poorly concealed grin while I searched the gathering for a pair of familiar friendly faces.

"We want everyone to have teams between four and six people by the time you leave the cafeteria today. Remember, we always have new students coming in. Try taking a chance on someone new today." The headmaster gestured that we get started, and the noise level jumped as kids got to their feet and called to each other in a scramble of movement.

This was a little too much for Chance, who hid in my

pocket. I didn't like how it seemed like I was going to miss out on the teammates I wanted if I just held still, so I ploughed into the gathering despite my instincts to retreat to a quieter area. Carmen followed me, glancing around and muttering to herself.

"No, they're full," she said as we passed a gathering of five girls with Sybella at its center. Amongst them stood a girl who'd come to RSI after me. Though I felt a sting of rejection, as Sybella had barely spoken to me except for the occasional snub and overlooked me in favor of this new kid, I recognized that at least I was lucky enough to have a partner, as prickly as she could be.

"They're not our speed," Carmen whispered of a pair of boys still looking to form a team. She had less kind things to say under her breath about a couple other pairings, until she tapped my shoulder and pointed. Fariq stood at the cafeteria's exit, his back to us while he leaned into the hall.

I looked up at her, hopeful something else uncharitable wouldn't leave her lips. "Vance is okay, I guess," she said. "Let's partner with them."

My eyebrow lifted. "Just okay?"

She scowled in reply, and I figured that was the best compliment she could muster. I was probably amongst the list of people that were *okay* to her and figured I should just accept it.

"Would you hurry up?" I heard Fariq snap.

"It was short notice, all right?" Vance's reply was in the same short tone when he appeared in the doorway. His uniform shirt was on backward. With an annoyed hiss, Fariq gestured him back into the hall.

Well, this was unusual. I cleared my throat, and Fariq jumped and turned, taking a brief look at my hopeful expression, hands clasped before me. "Yes," he said, and my insides flared with tingles of happiness. "But just give Vance a moment. He had to put himself back on right."

CHAPTER 15

LITTLES

VANCE STRODE THROUGH THE DOORWAY, his shirt now oriented correctly. "I wasn't expecting something actually important to happen today," he said.

"But classes are important," I pointed out. Not that he attended them sometimes. Still, he had some things going for him; he knew alchemy things and made tea that could clear up the winterbog. I appreciated that he had some skills, even if I barely knew him.

I was more relieved that Fariq was on my team. His smarts and willingness to help would make him an asset in any group, so I was glad he'd agreed to join mine.

Vance breezed by me with a scoff. "Sure. What do we do now that we're a cute little team of four?"

Fariq was the one to point out the adults circulating the room, noting down the newly changed or formed teams. It was Miss Barrios who came to us, a smile stretching her Tulari mark. "Are you four a team now?" she asked.

"Yes, ma'am," Fariq said politely.

She noted it down on her clipboard, expression shading to delight. "Congratulations. And I'm signing myself up as your mentor. The rest of this time is for us to get to know one another a little better, so if you'll follow me..."

She took us upstairs to one of the empty classrooms. I hadn't missed her glance toward me when she mentioned the mentorship and remembered that she'd wanted to be assigned the Big Sister of any team I'm on. *When I look at you, I see a young version of myself,* she'd said. I was glad. She was kind and smart, the type of person I wanted to be as an adult.

"Why'd we get assigned to the secretary?" Carmen grumbled in an undertone.

I glanced over my shoulder to defend Miss Barrios when I saw she was walking step in step with Vance, who replied under his breath, "Don't speak badly of one of the only Tulari on staff."

"Here we are," Miss Barrios interrupted unintentionally. She ushered us into a small alchemy classroom, made more cramped by the planters and pots taking up half the room. The plants within bathed in the rays coming off a tinted magelight, their leaves turned toward it like worshiping a mini sun.

I sneezed nearly immediately. Musty plants and their *pollen.* Why couldn't they keep it to themselves?

Miss Barrios looked around at the four of us, taking seats on stools at one of the high-topped tables, and nodded to herself. "I'll be right back with your last teammate," she said, walking out of the room.

I exchanged a glance with Fariq. "Was there another friend you made?" he asked.

I shook my head no, and Carmen scoffed.

"I think we're being *assigned* another teammate. Just another one of RSI's games," Vance commented.

We had a few guesses for who it might be, as there were a few stragglers here and there around the school who'd never gotten a partner. Five was the ideal size for a team, not too big and not too small, and I was cautiously optimistic about getting someone new to balance out the bigger, predatory personalities we had in Vance and Carmen.

When Miss Barrios returned, it was with a girl who was mid-sentence. "—just can't wait to meet them." She turned and waved to us as she walked in, her sunny smile of greeting fading to one of surprise as she flicked a few blonde curls over her shoulder. "Wait, is this the right room?"

"This is it. Margot, meet your new team." Miss Barrios dragged over two more stools to complete our circle, and the new person took a seat with slow, ladylike precision.

Her accent was refined and highbrow, the kind only the wealthy cultivated in their well-to-do circles and exclusive events. She sat with a straight back, the uniform clinging to the curve of her waist in a way neither Carmen nor I could compare to. Even though she had a full face of makeup making her seem even more mature, I could tell. She was still older than the rest of the group.

Miss Barrios cleared her throat as Margot opened her mouth. "Let's do some introductions," she suggested. To my relief, she went around the circle and named everyone before Carmen was...well, herself, and said what the rest of us must've been thinking.

"How old are you?" she asked Margot.

"Sixteen. And yourself?" she answered in a more polite tone.

"Thirteen. Like the rest of us, I think." She glanced around the circle, and there were nods all around except for the adult, of course.

"Margot here has had a tough transition, so she has not had a partner or team until now," Miss Barrios said.

Out of seemingly nowhere, Margot produced a lacy pink fan and unfurled it with a flick of her wrist. "Coming here was absolutely dreadful," she said in agreement. Carmen muttered and nodded.

"So, I told her I would find her a team where she could

excel. Teams don't *have* to have members of the same age and qualifications. In fact, we suggest you find teammates who can fulfill a unique role in the group," Miss Barrios said.

What role's that? Having money? I asked myself, really looking at Margot and then the rest of the kids around me.

There was me, the thief, the sneak. Fariq, with the brains. Carmen, with her fists. And I didn't even know what Vance was capable of, but he was the least awkward person at this table. Before Margot walked in, I would assume we'd make Vance the face of any operation, the one to talk to folk and distract them.

But Margot...she had the accent and presumably the family ties to get into places someone like me would only dream of. She had wide, expressive blue eyes with the kind of prey energy that told me she was uncomfortable meeting a group of strangers she was expected to fit in with as a teammate. The way she held her fan hid part of her face and thus any expression she didn't want us to see.

As Miss Barrios began to talk and warm us up for whatever bonding we were supposed to be doing, I watched Margot and the glimmer of smarts that came and went in her eyes as she listened with uncommon focus, like the adult was the only person in the room.

"If we haven't met, I'm Sasha Barrios, RSI's secretary. I'll be your mentor, otherwise called your Big Sister, while you are my Littles. My task will be to mentor you through the unique challenges coming your way now that you've been assembled into a team. I also handle the magical security measures at RSI and help the instructors with tutoring and scheduling. Quite the jack of all trades, but in any organization, a Tulari must be flexible. Isn't that right, Vance?"

I wasn't the only one whose gaze swiveled to the sputtering young man, who had no mark of magic on his face.

"If you want to be an effective team, the first thing you all have to do is trust each other with your strengths and past, even if they are your best kept secret," she continued. "You five are all noted to have high potential, so it's great you've found each other to be in this room together. Our first session together will be us reintroducing ourselves and breaking down those boundaries. Who wants to go first?"

There was silence amongst us. My gaze was on the peeling black paint of the tabletop. My skin was needled with discomfort at the idea of doing as Miss Barrios asked. She wanted us to talk about *before* RSI, where we'd come from, and what we brought to the team because of it. I never talked about that time, especially not with a stranger like the newcomer, Margot.

"All right. Fine. I *am* a Tulari," Vance said abruptly. He reached into the cuff of his uniform, retrieving a wand. He started drawing a spell midair, green magic flooding from its tip. I leaned in with my mouth hanging open as he threaded the wand's tip through the spell and tapped his chin.

His face…melted like the runners on a wax candle, features blurring together. I flinched away from him, horrified, but at least it formed back up again within a few heartbeats. "This is what I actually look like," he said, framing his face with his hands.

I sat in stunned astonishment, too amazed at what he'd just done with magic to have much more of a reaction. A green Tulari mark covered his left temple, the ends of its circle just barely wrinkling in the skin of his upper eyelid. Because of the unique marking, he had no left eyebrow, which did him no favors.

In showing off his real face, though, he'd gone from one with sculpted, symmetrical features to another just as flawed as the rest of us. I couldn't help but notice the weaker jaw, the pasty complexion, and the gray eyes set just a bit too close together. Even his hair had decided to lose its luster and get confused halfway between wavy and curly, turning into a frizzled brown mess.

On the side of his neck stretched half of an ugly tattoo, a black snake with an open mouth, bearing oversized fangs in menace. That hadn't been there before either, and I didn't fault him for hiding it with his magic.

Margot gasped, taking in the new him with astonished-looking eyes. Carmen masked her laugh behind her fist, a soft *heh* escaping instead.

"Wow, Vance," Vance himself said, holding his cheeks now and making an exaggerated expression of awe. "What an amazing and unique ability. You would make a fantastic spy someday."

He was really only revealing this to Carmen, Margot, and me, because Fariq seemed as unimpressed with him as always, and Miss Barrios nodded slowly as she watched us.

"How?" I asked. "Wait…that tea you gave me. It had magic in it?"

"You're welcome," he said.

"Thank y—"

"And to answer the how of it, well, I was part of a gang." He twisted his lips as he glanced at Miss Barrios, who circled her hand to encourage him to keep going. "Called Morashi Venom. Unlike the rest of you, I'm not here by choice."

Carmen scoffed. "What choice?"

"The Morashi?" I echoed, palms flattening on the table. "But they don't *exist*."

Vance flashed slightly crooked teeth in a grimace. "But they do. And I'm, well, the first member who got caught." He pulled his sleeve back and displayed his bracelet to the rest of us by clanking it on the table. It was a perfect copper circle like mine, but his had an engraving of mage runes on it. "I'm probably the only one here with a tracking spell, too."

"If that's what it looks like," I murmured. My head was spinning. To think Vance was one of the Morashi, a veritable legendary gang that made the rest of us seem like amateurs.

Uncle Jace had always told us Morashi Venom was an

urban legend designed to keep Tulari kids from staying out after dark. Jackie and I had been terrified of them when one of the older kids in the gang gave birth to a Tulari girl, just for her to disappear mere days after the outline of a magic mark started appearing on her face.

She said the Morashi had stolen her baby. Jace said the kid had been quietly adopted by a wealthy family, luckier than the rest of us because of her magic. And I'd believed him over her.

"Were you taken?" I asked quietly. New sorrow formed in my heart for that mother, who'd quietly moved up to Springfield's gang after it was obvious she wasn't getting her babe back one way or the other. She'd made the change a little early, being sixteen at the time, to get away from anything that reminded her of the child she'd lost.

"Yeah. I was five." Vance shrugged like it didn't matter. "Just old enough to remember my parents and my real last name."

"Taken? Like, kidnapped?" Carmen asked, sitting up straighter.

It looked like he struggled not to roll his eyes. "That's right. Tulari are rare, you know? And the magic isn't genetic. It's given when a god touches us. So, the Morashi recruits exclusively by stealing babies and kids marked by Lord Orion and teaches them some of the lost arts. I took to formshifting, which you won't find in any class at the Tulari Academy.

"That's why I have this." More reluctantly, he covered the face of his snake tattoo with one hand. A tremble of something like fear ran through his fingers. "The...boss, she wanted me to be a formshifter. To encourage my magic in the right direction, she had me marked with this so I'd be motivated to hide it."

"That's a brand, Vance," Miss Barrios said.

"Well, it worked, didn't it? I have magic no one's seen in centuries. That they know of," he said flippantly.

That explained some of the Morashi's effectiveness, I thought. The rumors I'd heard were that they ran the biggest cons, sometimes lying in wait for years to steal from prestigious institutions such as the palace. They stole the kinds of things that were then shushed by big money. Like Uncle Jace said, an urban legend. A gang made exclusively of Tulari mages that had the advantage of magic for any situation and were impossible to catch.

But apparently that hadn't been enough for Vance, since he was here. Maybe he overestimated his abilities or was betrayed by his crew…just like I was.

"How does your magic work?" Margot interjected.

He shrugged and spoke shortly. "Trade secret."

We must've reached the end of his patience, but I still had a question on the tip of my tongue. "What were the jobs like?" I asked.

He waggled his finger. "Ah-ah. I told you my secret, but I'm not squealing. I might be stuck at RSI forever because I will not talk about my gang or the cons we ran."

I immediately nodded in understanding.

"Well, now that you've shared, pick someone to go next," Miss Barrios interjected.

"I pick Heather. I've figured out you have some of the street in you, too," he said, nodding to me.

My mouth dried up like I was chewing on a rock of pure salt, rather than my tongue. My eyelid flickered a couple times. "Heather will go next. Then we'll save the rest for next meeting," Miss Barrios said. She smiled my way like she was completely unaware of the anxiety seizing my chest.

"I, uh…I…"

I almost mistook the slight weight traveling up the side of my uniform to be the path of some tickle or a lost bug, but it was Chance, popping up on my shoulder with a squeak.

"Aw, *misk*," Fariq said.

"I have a mouse now. His name is Chance," I blurted.

Carmen didn't conceal her scoff. "She found him at breakfast this morning," she snarked.

"You were just keeping the *misk* in your pocket?" Fariq asked.

"Mouse," I corrected. "And yes. I need to buy a new pouch to put him in."

"I make for you," he promised.

"I good distraction, yes yes?" Chance squeaked at me.

Bless that mouse. Somehow, he knew I'd been put on the spot and came scampering to my rescue. "Yes," I said simply, in answer to them both. "I'd really appreciate it, Fariq. It's not like I can go out and get one." I showed off the bracelet still encircling my wrist.

"May I hold him?" Unexpectedly, the question came from Margot. She placed her fan aside and held out her hand hopefully, a small smile cracking her perfect face of makeup.

Chance immediately gave her his best cute face, complete with the dark button eyes that belonged on a stuffed toy. I reached out, letting him transfer to her palm, and watched her pet down his back with a soft coo. "Aren't you the sweetest thing?"

Maybe she was faking the noblewoman's accent and was exceptionally good at mimicking the same rigid posture they all seemed to have, because I would've assumed Margot was more likely to shriek at the sight of Chance than find him adorable. It was an odd choice, but this was RSI. She had to be here for some reason.

I looked over at Miss Barrios and pointed to my bracelet. "When do we get these changed out or upgraded, by the way?"

She resisted the change of subject, I think, hesitating to answer. "In the next couple weeks, there will be a challenge for your team to complete so you can earn a bracelet upgrade to what we call tier one, when you have the clearance level to leave the school during daylight hours," she answered. "We like to rent Haladay Park for a field day when the snows melt. Most of you have our trust." I couldn't help but notice her gaze darting to Vance. His situation really did stand out...but I also figured one of the Morashi Tulari could remove his bracelet, and then we'd never see him again.

Then her dark brown eyes found me next, and she shook her head slowly. I couldn't help but think of my own circumstances and how I, too, was stuck here until I either aged out or somehow found the Eye of Acuity and returned it to the original owners.

A familiar resentment burned in my heart for Cartier and Rozma, the Weasel and Mongoose that'd stolen my freedom. Once I had a bracelet that allowed me to leave RSI, I could finally start planning to ruin them...if they were still in the city.

"The opportunity to come and go from RSI is a privilege. Remember that," Miss Barrios said.

"So, we're prisoners," Carmen muttered.

"Watch yourself," she said, her tone angrier than I'd heard from her. "I would hate for your candidacy to be cut short because of a bad attitude."

"Have you met Carmen?" Vance asked.

He chuckled until she elbowed him. They had a brief squabble, with Miss Barrios pitching her voice louder, trying to get them to stop before it became a fight. Margot watched them go with a frown and passed Chance back to me when they'd settled again.

Fariq sighed. "Come to the innovation workshop tonight with him," he said. "Just you and the *misk*."

I was nodding in agreement when the bells rang for class change. Miss Barrios muttered a curse. "You all will be needing to go back to class, but we'll meet again soon."

Vance scrambled to cast a new spell, returning his face to what it'd been when I'd first met him. His hair shortened and smoothed out as well. His borrowed face was a perfect sheet, not a blemish or a mark to be found. "That's what's odd," I blurted, seeing why I'd thought there was something off about him. "You're missing freckles."

He touched his face self-consciously, then shrugged. "I'll fix it later."

As we entered the crush of people that entered the hall during class change, I turned and realized it was Margot keeping pace with me. I flashed an uncertain look up at her, not sure why she was choosing to walk by my side.

"I hope I see you again soon," she said in that polite noblewoman's tone, raising her voice just enough to be heard despite the chatter around us. "I want to know your story too, Heather. Not just let your mouse distract us from it."

I bowed my head, not knowing how to reply to that. But when I looked back up at her, she was gone in the crush of the crowd.

CHAPTER 16

MORASHI

FARIQ HAD a new pouch made for Chance in a couple days. I sat with him in the innovation workshop, practically trembling with the desire to wander the odds and ends in the bins around us. But I had a bit of self-control, enough to know my belt was full for now and that some of my peers whispered about me. Between the mouse and the modified belt where I kept many things, just in case, my oddities were showing.

"I think he likes it," I said after Chance enthused that his new pouch was *very comfy, I sleep here, yes yes.* It was modified from a coin purse, neat stitches along the bottom and sides of the cloth giving more support to its structure. Fariq had found some leftover fur that now lined the inside and made a little bed for Chance. Instead of a drawstring top, it had a flap of loose fabric so he could come and go.

"Amazing how expressive he is," he said, watching Chance poke his head out of it and bobble in delight.

"Yeah," I murmured. "Hey, Fariq?"

"Hmm?"

I searched for a way to put the direction of my thoughts into words. I'd thought all my problems would be solved once I was properly in a team, but so far, all I'd noticed was that Carmen had lost a measure of respect for Vance now that she'd seen his real face. Over the course of the last couple days, Fariq and I spent our time working on the newly increased requirements for our group projects while the two of them bickered like kids half their ages.

And Margot, well, she was no help because she wasn't in any of our classes. I hadn't seen a single blonde curl since she pointed out how I'd wiggled out of sharing where I came from with the group.

"Do you think we're gonna make it?" I asked.

He regarded me for a while with a lifted brow. I suppose for someone as gifted as him, there was no question about his future. If he wasn't a spy, he could be any number of other things. I was asking for myself, because I didn't see a line of employers looking for skills like mine.

"What do you mean?" he said finally.

"Our new team. Do you think it will make it?"

"Ah. Seeing the future is for the gods." He shrugged. "Vance and Carmen are missing something…a reason to be here. Something to believe in when the going gets hard. Without that, they have not even taken the first step to, well, making it."

"They're going to bring us down with them," I said.

"Maybe they will. But our team isn't on the ranking boards, and no real jobs are at stake. Next year, or even sooner, there will be a new team. But I hope you're not giving up on them yet. We've hardly started working together. Vance has gotten a lot better."

"Really?"

"Mmhmm. He would change his face to a different person every day, trying to leave. When that didn't work, he made a deal with the peacekeeper…the one with, ah." He poked his cheeks, and I nodded in understanding. "Vance would become him and work his job while the peacekeeper left to do something else."

"That's what he was doing the other day, when his shirt was on backward," I guessed. He'd obviously donned it in a hurry and must've left a pile of the peacekeeper uniform somewhere.

"Yes. I got him to come back just in time," he sighed. "I don't like how dishonest he is, but he is my partner. Until I have another, I will work with him and encourage him to be better. Maybe with time, he will realize it's a mistake to protect criminals like those in Morashi Venom."

I bit my tongue hard so I didn't argue in favor of Vance. If Fariq heard me talking about gang loyalty, he'd realize I was more like his partner than he realized, with a gang family I'd left behind and missed dearly.

VANCE WAS willing to help me with alchemy, though he did so during my tutorial period while wearing the face and uniform of Brinsley, the pimply-faced guard. I hadn't gotten over the fact that it was Vance sitting next to me, pretending to be someone else, while still doing Vance mannerisms and speaking in his usual voice.

"Do you think the teachers know you hide from class like this?" I asked, gesturing to him.

He shrugged in a carefree way that left wrinkles in the pressed white uniform. "Probably. If RSI's taught me anything, it's that I'm not as clever as I originally thought. But they haven't fired him, so we're all happy. He sends messages for me sometimes. Perhaps I can convince him to carry one for you?"

I took in a sharp breath, and Vance smiled knowingly. "Tell me something first. What gang you from?"

"You wouldn't know it."

"Really? I guess I can't tell Brinsley where to take your message, then."

Musty devils, he had me there. "Jace's," I sighed.

His borrowed blue eyes sharpened with interest. "The Menagerie, huh. Which animal were you?"

I pointed to my shoulder, where Chance blinked with sleepy boredom. He seemed more interested in my alchemy homework than this conversation. "I was the Mouse."

"No kidding." He grinned, tapping my shoulder with the back of his hand. I almost flinched, but he was far gentler than Carmen. "To think we've had classes together and I never realized it. My boss is *furious* that you took the Eye of Acuity and disappeared. Even I've heard about it. She's putting your bosses through it to get the necklace from them."

"Oh, yeah?" I asked nervously.

"Yup. She had a job lined up, and you went in and took it mere hours before Morashi Venom did."

The thoughts spun in my head, and my gaze narrowed on him. "No, I mean, about my bosses...and how did she know it was me?"

He made a sweeping gesture to the empty cafeteria. "You got caught, of course. It's good you acted under your own kind of alias and hid out here until all that blew over. But what about freedom, hmm? With a little luck and planning, we could make our escape on that field day Miss Barrios mentioned."

I scrubbed the distrust from my face before it could answer for me. I noticed he'd avoided my question again. "What's waiting for you outside of the school?" I asked.

"My life. Everything I've worked for," he answered. "The person I'll kiss when I see him again." His cheeks flushed with some color.

I wished I could see his real face again. He'd seemed about my age, maybe fourteen at most. What had the mages in Morashi Venom done to him to have him be so eager to join back up with the people who'd kidnapped him from his real family? Or was his crush the real motivation?

Well, it wasn't really my business. "If you help me get a message to the right person, I can get some desda powder and then free you of that bracelet when we go to Haladay Park," I said. "But I also need information."

He cringed. "Hate to point it out, but I'm a Tulari under all this."

I threaded the cuff of my shirt under the bracelet I wore and raised a brow at him. "It only takes a couple grains. None of them will get on your skin. Then you can go back to what you had." I made a dismissive gesture over my shoulder.

He considered, staring at the far wall of the cafeteria. "What's the information?" he asked finally.

"Maybe someone in your gang has figured out how to disable a double-release spell. I need to know."

"All right." Still, he turned a curious look my way.

"What?" I grumbled.

"Would you want to return to the Menagerie? No offense, but Jace rooms the kids in a hovel by the sewage grates, right?" He wrinkled his nose meaningfully. "I could find you a better gig. If you cough up the Eye of Acuity, I bet my boss would take you in."

"I don't plan to leave RSI like you do." It felt odd, saying this out loud to someone who wanted to get out of here as badly as I had, originally. But it was as Fariq had said. I had a reason to be here, and Vance did not. "I want to get as many of my gang siblings here as possible, actually. Can't you see how great RSI is? They feed us. They give us new clothes. And no matter how good an actual spy you are, you get an apprenticeship for an honest job by the end of your time here."

He breathed a quiet scoff. "I guess that's the difference between our gangs."

I turned and looked at him, really meeting his gaze full-on for the first time. "Is it? You can't steal your way to success, Vance. Eventually, you're going to get caught, and the place they send you then won't be anywhere near as nice as this school."

His swallow was audible, and he broke eye contact first. "Of course you'd say that. You've never met a real Morashi mage."

"I've met you," I countered. "And one of the first real things I learned about you was that brand on your neck. You want to return to the ones who did that?"

Vance made a face like he'd tasted something bitter, his nostrils flaring. "Anyway, what's the message, and where's it going?" he asked gruffly, drawing out a new piece of parchment to jot it down with more force than necessary.

CHAPTER 17

MOVING IN

I WAS STILL WAITING ANXIOUSLY for a message from Jackie. She was the only person I'd send for, to let her know I was still alive and eager to take her to RSI with me. The days passed, and the real guard Brinsley gave me odd looks when I kept glancing over at him hopefully each time our paths crossed.

But one evening after a long week, I'd gotten washed and dressed down to my pajamas at the usual time and then flopped back onto my cot, playing fetch with Chance by tossing a ball of knotted yarn. Carmen lay face down in her cot next to mine, while most of our roommates were still out studying or attending clubs. Sybella sat propped up by her pillows and Nessa's, reading.

Of my roommates, only Harper had something to say about Chance, asking why I was willingly taking vermin into our room. I'd responded by holding him out toward her and saying, "He's not a vermin. He's small and sweet. Look!" She'd visibly recoiled and glared at me.

It was a surprise that Sybella didn't seem to mind him, and even now, she occasionally glanced up from her book to watch him scale the side of my cot to deliver the little ball of yarn back to my hand. He had way more energy than I did, zigzagging over the sheets in anticipation before I tossed the ball again.

There was a soft knock on the door. I sighed, hefting myself to my feet and going to answer it. Chance climbed me rather than the cot and sat on my shoulder, holding the ball of yarn handy. His little nose twitched. "Friend!" he squeaked.

I opened the door, and Margot was there, standing back from the doorway and looking at the wooden slat that displayed the room number. "Hello again," she said cheerfully. "Looks like this is the right place. I'm moving in."

"Right now?" I murmured.

"Miss Barrios let me know there was an empty bed in your room, and I'm taking it. I haven't seen you or Carmen or the boys since she put me in your team, so I'm fixing it." She nodded firmly and pulled a rolling cart away from the corner to show me she'd come prepared with her bags.

I could argue, or I could just step aside and let her see for herself that she was about to be rooming with seven girls younger than her. She breezed her way in and settled her bags at the foot of her new bed with a few *thumps* that woke Carmen from her half-asleep daze. She lifted her head and peered blearily at the young blonde humming away as she unpacked several carefully folded stacks of clothing.

"I'm Margot Connery, Heather and Carmen's partner," she said pleasantly to Sybella, who was watching what was going on over the top of her book.

To my surprise, the other girl smiled. "I'll find a quieter place to be," she said, leaving the room.

Carmen flopped back on the bed, this time face-up. "Hey, pipsqueak. Why's she moving in?"

"There's nothing that says I can't," Margot answered for me. "If we're to be teammates, I want to at least see you between jobs."

I glanced over at her, raising my brows. So she *was* pretending to be a noble. Her mimicry was so good she could easily run the Help Needed con, or even the extra difficult to pull off Stolen Valuables con.

"I work at an employment agency now," Margot said to fill the awkward silence that fell. "I've been a part-time governess for a couple weeks to a pair of sweet little boys."

I scratched the back of my head, shaking loose the ideas of cons and pretending. I settled on the conclusion that Margot, despite the vulnerable prey energy she gave off even now while she waited hopefully for one of us to speak, was the real deal. A real noble.

"How'd you end up here?" I blurted.

"That's a long story. Let me get my things settled and maybe we can have a chat, get to know one another better? I've so missed having companions," Margot said.

I nodded and nudged Carmen until she sat up with a great, big yawn. "Whatever," she muttered.

I really wanted to know how a noble had ended up at RSI, so I put off my nerves at the idea of a casual chat and waited for Margot to stuff her clothes to barely fit in the small space she had. Other than the clothes issued by the institute, she had several dresses, skirts, and blouses in every pastel shade I could imagine. Plus matching shoes and small boxes of what I assumed was jewelry. She had to sit on the chest at the foot of her cot to close it.

"All done. Now then." She sat cross-legged on her cot after freeing her feet from the boots and wiggling her toes with a soft sigh. "Both of you are the quieter sort, hmm?"

"Well, she is," Carmen said, hooking her thumb toward me.

"She always got her opinion," I said, pointing to Carmen.

"What's *that* supposed to mean, pipsqueak?"

"We like opinions," Margot interjected quickly. She looked

down in surprise. I realized Chance had given up on waiting for me to throw the ball of yarn, so he lifted it up toward her instead. "Oh, you like to fetch? I knew you were a sweet thing." He perked up from the sugary way she spoke to him before going dashing off once she threw the ball.

Well, if Chance liked her, then I could give her a chance too. "You were going to tell us what brought you to RSI," I reminded her.

"Oh, yes. So." Margot infused the syllable with all the intrigue of a good piece of gossip. "Are you familiar with the port town of Luccal?"

"Noooo?"

"What are they teaching in fundamental school these days?" she asked primly. "It is to the northeast, the next hub of civilization that side of Daramaine. The Connery family—*my* family—has held those lands for generations and raised that town up from doing good business with Rathi traders. My grandfather was named the first Baron of Luccal and my father behind him."

I breathed a soft *uh oh* the moment she mentioned Rathi, hearing the note of sadness in her tone.

"They flew one of their awful storm birds right over Luccal on its way to Daramaine. It threw so much seawater around that we all were bailing out all the cellars for days. I was so peeved." She rolled her eyes up and batted her lashes. "I just couldn't leave the help to save father's wine on their own. The Storm Front's existence delayed my debut at court, and this event just delayed me more."

"Of course," I said, finding it surreal that she'd even helped at all. Then Chance scampered back up to her, and she smiled brightly, holding him cupped in her hand for a minute, before tossing his yarn ball again.

"Meanwhile, my older sister, Serla, was so worried about her betrothed that she took the first carriage out to go to Daramaine, and it turned out he was hiding under his scribe's desk for days after the Rathi came for the other side of the city." She tittered a laugh. "Kissing on his scribe's neck the whole time and going further to violate his betrothal contract with Serla. She found them tangled up in each other. Can you believe it? If we weren't at war, it would be a huge scandal."

"She wanted to know why you're at RSI," Carmen pointed out in a grumble.

"I'm getting there, darling. Indulge me. My sister called the whole thing off and wed a different suitor right away. Oh, but the wedding was divine. And then on the way back to our home, my parents were…well, there's no graceful way to say it." She spoke as though forcing the words out. "They were murdered. The roads have been absolutely dogged by illegal activity of late, and a group of brigands set off explosives to force their carriage into a ravine. They were…"

Margot withdrew a kerchief from her pocket and dabbed at her face delicately. "I'm so sorry," I murmured.

She waved me off with a sigh. "It's…fine. It was a while ago, but I still feel so guilty. My carriage was just behind theirs. The horses must've sensed something off; they balked when they could've been caught in the blast. My parents had hired enough guards to fight off those blackhearts, but that didn't save them… They're gone."

All of a sudden, her face creased with anger. Carmen sat up straighter and turned her head to listen, suddenly intrigued. "My uncle inherited the Connery house and fortune. He and his degenerate son are why I'm here," she said.

"Your parents didn't leave the house to you?" Carmen asked.

"That's not the way of things when it's a barony. The next male heir was my father's brother, and his family moved in the split second they heard the news. Everything on the estate became their property, including me as an unmarried woman.

They threw my mother's jewels at an auctioneer and threw out the paintings my father made." Her fist closed around the kerchief like she could strangle the life from it.

Carmen glanced back at me. I read the disbelief on her face and had a feeling I knew what she was thinking. *Why didn't Margot fight back?* But again, she was a noble. She couldn't just raise her fists against her family over selling valuables that were technically not hers.

"Suffice to say, I didn't take well to the changes. They just…pretended my parents never existed and helped themselves to *everything*." Margot breathed a *hmph*, crossing her arms. "And my cousin decided to chase every girl around, including me."

Carmen's lip curled. "Your own cousin? He didn't…?"

"He didn't," Margot confirmed. "But he cornered me a few times and put his hands where they shouldn't be. He was the next lord of the house, and his dreadful parents turned a blind eye to every girl he was doing this to."

Carmen practically vibrated with secondhand anger, her fingers flexing into fists. Meanwhile, I nodded in understanding. I'd experienced grasping hands as a part of Jace's Menagerie when I was old enough to participate in jobs as the Mouse. It was just how it went and part of why I disliked the random pats and playful punches my companions tended to think were completely normal.

"One day, I had enough. I bashed him over the head with a candlestick holder when he reached for me and—"

"Yes!" Carmen exclaimed. "Did you make him regret ever trying to touch you?"

Margot breathed a sad chuckle. "I don't know about that. But I can tell you'd love to hear he had a huge black eye when he and his family sent me off to a woman's reformatory in Daramaine for my 'violent tendencies.'"

Carmen's expression pulled with confusion. "Oh. They

heard the whole story of what happened and still sided with him?" Her nose wrinkled with distaste.

"They did," she scoffed. "Eagerly, even. By sending me to a reformatory, they've disgraced me. There will be no debuting for me, no advantageous marriage, not with this mark on my history. I am *ruined*. And they get to keep the dowry my parents were saving for me."

"Married? You're way too young for that," I blurted.

For a moment, Margot fluttered her lashes with rapid blinks before she muffled a string of giggles in her kerchief. "Oh, it's such a relief to share all this. I forget you're still thirteen. I thought boys were gross at your age."

I wrinkled my nose. "They *are*."

"All right, darling. That is most of my story, but it turns out that RSI recruits spy candidates from reform schools across Altare. The headmistress saw something in me and transferred me here about a month ago, and I thought I'd done something *else* wrong." She rolled her eyes. "No, first I had to figure out this is an institute for spies and agree to take a part-time position at an employment agency while they train me in espionage techniques. My understanding is this team situation between us is temporary. If we get along, great. If my age ends up being a problem, oh well."

Carmen flashed a smile with her usual sharp edges. "I don't think that will be a problem," she said.

I nodded in agreement, noticing the knowing curve to Margot's lips. She'd shown the one side of her that would earn Carmen's approval...when she used violence to solve a problem.

"Good, because I need a solid group to help me get my dowry back one day. My uncle's family stole from me, and there has to be some way to get revenge."

I sucked in a breath. "You want to *heist* it back? Are you sure it'll still be there waiting for you by now?" I asked.

"I think some of it will be, and that would be enough for me. What do you say? Think you could help me?" She tilted her head, fixing me with the same kind of smile she'd given Carmen.

I scoffed, saying, "Of course," all the while realizing she'd already pegged me as the kind of kid that could help her one day. Who *wanted* to, after hearing what she'd been through.

CHAPTER 18

STORM'S END

By the next Monday, my new team gathered in the cafeteria together. We had to upgrade to a bigger table for this late afternoon meeting with our mentor.

"Hello again, Littles," Miss Barrios said.

Margot twinkled her fingers. "Lovely to see you, ma'am. Did I hear we might be doing something as a team soon?"

"Let her get a chance to tell us," Carmen muttered. Her lips were quirked to the side in a particularly annoyed line, but she'd been extra grumpy the last couple days, and I didn't think our new team member was the only reason why.

Laughing to herself, Miss Barrios said, "We are here to talk about that, yes. First, I wanted to say, your team is still unnamed. As soon as you think up a name, we will begin putting you all on the beginners ranking board."

I asked what I was sure some of us were thinking. "On the bottom?"

"Let's talk about that, shall we? Rankings are a combination of your grades, your scores in challenges, and how well you as a team are observed working together. We will be having our field day in three days—"

A violent rumbling interrupted her. I flinched, my gaze

automatically drifting toward the ceiling and my mind to another place. My old home had a soggy roof, especially during and after storms, and the mold that invaded would get Jackie sick for days. The crack of lightning and growl of thunder distressed her, knowing that ickiness was coming.

Rain tapped the roof over us, unleashing just as forcefully as the thunder. I hoped Jackie was somewhere warm and dry and that she'd gotten my message, even if her silence showed that she'd decided not to send one back.

"—Weather permitting, of course. We don't want to have you all traipsing around in the mud," Miss Barrios continued with a chuckle. "The challenge at this year's field day will be a rescue mission. You will be given a dossier at first light with all the information you need to locate an operative who has gone missing in the hostile land of Haladay Park. I suggest you look to Margot to take the lead."

Margot nodded. "Of course. I'd love to look after the group."

Vance shrugged to himself. "And the other teams of beginners will also be looking for this missing person?" he asked.

"Yes. In reality, a big mission that requires multiple spy teams would have each team working on a different part of the job, with everyone doing their part to ensure its success. But this is training, and we want to see your problem-solving skills. There will be a reward for every team that finishes before dark," she said.

I leaned forward eagerly. "The bracelets," I said.

"Certain placements get upgrades to their bracelets, yes," she answered.

My stomach dropped. "But…"

She held up her first finger. "It's an *opportunity*, and there will be more chances later. We have to keep up appearances as a reform school."

I had the feeling there was more that she wasn't saying, as

she was carefully avoiding looking Vance's way. It didn't surprise me that the school didn't trust him with more freedom, as they shouldn't. He was still a loyal Morashi Tulari, after all.

In a few short days, Jackie might be meeting me in the park with some desda powder to set him free. He'd fulfilled his end of the deal in getting my message delivered, and I had a response to my question about double-release spells burning in my pocket, as I'd stashed the note he gave me right before this meeting.

I suppose that meant I shouldn't be trusted, either. Did the school already know that too?

"It's not like we have anywhere to go," Carmen said through gritted teeth. "Family to visit."

"That's just the way things are. Play along to earn the rewards," Miss Barrios replied.

As soon as we went our separate ways, I pulled out the note Vance had slipped me. It disintegrated once I read it, but it was only a paragraph written in a woman's looping cursive.

Double-release spells are a recent breakthrough in defensive wizardry, designed with desda mushroom powder in mind. They are carved directly onto the surface of the item they protect. The powder starts eating the spell like normal, triggering the first release. But if the carved runes are not completely and evenly covered, it will still do its job and trigger a second release to catch thieves. It's easier not to trip a double-release spell at all.

I saw my mistake now, and it wouldn't happen again.

Field day was delayed because of the chilly rain pummeling Kaiamear. I was with Carmen, wearing kick pads over my forearms to help her practice, when the weather subsided with one final boom of thunder. "It's over," I sighed with relief.

Carmen paused and swiped at her head and neck with a towel as we listened to the patter of the rain grow lighter than our breaths. "Know what I realized the other day?" she asked me. She slung the towel over one shoulder and put her hands on her hips, a sign we might be done for now.

"What?" I asked.

"I haven't gotten any mail from my dad or uncle in over a month. This huge storm has been reminding me of them and those eldrafn they must be fighting." She turned her head, ducking to hide a troubled frown.

Oh. That explained the funk she'd been in, her tongue sharper than ever. "I'm sorry. Maybe there was a delay getting mail out of the Storm Front," I said.

"I keep telling myself that every day." She tilted her head one way and then the other, causing her neck to pop several times. Though she hid it well, there was fear in her eyes, the glimmer of which I could recognize anywhere. "Let's switch you over to punch mitts."

"Y'sure?" I asked, since I knew she came away extra sore and tired every time she practiced her punching.

"Let's go, pipsqueak," she grumbled.

For someone so determined not to teach another person Tosh Zorena, in having me hold the pads for physical practice, she'd taught me a lot about stances and blocking. She'd even called me a natural at it.

I switched into the broad red mitts and started catching her fists, moving with her in slow circles backward on the mat. We hadn't gone more than a quarter bell before we heard the horns. Carmen's next strike faltered, and we both lifted our ears at the unusual brassy sound infiltrating the walls of RSI.

"Oh, my gods," she whispered.

It was the Altarian anthem playing, so loudly it had to be

amplified with magic. The upbeat music wove around the first peal of the city bells, ringing in a pattern every citizen knew by heart. Even I'd learned it, in my limited fundamental education.

The bells rang with Altarian victory.

Carmen shook out her hands, her face splitting into the biggest toothy smile. "It's over. Pipsqueak, it's over!" She grabbed me into a crushing, sweaty hug. "I'm getting out of here! My father is coming home!"

The anthem started over for a second playthrough while I struggled to breathe. "That's great," I gasped out.

I was sure, outside of RSI, most of the city celebrated that night. It would be the perfect night to steal something valuable—if I were still in that business.

CARMEN WAS STILL GRINNING when the school's leadership decided it was dry enough for us to have our field day. She didn't argue or pick a fight with Vance, who was equally easygoing as our unnamed team sat at our table in the cafeteria with the other beginner teams all whispering over their dossiers.

Margot, Fariq, and I were the only ones paying much attention to what was in the folder we'd been given, even though my thoughts kept drifting too. The headmaster had confirmed that Altare had won the war over the Storm Front but warned us to stay focused on our academics, as the Crown was planning for a big celebration to start when the soldiers finished marching their way home to Kaiamear.

Once that happened, Carmen would be leaving, if not sooner. I'd miss her, attitude and all. If Jackie got the second message I'd sent off with Brinsley, she'd meet me in Haladay

Park today, and we'd have a gaping hole in our team with Vance also gone.

We'd be defeated before we even started, but I'd always known the two of them were the least engaged members of our team. I had high hopes for Margot, who was doing her best to come up with a plan as our appointed leader.

The folder included a map of Haladay Park, but someone had written overtop it. The walking trails were now "roads," the forested northern section "no man's land," the cultivated garden with its family tables "the city," and landmarks along the trails considered towns and villages.

"We need to pretend we are going to the country of Haladay Park," Margot began after double-checking a few last details on the map and report. We all turned to her expectantly. "Miss Barrios failed to return after being assigned a mission there, so it's our job to find her."

"Without making the older kids acting like Haladay Park citizens suspicious that we're spies trying to rescue her," I added.

"We're starting in the garden, where Miss Barrios was last seen. We have to seek out information about where she went, it looks like," Margot said.

"Wouldn't that make us immediately suspicious?" Vance drawled. "Hey, more importantly, what do we do if a normal family walks by and notices all this?"

"Park closed today. Should only be us there," Fariq said.

Carmen shrugged. She didn't have a care, so she was at her most relaxed. "Whatever. Let's go have fun or something."

CHAPTER 19

FIELD DAY

I FLASHED a look over at Miss Barrios, who kept the school's front door open for us. She held her wand up, glowing blue at the tip. "First place. We found you," I joked.

She smiled back warmly. "If only it were that easy, right?"

While I agreed, I practically bounded down the steps away from her and lifted my arms and face to the sun. It bathed me in watery spring light, not a cloud in the sky to shroud it. How I'd missed the kiss of warmth on my skin! Glimpses of the sun from the windows just could not compare.

Now that the weather was better, I hoped they would let us take our meals in the Square, the grassy yard in the middle of RSI, just as Miss Barrios had promised during her tour.

Vance fell into step with me for the walk to the park. "Think your contact will be there?" he murmured.

"Brinsley said he delivered both of my messages," I replied in the same low tone.

"That's not a yes."

"She didn't reply. It could be that she can't." I'd worried over every possibility when no message came back both times. "She's ten now. Maybe she's out on a job."

He raised a skeptical brow. "Maybe," he echoed.

Truth was, her silence mixed with the fact we were going to Haladay Park had me in a haze of memory. I had an older gang brother once named Thylacine. He was nearly an adult when I was a little kid. Sometimes I suspected Thylacine was my otherwise unknown father, as he'd had no shame in treating me special.

Thylacine was the only older kid who'd ever taken me to the park. Often, we'd go there surrounded by a pack of our little siblings, but he would take my tiny hand and walk by my side. But as I got older and took on more responsibilities in tending to the squalling babies and needy tots, plus my own little sister, he'd find some time to go to Haladay Park with just him and me. He'd flick a couple copper clorets to a street vendor who sold smoked sausages on a stick.

I could practically taste the tangy mustard and the sense of loss. One of those days, Thylacine had turned to me and said he was enlisting. "There's gonna to be a war, Heather. They's need big, strong boys. But don't worry, I'll send home every cloret I can. You 'n' the others won't be hungry no more."

"Can't you take me with you?" I'd replied.

He didn't, but a few of the other boys followed him to the recruitment office and were eventually posted down south to protect our border against Lithosian forces. Thylacine wrote, but there was no money. Uncle Jace said foot soldiers like Thylacine didn't make more than *a couple coppers to rub together*, in his completely scornful voice. He'd been so mad when all those boys left.

Thylacine only visited once, when he had leave. Before he knocked on the door, Jace coached me up on asking him for money. I'd never seen such sadness on my gang brother's face when I did, sitting next to him at one of the family tables in Haladay Park.

"I wish I'd taken you with me, Heather," he'd murmured.

"It's Mouse now," I reminded him. At the time, I'd been so proud to wear my late mother's title, like I'd proven myself to Jace by inheriting it.

That expression of heartbreak didn't change. "Right...my mistake."

He'd returned to the Lithosian front, only this time, there were no letters. He must've died horribly, Uncle Jace said, as sometimes rozash attacks don't leave behind identifiable bodies. I tried sending a few letters like he wasn't dead, only for them to return unopened.

I cried for Thylacine for weeks, taking it as confirmation that he'd met a gruesome end.

I drifted around lost in thought before Margot grounded me. She singsonged my name a couple times and fell into step beside me. I blinked in surprise, but that moment chased away the ghost of Thylacine from my mind.

"Isn't it a nice day, Heather? I wish I had my parasol. Oh, I used to have a lovely one in a shade of blue that matches the sky like this," she said, a haze of memory over her expressive eyes. "I matched it to an outfit that was the envy of my friends when we would promenade on spring trips to Daramaine."

I hummed in realization, coming up with what animal she reminded me of. A cat, and not the independent type that roamed the streets and found temporary refuge in places like my gang's old home. She was a noble's cat, bred to be meek and too fluffy. Events had sliced her metaphorical front paws and removed the defense of her claws. But she still had a streak of viciousness to her somewhere inside, as I'd discovered from her story about her cousin.

But I did like cats, and her fluff kept me from darker thoughts. Margot had something endearing about her that lifted my spirits. "What's *promenade* mean?" I asked.

She glanced upward and fluttered her eyelashes. "Oh, you know, a walk."

"Like this?" I gestured to the group of RSI kids all traipsing to the park.

"Not quite. A walk where you want to be *seen*," she said primly. "To show off your newest dress or turn the boys' heads. I'd never want to promenade wearing this." She plucked at her RSI uniform with poorly disguised distaste. Apparently, wearing the same outfit too often was "gauche," and she had to explain what that meant to me too.

Nobles, I decided, were an odd bunch. At least Margot left her pink fan back at the school today. She'd be likely to get it snagged on a branch and ripped in half.

We passed the weathered sign welcoming visitors to Haladay Park as the city bells rang the hour of ten. That left about seven hours to find Miss Barrios before our competitors did so we could get those bracelet upgrades. Assuming the teachers and older kids would give us until the sun set—it sounded like we'd be going back earlier, for safety's sake.

A young man wearing the RSI uniform stopped the group in the park's campground area, having us amass into a semicircle. "Visitors!" he proclaimed, throwing up his arms. "Welcome to Haladay Park. We're so happy to have you today." He wore a bright yellow sash over his black clothes, as did some of the other kids who dashed past us.

Also, more strangely, he was speaking with a pronounced and unusual accent that sounded completely made up. Some vowels were replaced with a different one, making *visitors* sound like "vis-ee-tars" and *Haladay* into "Hell-ee-dee." The dossier had mentioned the accent, suggesting we pay attention to it.

Vance crossed his arms, looking unimpressed. "Why's he talking like that?"

"It's silly, right?" Margot giggled.

"Shh," Fariq hissed at them. He tilted his head, eyes closed, concentrating on listening.

"Very soon, we will start a tour of our city. Try to keep

hands to yourself. Our people have seen many troublemaking Altarians in the past and are wary of visitors," the older kid was saying. I recognized him as one of the eighteen-year-olds who'd starred in RSI's latest play. He even had the acting chops not to grin as he delivered his lines in that goofy accent.

He walked us backward, tour guide style, labeling some of the "shops" as we passed the lunch tables. Each was now covered in junk and manned by older kids, all wearing a yellow sash to identify themselves.

"The folder said to check the wand shop," I murmured to Fariq, pointing it out as we walked past. The young man standing by his wares—piles of sticks—was none other than Davit's friend and teammate, Wyatt. The one whose journal I'd damaged. He spotted us in the crowd, and his lips twitched before he hid his reaction behind a mask of professionalism.

Fariq saw it just as much as I did. "The rest of you go talk to him. I'm going to try to pick up the accent and see if those are really for sale." He gestured to a different table, which had the yellow sashes displayed.

"Good idea," I said, a little surprised. Here he was, already thinking like a spy and looking for a way to blend in with the "locals."

As soon as the tour was done, the crowd split into our separate teams, each wandering to a different table. I took Margot, Carmen, and Vance back to the table where Wyatt waited with his hands behind his back. "Hallo, Altarians. What can this humble shopkeeper do for you?" He shot a mean smirk at Carmen and me.

Margot seemed to pick up on the tension between us and stepped forward. "Nice weather we're having. Do you sell many, err…" she glanced toward his sticks. "Wands?"

"Only for the most discerning!" He held out his hand like he wanted to shake hers and grasped her wrist at the last second, stacking random sticks into her palm. "We have ash, spruce, mahogany and many more."

Carmen's hands balled into fists as he spoke. "We're looking for someone," she blurted. "Have you seen another Altarian? Tall, with a mark right here?" She poked her cheek.

I *tisked*, feeling like asking after Miss Barrios in such a bluntly direct way wouldn't get us far. Wyatt glanced her way and said, "Can't say I have."

"Really? Maybe you could think back," she gritted out.

"Sorry you're so stupid that you can't take my first answer," he replied.

"We're just looking for our, ah, friend," Margot butted in, her eyes widening at their exchange. "Surely you'd understand us getting lost in such a big city."

He considered for a moment. "Hey, are you new or something?" he asked without the fake Haladay Park accent. "Did they really partner you up with these losers?"

I stepped into Carmen's path when she took an aggressive step forward. "Keep your cool," I whispered. I glanced to Vance for support, but he was just watching us like we were putting on a show just for him.

Wyatt sneered. "Didn't they partner with that Lithosian geek, too? You deserve better than that."

"Get out of my way, pipsqueak. I'll solve this the same way I fixed the leader of his team," she muttered back.

"Guards!" Wyatt called when she brushed past me and started toward him. Two of the larger kids wearing sashes came over at his call and converged on Carmen's hostile posture without Wyatt having to say another word. They stood in her way just as I had and then herded our team away from him.

The guards explained that we'd received a time penalty since a shopkeeper had called for them. We'd have to start the conversation over again once we were released. They led us to a table where we could sit, and we picked up Fariq on our way by. "What happened?" he asked. His gaze darted between Carmen's murderous expression and mine in concern.

I scooted over so he could sit next to me. "We have to wait half an hour because we messed up our conversation with Wyatt," I told him without adding how exactly it'd gone sideways. While I wasn't happy about Wyatt insulting Fariq, I found it interesting that Carmen's temper was so short when it came to insults against him. Had she really found a sense of team loyalty just as she was going to leave?

"Let's just say it didn't go so well," Margot sighed, rubbing the back of her head with a tinge of pink dotting her cheeks.

We weren't the only group that'd received a penalty, but most of our peers were off running down the maintained paths into the park. I sat with my back to the table, watching one interaction that ended with a shopkeeper giving one of the other groups a note from her back pocket.

I didn't say it aloud, but I had the feeling Wyatt would stall us as much as possible so we'd lose this challenge.

"The sashes aren't for sale, by the way," Fariq said, motioning to the far table where they were laid out.

"They're for stealing, then," I said absently.

"What? We can't just take…"

I slanted a look his way. "It's just a game, so we'll give them back."

He was the very image of disapproving as he said, "I suppose. Well, we need a plan."

I turned around so we could all put our heads together over the table. "We're getting a sash and the clue for the next step, no matter what," I said and realized the other four were looking at me expectantly, Margot included. So much for being our team's leader. My eyelid twitched. "Um, Carmen, Vance, and Margot are going to go talk to Wyatt again. While you distract him, I'm going to pick the clue out of his back pocket."

"Easy," Vance said with an approving nod.

I nodded too. It should be, at least. "One of us is going to knock a sash to the ground," I said to Fariq. "You'll pick it up pretending to tie your shoes."

He frowned but didn't argue. Finally, I scooped up the mouse who'd just woken up leisurely in his pouch and muffled a yawn at the same time his jaws gaped. After that, I pulled Chance close to my mouth and whispered instructions to him. He perked up and stood on his back paws. "Yes yes, I do! I be good spy too," he squeaked, darting off when I placed him in the grass.

I tapped on the table as the seconds passed before realizing my whole team was all still looking at me. "What?" I murmured.

"Did you just give Chance *instructions*?" Margot asked in a low voice, leaning in further like I was about to whisper juicy gossip in her ear.

Carmen rolled her eyes. "She was probably just saying goodbye to it and letting it go."

I hesitated and faced away from all of them, watching Chance scamper up the far table and tug a sash one painstaking knuckle length at a time until gravity took over and sent him and the brightly colored cloth down into the grass.

Margot smiled my way with a little nod of approval. I just might have to tell her Chance's secret since she'd clued in so fast.

Chance was back on my shoulder and cleaning his face meticulously by the time we were released from our time penalty. We went our separate ways, Fariq stooping down next to the table of sashes, while Carmen approached Wyatt and quickly reentered an argument with him. I snuck up behind the young man and slipped my fingertips into his back pocket, retrieving the clue he was supposed to hand us.

At the same time, one of the guards noticed Fariq walking away with a sash. "Thief!" she shouted.

Wyatt turned abruptly and caught sight of me behind him. "Thief!" he echoed, lunging for me. I hopped backward and went racing away into the tree line with him on my heels.

He said curses that Uncle Jace would beat me for as I used my smaller, nimbler body to outpace him amongst the tightly spaced bushes and undergrowth. Greenery whipped by as I twisted, dodged, and ducked. Thinking fast, I realized my options were to find a large bush and hide under its foliage or climb a tree. I picked the latter, scaling one like an overgrown squirrel and I picked a sturdy branch to sit on while Wyatt went crashing by below.

"You outsmart him. Good job," Chance said, the two of us watching the ground for any sign of him doubling back or looking up. The branches around us were only starting to bud with new life, ideal for hiding with the dark shades of my uniform.

I held my breath as he walked by again a few minutes later, body language clearly angry. When he was gone, I offered my fist to Chance, who bumped it with his tiny paw like I'd taught him. "You did great, too," I whispered. "They didn't expect a thing."

Unfortunately, there was no sign of the rest of my team from here. We were alone up this tree and probably far from the park's walking path.

CHAPTER 20

HIDDEN IN THE WOODS

I CAUGHT my bearings by the trail of broken branches and mud that marked an obvious trail to take us back the way we'd come. Even though I wasn't much of a tracker, I still saw three distinct sets of footprints—my smaller ones, then Wyatt's long stride in pursuit, and finally the same boot marks walking away from this spot. If I followed, he might be waiting to ambush me.

It was Thylacine's voice I heard in my head as I considered what to do next. We'd come here enough that he had made sure I knew exactly how to find the exit to Haladay Park if I got lost.

Don't panic. Remember to check where the sun is and walk east. You'll find a path or the street eventually.

I faced back the way we'd come and closed my eyes, picturing the park's map in my mind's eye. Though I hadn't run in anything that looked like a straight line, if I headed east, I would eventually cross one of the walking paths and hopefully find one of my friends along the way. Thanks, Thylacine.

"I scout?" offered Chance as I started walking that way.

Now that I was done bumbling through the undergrowth,

I heard the singing of insects and other wild creatures surrounding us. Any of them could be a hawk or a wildcat who'd see Chance as a juicy morsel. "That's okay. I prefer you safe and sound, right here with me," I said.

He made a frustrated little snuffle but didn't argue when I cupped him in my hand and petted his silky fur. "Good mouse, sweet mouse." With no one around to see, I cooed over him and kissed his little pointed head. He was still my Linked friend, and I wasn't going to let anything happen to him.

It wasn't too long until he turned his face to the right. "Hello? Anyone?" I heard Vance call a few moments later, plus the rustling of him stomping around.

"Over here!" I called back.

We met up somewhere in the middle, Vance looking worse for wear with a couple rips in his shirt and his perfectly glamored hair in a tousle. "Have you seen the others?" I asked.

"I was hoping you had," he answered.

"Let's head back to the tables. Maybe they're waiting for us there," I said. Knowing Fariq, he'd probably turned himself in the moment he was called a thief. And I couldn't see Margot running anywhere.

Vance followed me, as he had little sense of direction and kept either tripping over branches and rocks or snagging his clothes in the underbrush. I found the trail, which we followed until we came across a sizable rock about hip-height leaning against the bulk of a tree. Chance turned his twitchy little nose toward it.

"Told ya it was 'er," someone whispered.

"Y'sure?" came another voice, this one clearer as a head of red hair peered over the shelf of rock.

I stopped dead, recognizing the girl who spotted me and waved. She had a thin face, her head a small circle on a long neck with a mane of flame red hair she was incredibly proud of. In a ray of sunshine, her green eyes were just as bright. It was Wildcat, a girl about my age and my biggest rival for sneak jobs in Jace's Menagerie. She looked smaller than I remembered, her bones fragile outlines under her pinkish skin. She burned fast when out in the sun.

"Mouse!" exclaimed the boy who popped up next to her. Unlike Wildcat, whose keen predator eyes landed on Vance next and narrowed distrustfully, Bear was already on his feet and charging toward me with his arms out.

Bear was still ten. He'd asked me to name him after something brown and fierce and had been overjoyed when I suggested his title. Of course, I never told him it was because he was like a teddy bear, with his innate sweetness and how he was rounded with baby weight that clung stubbornly even during the leanest of times. It meant he gave great hugs, and I met him in the middle for a long Bear hug.

"Mouse, you's alive. We thought…" he murmured, burying his face in my shoulder. Someone had helped him with his hair while I was gone, as it was freshly braided into a few big rows along his head.

"We thought you were dead," Wildcat said bluntly.

Bear sobbed and clung harder. I patted his back, getting misty eyed. "But you's not! We got your messages," he said.

My lips turned down as I glanced between them. If they were here instead of Jackie, did that mean…

Wildcat crept out of her hiding place silently and jerked her chin toward Vance. "Who's that?" she asked me.

Vance seemed a little lost, but he stood back and watched with an air of curiosity, just as he had when Carmen was about to get into another fight. "He's a friend. This is Vance, the reason I needed desda powder," I said. "And Vance, this is Wildcat and Bear, siblings from my old gang."

Wildcat thrust a small cloth sack at me. I separated from Bear and took it, peering inside carefully and seeing a few pinches of crimson dust. "All we could spare," she sighed. "Can we trust 'im?"

"Yeah," I murmured, gesturing for him to follow as she and Bear ducked into the woods. They led us to a small clearing out of earshot of those who could casually pass us by on the path. As they did, I tapped Bear on the shoulder and offered him Chance. "Looks what I got." I fell into the old cadence of gang kid speech with ease, like I hadn't had half a dozen adults correcting me constantly for the last couple months.

He took the little critter with a gasp. "A real mouse!"

I let Chance charm him as we stopped moving away from the path. "Where's Jackie?" I asked Wildcat in an undertone.

She grimaced. "That's why we came t'find ya."

Rather than getting distracted, Bear looked up with a teary expression. "Boss Springfield's got Jackie!" he blurted. "We need your help!"

The whisper of the wind and all the birdsong and insect calls around us faded to pinpricks of noise. My heartbeat was the loudest thing in my ears. "What?" I breathed.

"Cartier and Rozma told Boss Springfield that you stole the…" Wildcat drifted off and glared at Vance.

"He knows about the Eye of Acuity," I said.

"Oh. They says that you took it and gave it to Uncle Jace. Uncle says no, you didn't come back, so you's dead, and if you's not, you might as well be. He came back to the house with Springfield's big men behind him."

I listened to her talk with a stone of dread sinking in my stomach. "Then they took Jackie," I murmured.

"No, they's just destroyed all our things looking for the fancy necklace. Uncle told us to let it happen so Springfield sees that we don't have it. After they's done, Uncle said again that you's dead and…" She shrugged, her shoulders falling. "That's what we thought. But Springfield didn't believe any of us and declared war against the gang."

I gasped. "No. He wouldn't!"

"He did," Wildcat said grimly. "We found your messages

shoved under a rock 'cause the house was abandoned and boarded up months ago. We moved into smaller groups in harder-to-find places and kept running jobs to keep us alive. If any of Springfield's adults find us, they's taken for ransom and dead within a week and we never see the bodies again. He says it'll all stop of we give him the Eye of Acuity."

"But Uncle doesn't have it," I said. I shook with a mix of rage and fear and shame, my belly twisting into knots. "Cartier and Rozma do!" And because I was hiding all safe and comfortable in RSI, my old gang was paying the price of their decision to take it. "How long have they had Jackie? How much time do we have?"

"Weeks," Wildcat sighed. "Springfield knows Jackie is Uncle's favorite. He's holding her at The Last Stop until Uncle pays up."

I hunched over, holding my middle through a dizzy spell. Springfield wasn't the most patient of men, and he'd had Jackie captive in his club for *weeks*. I was the worst sister—I hadn't even known or tried to return, assuming my gang would be just fine without me. With that thought, the queasiness won a war within me, and I rushed away from the group to be sick behind a bush.

"Hate to interrupt, but I think you all have a bigger problem," Vance was saying. I pictured Wildcat shooting him a dirty look as I struggled to spit up the last of a flood of bitter bile.

Truly, how could I have abandoned my gang? I'd realized staying at RSI was the selfish choice, but I hadn't considered how big the price would be. How I'd truly failed the other kids who needed me.

Still feeling ill, I returned to the clearing. "How many have died?" I murmured.

"'Bout a dozen," Bear said, still sniffling. "Mostly at first. We wised up right quick."

Vance held his palms up while I focused on my breathing,

taking deep breaths through my nose and out through my mouth. He said, "Look, I can't share a lot directly, but I'm in a gang run by someone who has a use for both dead children and rare magical artifacts."

I gasped. "You think the Morashi are part of this too?"

Wildcat's pointy nose wrinkled up. "They don't exist."

"They do. And I know for a fact the Eye of Acuity was one of our targets before I got taken to RSI. Think about it—this boss that declared war on your gang isn't acting all that reasonable. He should've backed off when he turned over your home and realized you all really didn't have it," he said.

"Yeah," she said, still looking at him with distrust.

"But instead, he's biding for time because Morashi Venom has demanded the Eye of Acuity and he cannot find it," Vance continued. "My boss threatened him with a fate worse than death. You...have no idea how motivating it can be." With a shiver, tiny bumps appeared up and down his arms.

"Like the food chain," I said to myself.

It seemed he'd heard me, as he raised a brow my way.

"Jace's Menagerie is a small fish compared to Springfield's gang," I said. "But compared to the Morashi..."

"It's about to get eaten alive. You're right. Good analogy there. So what really has to happen is that those two people that stole the necklace had better cough it up before both gangs in question get crushed under Morashi Venom's boot heel," he said matter-of-factly.

Wildcat turned to me. "Y'sure Cartier and Rozma have it?" she asked.

"Cartier was the one who pried it out of my hand after I got caught in a magical trap," I said. I was definitely squealing, but it was past due. For Jackie's life, I'd squeal straight to the peacekeepers if I had to. "He says to me it's too valuable to sell because it can see people and places when you look into it. He says, imagine what he and Rozma can steal with it.

They wouldn't need anybody anymore, not even Springfield."

"Yet they's working with Springfield to catch us now." Wildcat's expression twisted with hate.

"But why?" I murmured, scuffing the grass as I thought aloud. "Why do all this instead of giving the necklace to the Morashi boss?"

"Maybe they sold it anyhow," Bear pitched in.

"The only way to know is to ask them." Vance stroked his chin thoughtfully. "Do you know where to find them?"

"Yeah. Them two live together," Wildcat said.

"Let's send them a message. I'll deliver it and see if I can arrange a meetup." His gaze cut to me, like he was asking if I was thinking what he was.

"We have a lot to talk about," I agreed, doing my best Carmen impression when I made a fist and cracked my knuckles. Then I shook out my hand with a little *ow*.

"Can we also come talk to ya at RSI?" Bear asked hopefully.

"No," the rest of us said at the same time.

Not to be left out, Chance echoed, "No no!"

"They'll enroll us if they see us," Wildcat sighed. "And you can't leave, right? Innit what your letter said?"

"But...when will I see you again?" Bear turned such a sad look my way that I hugged him again.

"We're going to figure it out, Bear, I promise," I soothed, even though I felt anything but confident in that statement. Jackie's life hung in the balance, and I had no idea how we were going to save her, not before I had a long overdue conversation with Cartier or Rozma.

"I'll come with you," I said to Vance.

He shook his head. "There are some people I need to talk to in Morashi Venom. You should stay, get your team to help you."

I didn't miss the emphasis. My team, because once I sprinkled desda powder on his bracelet, he was gone. He had no intentions of helping us because he was on the Morashi's side, crawling back to his old life like he said he would. I didn't hide the dirty look on my face as I opened the pouch with the crimson powder and said, "A deal's a deal, then."

He'd worn the long-sleeved uniform for this but didn't move to adjust his sleeve to protect himself. "No, Heather, I —" He blew out a frustrated breath. "—I'm not taking everything I just heard and running away. But I can do some things away from RSI to help your gang that I could never do with a tracking spell on me. And you have…well, the brilliant guy who thinks of everything, a girl who will punch any problem you ask her to hit, and another girl who certainly sounds like she has money and connections. Plus a surprisingly smart mouse." He raised an eyebrow toward Chance, who at some point had scaled my clothes unnoticed and was cleaning his fur while sitting on my shoulder. "What a great crew, right?"

Crew, not *team,* what he and I would call a group we could call on to help us with anything.

I straightened with a nod. I needed a solid crew to save my sister, and as long as the others agreed to help, I had one. "We don't call the peacekeepers, and we don't tell the staff at RSI. If the authorities move, the first thing Springfield will do is hide his wrongdoing," I said. He'd kill or hide Jackie, and then it would be over.

"Agreed," Vance said. My two gang siblings nodded.

I beckoned him over and smudged my thumb with desda powder. He turned his bracelet around to show the part etched with a tracking spell and stuffed the cuff of his shirt under the bracelet.

"Promise you won't disappear?" I asked, feeling vulnerable in that moment because I knew no matter what he said, this might be the last time I saw any form of his face.

The ball of his throat bobbed. "Promise," he answered quietly.

I touched my thumb to the tracking spell and then the other side of his bracelet, which fell off him in two pieces and melted into a sizzling coppery puddle. Wildcat and Bear took him with them one way, and I went another, pretending to wander further into the forest. I entrusted Chance with the pouch of desda powder in his pocket on my belt. When the sun began to set, I found the rest of my team in the family area, sitting together with expressions that ranged from Fariq's concern to Carmen's irritated.

"Sorry, I got lost," I said as I joined them. It was a relief to get off my wobbly legs.

Margot eyed me, wringing her hands. "Are you all right? We've been waiting for ages for you to come back."

"Good to see you," Fariq said.

"We definitely aren't getting better bracelets after all this," Carmen muttered.

Fariq had turned back to the woods expectantly. "Did you see Vance?"

I called on what little scraps of acting skill I'd picked up as I feigned innocence. "Uh, no. Did he get lost too?"

CHAPTER 21

MY CREW

HEADMASTER RADCLIFFE CALLED me into his office the next morning. I hadn't slept a wink, knowing Jackie was being held at Boss Springfield's club and that I needed to come clean with my friends about needing their help and why. There were some details of my past that I never wanted them to know, but sharing them was now unavoidable.

I had been expecting some questions about Vance's disappearance, though. I'd rolled up the pouch with its pinch of desda powder and given it to Chance to put it in a hidey hole. He'd assured me that there were many places only those really low to the ground knew about, so after a long bath, I hoped there was no way to know I'd handled some of the red dust.

The headmaster was alone in his room when I entered and ducked my head, sneaking a long glance at the glass case and the crown on display. It was as I remembered, made of platinum and glittering with jewels. The double-release spell was etched across the whole plane of glass protecting it behind the curio doors. Without the spell, it'd be easy work to pick a simple lock to open the cabinet and steal the crown.

Sighing, I slumped into the seat across from the headmaster. "Good morning, Miss Mouse," he said. He was still stuffy with a head cold of some kind.

"Winterbog, sir?" I asked.

He dabbed at his nose. "It's that terrible time of year when the winterbog meets the first blooms of spring." He sounded at ease, at least, which gave me some hope that I hadn't reported to an interrogation.

"Sorry to hear," I said politely.

"I'll be all right. I'm not here to take up too much of your time today, by the way. Were you aware that your teammate, Vance Bradford, has gone missing?"

He tapped the end of a quill on the table, his keen predator eyes watching my reaction closely. "I…didn't know he was still missing. I got lost in the park yesterday, and when I found the rest of my team, they said Vance hadn't returned." Hoping this was good acting, I let him see some of the genuine concern and fatigue I felt as I lifted my gaze toward his, even if little of it was for Vance.

"Is that so?" he asked with little inflection.

Panic started to claw up my throat. What else did he want to hear, with a question like that? "Uh, yes?" I mumbled. "I didn't see him in the woods or anything."

"How concerning." The headmaster leaned back, pinching his brow. "He was our only link to an incredibly dangerous gang. I fear we'll never see him again."

I was afraid of the exact same thing, despite his promise. Vance didn't strike me as the type to have a sudden change in alliance and he'd never been ashamed to admit his loyalty to the Morashi.

"Well, you may go, Miss Mouse. That's all I needed," he said.

"Wait."

He lifted his hand, an almost knowing look on his face. I didn't like that, recognizing that some of this conversation had been an act to bait out information. "Will you tell me about this?" I pointed to the crown in its glass case.

"Ah, considering the challenge for it?" He transitioned smoothly into a proud smile. "That is Stone's Crown. One of the original founders of RSI was Princess Stone, who donated much of her wealth to establish a place in Kaiamear for us to educate and reform troubled and less fortunate children. She insisted the crown be kept here in case the school fell on a time of great need and instructed that its precious stones be sold one at a time to maintain RSI for as long as possible. If you look closely, some of the smaller settings are empty now. Go ahead."

When he motioned for me to go over to it, I didn't hesitate to squat down and nearly press my nose to the glass. The magelight in his room shone just right to make the gemstones that ringed the crown sparkle, but a few of the smaller ones were gone, just as he said. The empty prongs were tucked, but now that I was catching more than a passing glimpse of the crown, the dark squares gaped.

Still, it was a beautiful and heavy-looking piece of jewelry with many thousands of clorets worth of cut gemstones glittering tauntingly at me from behind the protection of a double-release spell.

"If your team intends to take the challenge, we would need the crown back, of course." Headmaster Radcliffe startled me; he'd joined me beside the cabinet as I took a moment to inspect how it was made.

"Of course," I echoed, standing straight. "My team was really disappointed we didn't have much of a chance with yesterday's challenge. We all really wanted the chance to come and go from the school."

"Then I suggest you all finish one of the extra credit challenges. The first one is easiest," he said. "Run along back to class now."

A FULL DAY of classes was torture with Jackie's fate still weighing heavily on my mind. I wasn't able to catch a quick nap either. Any time I put my head down and drifted, my anxiety would strike with its claws out, reminding me that she'd been Springfield's captive for far longer than he let any of the other Menagerie kids live.

If I wanted to save her, I'd need to figure out why. And if I wanted to do *that*, then I needed to muster myself for one last conversation after dinner. My team sat together at a smaller table again, one of the ones that seated four. "Could we have a meeting in the library?" I asked. Three sets of eyes turned toward me. I recognized the hesitation in Carmen's, as she saw little point again to the endless projects and work at RSI when she was leaving soon. "Please?"

"Is this about Vance?" Fariq asked.

"Partially," I said.

With that, they all agreed, and we relocated to the most private part of the library I could think of, a study room hidden behind the second floor's stacks. Patches joined us, curling up in Margot's lap since I stayed standing and paced around the worktable placed in the middle of the small space.

"You're going to make me dizzy, darling. What troubles you so?" Margot asked.

They were all looking at me expectantly, including the feligryph in disguise. Well, here goes...

"I came from a gang, before I, err..."

Vance had made this look so easy, talking about his past even when put on the spot. I tried not to look at Fariq, to see the moment his opinion of me changed for the worse.

I took a deep breath and tried again. "It was called Jace's Menagerie. All of us were given a title and a job to help make money. The house had kids...a lot of really young kids, who relied on the older kids like me to get clorets so we could all stay alive. Most of the jobs weren't really…legal." I scuffed my foot sheepishly. "I worked with adults mostly from another gang led by Boss Springfield. I was a sneak, one of the best thieves, until I got caught. And that's why I'm here."

It wasn't the best explanation, and I had mostly sympathetic looks staring back at me. They were waiting for me to come to some kind of point, I thought, fumbling toward it in a rush of words. "Look…I don't have parents anymore, but I have a sister, Jackie, and a bunch of kids as close as siblings that I left behind. I chose to be here, and it was selfish because they needed me, but I saw the food and the clothes and the opportunities here and wanted it. I wanted to be a spy, to be someone…someone *better*." I felt my voice threaten to crack with emotion and noticed Fariq nodding. "And I had the headmaster and Miss Barrios agree that Jackie could join me at RSI someday, when I had the freedom to leave the school and explain everything to her."

"Ah. We left yesterday," Fariq said, mostly to himself.

"We did, and I learned that my gang and my sister are in a lot of trouble." I sagged with the burden of everything.

"Maybe you should have a seat," Margot suggested. "This feels like it will be a long story, yes?"

"Yeah," I sighed.

Carmen nudged the chair next to her backward by the leg, indicating I sit with a jut of her chin. "Gotta say, I'm not surprised you were a thief, pipsqueak."

I sat and realized Fariq was also nodding in agreement with her. "It's pretty obvious," he said. "I watch you take and hold on to anything that might be useful, even if it's junk."

"Junk?" I repeated, a little offended.

"You've got a screwdriver on your belt," he pointed out. "But next to it is a pouch. What's in it?"

Absently, I undid the drawstring of that pouch and lifted

out a palm full of the metal spheres I'd taken from the innovation workshop.

"You see?" he said.

"These are going to be very useful someday," I replied.

He turned to Carmen and Margot, exaggerating a gesture toward me.

"Yes, you've proved your point," Carmen drawled.

"But what is this trouble your sister and gang are in?" Margot prompted.

I thought of all the talking I needed to do to catch them all up. Maybe my fatigue would overpower my anxiety this evening, once the tale was done. That thought motivated me to begin with Yule and the failed heist, to introduce them to the two adults who'd taken advantage of me and left me in a magical trap so they could have the Eye of Acuity.

Then I laid out the gang food chain for them, repeating everything Wildcat and Bear had shared yesterday. Springfield's gang ate Jace's, but the Morashi were lurking too, somehow interested in both the Eye of Acuity and the kids that were going missing after a week's ransom and presumed dead.

Even Carmen listened, occasionally cracking her neck or knuckles as her gaze flickered. I think she was imagining throwing punches and kicks, saving the day with the art of Tosh Zorena.

Margot had produced her frilly pink fan from somewhere and fanned herself, getting emotional when I did as I spoke of my sister's uncertain fate.

Fariq was completely still on the outside, but that probably meant he was thinking through the problem before he spoke.

"Sorry sister in trouble," Chance said from my palm. "We save, yes yes?"

"I hope we can save her. I hope we can stop all of this," I said. "But in the meantime...I set Vance free because he promised to help. He's going to go talk to people he knows in Morashi Venom."

Carmen snorted. "Fat chance he's ever coming back."

"I know he's not the most trustworthy," I mumbled. "But he's the only one with connections to a gang none of us thought existed. And he also was thinking we could meet with Cartier and Rozma. They might know where to find the necklace if they don't have it."

"Releasing him was the right thing to do," Fariq said, surprising me. "And telling us all this is good too, even though it's hard." He reached across the table, squeezing my hand in sympathy.

"I just don't know what you expect us to do when we're stuck here," Carmen said.

"Well, I'm not." Margot twisted her bracelet as she spoke. "I have a part-time job at an employment agency. Tell me what you need, and I will do it," she said fiercely, like a pampered cat showing her teeth.

I nodded in gratitude. "We can use you to deliver messages and go where we can't. The rest of us need to get that freedom, though." I produced my battered schedule and turned it over, displaying the three extra credit challenges to the group. "We have to finish at least one of these, and the headmaster thought the first one would be easiest."

"Deliver a properly coded message to Altare's Spymaster," Margot read aloud. "Hmm. Doesn't seem too hard."

"But who is the Spymaster?" I asked.

For a moment, the table was silent.

"Wouldn't it be the headmaster?" Margot ventured.

Fariq shook his head. "The wording says Altare's Spymaster. They would be too busy to run a school."

"Well if they're outside of the school, how are we supposed to get a message to them?" Carmen grumbled.

"That's not the most pressing problem." I almost said *our* most pressing problem, as I was getting the feeling these three people were in. They would really be my crew and help me save my sister. But their reaction to my next question would be most telling. "If Vance did convince Cartier and Rozma to a meeting, how do…we convince them to give up the Eye of Acuity?"

Margot didn't even pause this time. "Why, you offer them a trade. If they have this magical necklace in their possession still, they'll want to be rid of it discretely," she reasoned. "Imagine if you had something of equal monetary value. If it doesn't have the baggage of a gang of Tulari killing for it, they should be eager to agree to the trade."

"If only we were rich, right?" Carmen said dryly.

I sat there, momentarily stunned with realization. "We don't have to be," I murmured. "I have half of an idea."

Fariq's expression was lined with concern. "That's the most dangerous kind of idea," he said.

CHAPTER 22

SPYMASTER

THOUGH I PASSED out early that night, I woke the next morning before the first bells. The nerves in my belly didn't help me do more than toss and turn, so I eventually tiptoed out of the room. I found the nearest magelight in the hallway and set up under it, writing out four identical messages in the basic code Miss Liang had taught me.

I tore them out of my journal and set them aside in favor of making a list of every adult I'd met at RSI. My half-formed idea hinged on finishing the first extra credit challenge and having a direct line to the Spymaster, just in case. He, or she, had to be on our side if I wanted to successfully pull off what I was thinking.

It was in those early hours that I started piecing together my thoughts, doubts, and fears into a plan so ambitious I didn't dare to write it down. Instead, I distributed copies of the coded message to my crew and told them to give it to the person they thought was the Spymaster. I kept mine in my pack and waited to see the person I wanted to give it to.

Days passed. I said nothing of the plan... I said almost nothing at all, my tongue weighed down and my mind paralyzed with the crushing weight of uncertainty. My sister was in trouble, and any moment could be her last. I'd answer to the Gatekeeper if I waited too long behind the excuse of timing.

The only person able to coax more than one or two words from me ended up being Margot, who spent as much time with me as she could, considering our different schedules and her job, which she'd taken an emergency leave from to spend her time following me. "Sisters are so important. Trust me, if it were my dear Serla, I'd be begging you to look after me," she said one afternoon after my classes were over.

I was on the hunt for a specific man. He'd never been too hard to find when I wasn't looking for him, but we'd had little luck walking the halls like this. "Is she like you?" I asked quietly.

"Hmm?"

"Your sister," I said a little louder. "Is she...nice? Easy to talk to?"

That was my impression of Margot through the short time I'd known her. She was almost too easy to talk to, and I wanted to chip off the top of the boulder of worries lodged in my gut to tell her all about it even after days of queasy silence.

Margot smiled to herself. "I suppose you could say that. You can't get much of a word in edgewise when we're in the same room unless we both want to know the same thing from someone else." A wistful look stole into her happiness as we turned down Stryker Hall, headed for the gym. "I miss her dreadfully. We were pushed to be perfect and marriageable young ladies our whole lives. Securing a good match was supposed to be our number one goal before we grew too old."

I pulled a face. Marriage at sixteen—*yuck*.

"What our mother never said was how lonely it is. Serla had her happy day, and I have not seen her since. She had her husband's support for our parents' death, and I have..." She shook her head of curls. "Well, I have RSI and the chance at a life I never thought I'd have. Without it, I think I would crumple, if I'm honest. I'll never have what Serla has, and many of my fair-weather friends have since abandoned me with the disgrace that follows being sent to a reformatory in the first place."

I stopped walking and turned to her. She did the same, cocking her head at me curiously. I took a grounding breath and threw my arms around her for a fierce hug. "Oh." She laughed, hugging me back.

"It'll get better," I murmured, speaking from experience. I barely thought of my mother anymore, even though her death had devastated me when I was tiny and vulnerable. And Thylacine...well, he was coming up more in my thoughts lately. I wish he were alive too, to tell me if he really was my father as I suspected. But they were both gone, and I had to somehow plough ahead to make sure my sister didn't join them.

"Thank you, Heather. I'm happy to have new friends like you and something to do in the meantime," she said. "Ah, do you think we'll find this janitor of yours in the gym, perhaps?"

I sniffed, appreciating the change of subject. "Let's see," I said, opening the door and walking both of us into a self-defense class in session.

My eyes widened immediately. Five people were in motion on the mat while several older kids sat against the far wall, watching a young man defend himself with his fists while the other four rushed at him with daggers in hand. He deflected and dodged, leaving one girl on the floor, clutching her wrist.

I was too busy gaping to look for Manny, the janitor. The defending fighter was good, probably cracking a few bones in the process of defending himself, but eventually, one of the other people fighting him jabbed their dagger into the side of his neck. Margot released a shrill shriek, and I was sure we were about to see a fountain of blood right there on the mat.

He turned toward the door. "It's a prop!" he shouted over at us, pulling the dagger free and tilting his neck to show that there was no damage.

One of the Coach Strykers, the lean woman, came over to shoo us back out the door. "You shouldn't have seen that yet," she said, eyeing us sternly. Margot was still shaken and pale next to me.

"Sorry," I murmured, my shoulders folding in.

"Have you seen Manny today, Coach?" Margot asked her in a smaller voice than usual.

She shook her head. "Come around again tomorrow. He has more jobs than just cleaning up after you kids."

I glanced over at Margot, raising my brows. She gave me a shrug in return, not yet convinced I'd found the elusive Spymaster.

How could one man be so mysterious?

The next time I saw Manny, he was carrying a mop and bucket upstairs to get to work on the mess left in most class-rooms once they were used for a whole day. For a moment, I thought he looked over his shoulder and saw me tailing him. When I sped up so I wouldn't have to yell after him, taking the steps two at a time, I'd turned to see which hall he'd gone down, just to be looking at empty air.

Now, I'd already found out the hard way that the hall-ways had nowhere to hide. It was at that moment I knew for sure. I was tailing either a ghost or the Spymaster. And to deliver my coded message, I needed to run into him by acci-dent, like I had before unknowingly, or find a situation where he had to stand around and wait to clean. The gym was a good choice, if they weren't going to kick me out again.

As luck would have it, the next morning, the headmaster called a special meeting after breakfast. I was giddy when I turned in my seat and spotted him standing against the back wall with his broom, mop, and bucket at the ready when we cleared out the cafeteria. While the headmaster explained that the Crown was calling for a parade next week when Altare's troops returned from the Storm Front and their long walk home, I was creeping over to Manny's side and extending out a roughly ripped sheet of paper.

His fingers closed around it, and he cocked his head. "What's this, young miss?" he asked.

Doubts needled me, despite his disappearing act earlier. The other three messages had come up duds; my crew hadn't given them to the right people. But they'd given them to teachers or staff members, all of whom spent whole days teaching at RSI.

Manny was only here every once in a while.

It was rare to see him alone. He was popular with the older kids especially, who looked eager to speak to him.

He was good at arithmetic. Well, better than me, and a patient teacher. That had to mean something, right?

"A message for you," I said.

"How intriguing. I'll read it later." He folded it and slipped it down the front pocket of his overalls.

My lips twitched downward. Was that it? He wasn't going to tell me if I'd guessed right or not?

"You should listen. You're getting time off your school-work," he added with a jut of his chin toward the headmaster.

I stayed where I was and caught the end of what was being announced. Not only were we getting *some* time off, it sounded like we might be released from the school to celebrate for however long the Crown called for it. For a moment, I cursed the timing. Big events were great for stealing things.

Maybe they'd be great for stealing...*people*. I could pay a visit to The Last Stop personally and see about freeing Jackie from the club.

Then Boss Springfield and his adults would recognize me and hold me captive right next to her.

Stick to the plan.

Unfortunately, the plan involved waiting some more. I turned it over in my mind until its sides were sanded clean, like a river stone tumbled smooth in the stream of my thoughts. The only missing variables were the Spymaster... and Vance.

CHAPTER 23

TIER ONE

BRINSLEY SAT down across from me as I spent another tutorial period in the cafeteria. Miss Barrios had gotten frustrated with me staring blankly at my work yesterday after passing Manny the coded message. She said I'd be here, and so I was, still surrounded by untouched assignments.

I looked up at Brinsley with my heart in my throat. "Can I help you?" I murmured.

"Maybe I can help you, actually," he replied in Vance's voice.

The relief I felt was so heady I nearly passed out on the spot. "You came back," I said with a little disbelieving laugh.

"I promised. Here, hide these." He slid a couple sheets of parchment over to me, and I stuffed them into my bag. "I need you to do me a favor. You still got that desda powder?"

"Yeah."

"Can you destroy this? Quickly?"

He placed another piece of parchment on the table, just out of reach. I woke Chance from a nap by lifting him out of his pouch, and he blinked up at me sleepily. "We need the powder," I whispered, scratching down his back with one fingernail in apology.

"I get for you," Chance squeaked before opening his mouth wide in a yawn. I muffled one of my own and placed him on the ground to scurry off.

"Smart mouse," Vance commented.

"What's with the paper?" I countered, gesturing toward it. He tapped the table next to it, leg bouncing with the kind of anxiety I recognized.

"Can't tell you 'til it's gone," he said.

I didn't like that answer, but I didn't ask further. The fact that he'd really returned worked wonders for my trust. You never betray your crew, and he proved himself part of mine just by showing up.

"Anyway, I've got news." He lowered his voice, and I leaned in. "I visited The Last Stop wearing a different face and scoped out the place. I drew you a map and also got eyes on your sister. At least, I think it was her."

"She okay?" I burst out.

He nodded once. "She's fine. They put her to work serving drinks and food. Thing is, she was wearing a tethering band. You know what those are?"

I shook my head and glanced down. Chance was tugging on my sock. He'd tied the little pouch of desda powder around his neck and gotten back here really fast. "Who's the best mouse?" I cooed, scooping him up and freeing him from the pouch's strings.

"I am! I am!" Chance exclaimed, trembling with unrestrained happiness. He held out his tiny fist for a bump, and I obliged, knowing Vance was watching with obvious intrigue.

"You were saying?" I asked Vance while taking out a small pinch of powder. He changed seats to be farther away from the paper as it started melting from the sprinkling of red dust before it burst into flames.

I jumped to my feet, ready to dash it to the ground and stomp on it. "No!" Vance grabbed my wrist, and I flinched hard. "Let it burn."

I snatched my hand back. "The table…"

It was fine, actually, as the flaming piece of paper became a pile of ash without the fire touching either the table or the very flammable fan of homework I'd set out. Vance breathed a deep sigh of relief, his head lolling back as the last of the fire sputtered out.

"Right," he said, shaking off whatever that reaction was and brushing the ashes out onto the ground. "A tethering band is a magical device for criminals, to make it impossible for them to escape their jail cell. I sensed one of the Morashi's extra-strength ones around her ankle. She's stuck in The Last Stop, but that's not all it does—"

Miss Barrios dashed into the room, her wand raised and a magical breeze blowing through the room behind her. "Where's the fire?" she demanded.

Vance and I exchanged a frightened glance before he leapt to his feet. "I took care of it, ma'am," he said in his best impression of Brinsley's wavering voice.

She turned toward him, eyes narrowing and sparking with blue magic. *Musty devils, she's caught us.* There was no way she didn't realize that wasn't Brinsley standing there.

Then her attention went to the obvious trail of ashes from the table to the ground. She lowered her wand and shook her head. "Thank you, Brinsley. You can go back to your duties… I needed to talk to Heather anyway."

"Yes ma'am," Vance replied, turning and leaving the cafeteria with our conversation hanging there half-finished.

I palmed the pouch of desda powder, hiding it under the table. Tiny paws tugged on it. "I take back," Chance offered. As I released it, I hoped he waited a moment for me to distract Miss Barrios.

"What did you want to talk about?" I asked nervously, standing and going over to her, hoping she didn't look too closely at the ashes.

She flashed her usual warm smile and extended a folded

piece of parchment to me. "You should take a minute to decode this before I tell you the good news," she said.

I tried to ignore how she sat where Vance had been and muttered something under her breath while I worked on figuring out the coded message she handed me. Miss Liang had taught a couple of basic cyphers in language club, and after some time and sweating about the ashes, I recognized the code and wrote out the real message on the bottom of an untouched assignment.

Congratulations, Miss Mouse. Sasha will take care of your request.

I smacked my palms on the table. "He *was* the Spymaster!" I exclaimed. I glanced up at her, and my lips twitched upward. "You know of a way to contact the Spymaster quickly?"

"There's a much more direct way, since he only comes around when he has a spare moment to speak to spy candidates. It'll be on your new bracelet," she promised. "Why don't you pack up your stuff and come with me?"

I did so eagerly and presented my wrist in the same room where I'd first been shackled with this copper bracelet in the first place. With a tap of her wand, it was a straight piece of metal again and going back into storage for the next new RSI kid.

"This upgrade will stick with you a lot longer, so we usually offer a choice of materials for your next bracelet," she said, laying out the possibilities. Nothing was as fancy as Margot's pearl-studded piece, which I suspected was from her collection of jewelry, but some resembled the silvery metals that almost everyone else seemed to wear, older kids and teachers included.

Still, my fingertips landed on a strip of chocolatey brown leather that would close around my wrist with a little metal clasp. It was perfect. No one would try to steal it off me for being flashy, and it wouldn't catch the light when I didn't want it to. "This one," I said.

She wove a spell over it, and it secured itself to my wrist. "Your bracelet is now upgraded to tier one. RSI's outer doors will now unlock at your touch during daylight hours. However, the spell coded to them will communicate with a ledger that will record the time you leave and the time you return. We look at it regularly for any suspicious behavior," she warned.

She turned over the band and pointed to a little circular symbol that resembled a tiny version of Lord Orion's holy symbol, a spell circle. "And here is the spell that will help you communicate with the Spymaster. You touch any correspondence you want to send to him to it and say 'no locks.' The parchment will disappear from your hand and reappear in his inbox. The Spymaster's secretaries check his mail at least once a day."

"Perfect," I breathed. "Why that phrase, though?"

"It's half of an old saying." She shrugged and leaned against the wall, the picture of ease. She really wasn't suspicious. But that was a close one, too close for what was at stake. "Personally, I think it is 'no locks, only keys.'"

I nodded, twitching with the need to be in motion again. I was eager to see the map Vance said he'd left me and maybe catch up to him before he traded places with the real Brinsley. "Well, thank you for this," I said, holding my wrist up as I backed toward the door. "I'm sure there will be a class change soon, and I better go…"

She followed me back to the cafeteria, unfortunately. I was starting to wonder if she was suspicious after all as she watched me pack away my things. "Heather, is something troubling you?" she asked.

"Hmm? No," I said, hoping I sounded innocent.

"It doesn't seem like you've gotten much done," she continued in the same concerned tone, turning over a piece of parchment. I pulled that one away from her before she got a good look at the doodle on the other side of a wart-covered weasel sitting behind a begging bowl. That would require too much explaining.

I blurted out the first thing I thought of. "I've just been a little distracted. My team. I mean, with Vance gone…"

She gave me a sympathetic smile. "I understand. It must be hard to lose someone you thought you could rely on, but look what your group has accomplished without him. Finishing one of the extra credit challenges is something to be proud of."

"I don't know if we'll be able to finish the other two," I murmured.

I checked under another assignment and packed it away before she could spot the mongoose I'd shaded in with rapid scribbles of my quill. The furry beast stood out as parchment colored in a block of black shadows, with a pitiful expression turned toward the perspective and the shadow of bars across its body.

"Well, you are my Little. If there's anything you want help with, I'd love to plan with you," she offered.

"Yes, of course," I murmured, wishing for a moment that I could trust her. But she was an adult, and I knew she'd have to stop me if she was aware of what I was thinking.

It was toward the end of my Lithosian language class that I finally felt it safe to pull out what Vance had given me. The map of The Last Stop was surprisingly detailed, but I tucked it aside in favor of reading the note that came with it.

At the top was a doodle of a mouse, before the message was scribbled in shorthand. Any one of the teachers here would call it lazy, but I recognized the small pictures and abbreviations as well as if they were words.

Mouse,

Cartier and Rozma agreed to meet in neutral territory. Crossing of Doranwood and Trade Street, this weekend, after the eighth hour bell. Your friend says you can't come, but we hope you can make it anyway.

Bear wants you to know he misses you lots.

Love,

Ram, Dexis, Wildcat, Bear, and Needlecoat

At least, I thought that was a doodle of a pointy needlecoat at the end. It had to be one of the younger kids who'd named him or herself since I was gone. I turned the parchment over, wanting more than just a quick note from a few of my gang siblings. I needed to know they were all okay and safe, because there were a lot more than five that I wanted to check in with.

There was another note, though, this one in Vance's handwriting.

In case I did not get an opportunity to tell you everything:

1-I've secured a meeting with the married couple you say have the necklace. A group of kids from your gang and I will be at the meeting place extra early if you have a plan you want to suggest. In the meantime, I told the couple I wanted to hire them for a job. If you're not able to make it, I will reveal that I'm a member of my gang and intimidate them into returning the piece.

I snorted, thinking that was unlikely to work. Rozma especially was not intimidated by anything. Good thing I'd be able to attend this meeting and change Vance's plan. I skimmed over him specifying the time and place, as it was the same as what my gang siblings had said.

2-Brinsley wants a full day off next week to party with his friends. See if you can secure the detention hall for a day and let him know which one. I have an idea!

3-Your sister is not in direct danger, but she is wearing a teth-

ering band that's preventing her from leaving The Last Stop. It is designed to kill her if it's deactivated incorrectly. Save up your clorets to rent a Tulari's all-key or see if Miss Barrios will lend you hers.

Hope to see you soon.

He didn't sign it with his name, and I frowned at the message about my sister. So that's what Vance was trying to tell me earlier...and hopefully some information on what an "all-key" was. It sounded important, but since I didn't know what it was, I had no excuse to explain away why I needed one to Miss Barrios.

Even more concerning was Boss Springfield holding her for ransom with Morashi Venom's help. There had to be a reason other than her being one of Uncle Jace's favorite kids. I needed to find out why before it was too late.

CHAPTER 24

MORNING DEALS

THE CORNER where Doranwood and Trade Street intersected was shadowed by two-story shops where the wealthy go when they want a fashionable wardrobe upgrade. Or so Margot told me as we walked down Doranwood, huddling together in the early morning chill. There were plenty of folk in plain clothes working on deliveries, as this was considered a back road that wound behind many of the major shops in Kaiamear.

I decided to only take Margot to this meeting. Fariq and Carmen were aware it was happening but didn't change their weekend habits from usual. I figured it would be less suspicious if the ledger showed that two of us went out early rather than my whole crew.

Plus, there was less of a chance that straightlaced Fariq would interrupt the meeting by arguing that I couldn't barter away something I didn't own. Or for Carmen to get mad and pick a fight.

We'd ducked into a bath house to get Margot changed into one of her old dresses, which we'd smuggled out along with a few pots of cosmetics in my pack. The dress was dark green and uncomfortable-looking. She'd wanted it tight around her ribs in a way that required me to yank on the ties behind her back. Once it was in place, she'd quickly painted her face and outlined it expertly to make herself look a little older.

After she was done, she turned to me and motioned with her brush. I shook my head sadly, because I did want to see what her cosmetics could do to make me look older too. "I don't want to get fancy for them," I'd explained.

"Later, then," she'd said.

Even with the detour, we arrived early and waited in the shadows of a red brick building. "Remember, we need at least until Wednesday," I murmured. We'd booked out the detention rooms for that day under the excuse that we wanted to attempt the second extra credit challenge. Vance would presumably be joining us as Brinsley for whatever idea he had up his sleeve.

"Right," Margot said patiently. We'd been over this a couple times already.

"We want them to bring the goods next time we see them," I said.

It was a big assumption, considering the circumstances, that one of them would come to any meeting *wearing* the Eye of Acuity. But Chance had agreed to take a huge risk for me just in case they didn't want to answer that demand.

"And we're offering them something of greater worth," she added, still disbelieving. She'd said that all the jewelry and fine clothes she'd been allowed to take from her parents' estate combined didn't come close to equaling the magical necklace's value.

I wasn't concerned. I knew Cartier and Rozma and how they worked. "Yeah. We're *offering*," I said meaningfully. Margot, who'd never stolen a thing before in her life, didn't seem to understand the emphasis.

We didn't wait much longer for another group to join us like five lean shadows. Bear broke out into a big smile, and I held my arms out for a hug automatically as he came over.

My gang siblings had donned cloaks to hide their faces, but they pulled them back a moment to say hello.

Ram and Dexis stood at the back of the group and kept a cautious eye out. They were both about Margot's age. I hadn't named Ram; Uncle Jace had for his tendency to go into problems head-first, without an ounce of caution.

But I'd convinced Dexis to take her current name when I'd become the keeper of the book of animals. It took some work, as she hadn't understood why I suggested Dexis instead of Widow if she was going to be a spider. She was curvy and pretty and used her charms to steal men blind, but *Widow* was an obvious tell, while *Dexis* could be a last name. Besides, dexis spiders only maimed their mates rather than ate them. It was nicer.

I smiled with delight when I spotted Needlecoat's face. He was freshly ten, as I'd suspected, and the name couldn't be more perfect. He liked practicing with sharp objects and was probably carrying a few.

After a round of hellos and introductions, in which Margot was terribly confused by my gang siblings' animal names, I turned to Dexis, who was most likely the leader of the five of them. "I came with a plan. I need you out of sight," I said.

Her brow furrowed. "Why?"

Well, Ram was just as likely as Carmen to want a fight, and little Needlecoat was probably eager to reinforce his title by drawing whatever sharp objects he'd brought. It would be a disaster. But I didn't say that. "I just need them not to be intimidated by all of us, plus Vance." I glanced around for a moment. "Where *is* Vance?"

Four heads turned toward Needlecoat, who grinned broadly. "You didn't really think we'd bring a newly titled boy, did ya?" Dexis snorted.

"I was wondering how long it'd take," the boy said in

Vance's voice. He must've avoided talking to make sure he didn't give it away.

"You're shorter," I commented.

"Spinal compression," he answered. "It's not fun."

Ram pulled out a stick of chalk and a pair of dice from his pocket. "We'll be over there," he said, jerking his chin around the corner to the shadowy alley between buildings. "Give us a holler, and we'll bring the force."

"No force necessary, I hope," I murmured.

He took a few steps toward me and leaned down, cupping my cheeks and forcing me to look up into his gray eyes. "Don't get intimidated, Mouse. Or I *will* do this my way."

Dexis nodded and punched her palm with her fist. I blinked slowly as I realized none of my gang siblings knew how much I'd tried to change since going to RSI. I was a meek Mouse but not quite as helpless in a confrontation as they remembered. They were still ready and willing to protect me, though, and that gave me a warm feeling in my chest.

It was short lived. My eyelid flickered, and nerves and the trembles took over twice as bad when the five of them hid around the corner and pretended to play a dice game. Margot waited with her hands folded over her middle, the image of poise if not for how she rocked back and forth on the balls of her feet.

"Oh, Heather, I don't know about this..." she was saying when I spotted a pair of folk headed toward us, hoods drawn. Their shape and gaits were right. I'd seen Rozma's confident march and broad shoulders dozens of times, just like the pained, bowlegged way Cartier limped alongside her like his joints popped with every stride.

When they saw me, their reaction was more than I hoped for. Their hoods moved toward each other in a fast whip of disbelief, but they didn't approach with the hostility I think Ram was expecting.

"Mouse! It's really you," Rozma exclaimed. I braced

myself a moment before she swept me up in a hug with all her strength, like she wanted to crush my ribcage with her affection.

"Good t'see you, kid," Cartier said.

Rozma released me, and I refilled my lungs with a gasp. "I just couldn't believe we had to leave you at the Gladbeck job. He told me there wasn't no other way, and I was real sad, Mouse," she said.

"Real sad," he echoed.

"We've been filled with all the would-a's and could-a's." She slung a heavy arm over my shoulders.

"But you's alive, obviously." Cartier eyed my clothes and scoffed. "Oh, they put you in that school."

"Gods-awful place, I've heard. Gotta do what you gotta do to survive, though," Rozma said.

"Too bad, really."

"Jace was so upset when he thought you'd died."

Cartier's smile was turning into a grimace. "Ya tell 'im the good news yet, or just decide to surprise us first?"

I opened my mouth, but Rozma rushed in to say, "So, what's this job, huh?"

I recognized their tactic, filling the air with false apologies until, when they finally let me get a word in edgewise, it was assumed I had forgiven them. Which, there was no chance of that, but I hadn't grown up in Jace's Menagerie without learning how things like this went.

They needed clorets, so they were just as tempted as always by a job. That was the only reason they'd come here this morning. "I'm here with my friend to propose a trade," I said, gesturing to Margot.

"A pleasure to meet you." She put the noblewoman's accent on thick, by my request.

Rozma's arm tightened around my shoulders, becoming more of a chokehold. "What ya mean, a trade?" she demanded.

Margot answered for me. She drew some of her blonde hair behind her ear, rattling the large earrings she wore, which glittered with cut emeralds. I owed her big for taking out her finery for this, especially since the pair were the most expensive she owned. "I'm a collector, you see. I have dozens of magical items in my collection."

Cartier pulled his wife away from me, and I breathed a little easier without her arm that close to my neck. While she was fully in a defensive posture, he was nudging her, a hint of greed crossing his weasel-like face.

"I told her you might have a certain necklace," I said.

Rozma's nostrils flared, and her pale cheeks reddened. "Such a rare item never changes hands," Margot butted in before the other woman could snap at me. "I do not have the raw currency to buy it off of you, but I *do* have something I think would be worth your while..." She simpered and placed her fingertips on her jaw. "That is, if you still have the necklace."

"We do," Cartier answered immediately. My heart leapt in my chest. They really hadn't sold it, so now we had to offer them an exchange they couldn't refuse.

Rozma flashed a tight smile at Margot. "'Scuse us for a moment," she said, drawing her husband forcibly to the other side of the road.

I glanced over at my friend before watching the two adults argue in low tones. "You tell them that you have an ancient crown that once graced the head of Princess Stone," I whispered to her. "Made of platinum and kept museum fresh, heavy with giant glittering gemstones worth thousands of clorets each."

I felt rather than saw Margot's disbelief. "No, I don't," she hissed.

"You will in a few days," I said with about as much confidence as I could muster.

Chance peeked his pointy head out of his pouch. "I spy now?" he asked me.

"Not yet," I whispered, seeing the couple coming to some resolution in their argument. They'd be coming back over here at any moment.

Rozma took the lead on their negotiations, standing far too close to Margot. "We wanna hear about your item," she demanded.

"It is a keepsake," Margot responded. She craned her head up to meet the larger woman's gaze. "A beautiful and well-preserved crown that a royal princess once wore. Its weight in gemstones alone equals the worth of the necklace."

"What's it made of?" Rozma asked in the same aggressive tone, no hint of interest in her bearing yet.

But I knew they'd take the deal. They didn't want to be caught holding something like the Eye of Acuity when Morashi Venom was literally killing to get their hands on it. And if they thought they could take advantage of us rather than hand off the necklace, all the better.

"Platinum. Once you remove the stones, I'm sure you can have it melted down," Margot sniffed.

"We'll take it," Rozma said gruffly. "You got it now?"

My friend released a high, tinkling laugh that she covered daintily with her fingers. "Gods, no. I don't just carry such valuable things around," she said. "We weren't even sure if you still had the necklace. The coming festivities will make timing the exchange more problematic. I can bring it to this location in a few days?"

Cartier hid another grimace poorly but left the talking to his wife. "Here, after nightfall, four days from now," she stated.

I exchanged a glance with Margot. That would be the same day as when we'd booked the detention rooms. It'd be tight, but…I dipped my chin in a subtle nod. It was doable.

"Very well," Margot said with barely a pause and held her

hand out to shake. She cringed from the force Rozma no doubt used to seal the deal.

"It was good t'see ya again, Mouse," Rozma said, turning back to me.

I couldn't find it in me to smile, so I just bared my teeth. "Likewise," I gritted.

She didn't linger, no true warmth there. "And a'course we'll be trading with ya shortly, Lady…"

"Norston," Margot lied smoothly. A duke family name, she'd told me in advance. The Norstons were apparently both numerous and eccentric, the perfect cover.

As they turned away, I took Chance out of his pouch and placed him low on my uniform pants. He scampered to the ground and took off after the two of them, catching the edge of Rozma's cloak and flashing a tiny thumbs up at me as she carried him away. I watched him go with my heart thumping away within my throat, afraid either they or any number of hungry predators would spot him between now and when I'd see him again.

"Let's go," I murmured, turning down the alleyway where my four gang siblings plus Vance were listening in. They patted my shoulders and ruffled my hair before they went one way, while Vance fell in beside me, heading back in the direction of RSI. Margot avoided a produce cart in the process of crossing the main road, going back to the bath house without me to change.

I drew the hood of my cloak up, slouching to match Vance's disguise. "So, what's an all-key?" I asked quietly.

"That's a more complicated question than you think," he answered. "Most Tulari wizards possess the ability to make a unique spell called an all-key that can undo spells cast by any wizards. In the case of a certain tethering band that we need to open, an all-key is the only thing that will unlock it without triggering the deadly magic inside it."

"Okay," I said with trepidation.

"Wizards only ever get one all-key. They either have to trust you a lot to lend it to you, or you have to steal it."

I had a sinking heart, because I couldn't see myself convincing Miss Barrios to lend me hers. "What's it look like?"

"Guess."

"A key?"

"Yeah. Practicing wizards always have theirs around just in case something goes wrong with a spell. There's…one more catch. The tethering band will record the magical signature of any all-key that's used on it."

"What do you mean?" I asked. He'd said that like it was a very bad thing.

"The boss…" he sighed and breathed her name. "*Madam Morashi* will then know the identity of the all-key we use on the tethering band. She could and would use it to track down the wizard who made that all-key. Trust me, she's not the forgiving type when she feels she's been crossed."

I shook my head slowly, my palms sweating at the thought. "I'm not bringing Miss Barrios to your gang's attention," I said. "There has to be another way."

"Got a couple thousand clorets to borrow one?" he asked dryly.

"Don't you have a whole group of mages you could steal one from?" I asked in the same tone.

He ducked his head further, hiding in the recesses of his cloak and mumbling something.

"Hmm?"

"I…I can't go back there," he whispered. "You know that paper you helped me burn?"

I recalled the look of relief on his face when it was destroyed and nodded cautiously.

He was practically sheepish. "That was my magically enforced contract with Madam Morashi. I can tell you gang secrets now, but the others will know something's wrong if they see me again. Th-they would take me t-to her and…" He shuddered, something clear and bright in his eyes like the level of fear only a cornered animal would have.

"And what?" I breathed.

He forced a nervous laugh, shaking himself off. "I mean, don't get too cozy without me at RSI. I'll be coming back before you know it, because I'm not a member of…that group anymore. I'd receive the maximum c-consequence if I were taken to Madam Morashi."

I stared at him in blatant disbelief. "Did you kiss that boy on your way out at least?" I asked.

He barked a laugh like I'd caught him off guard. "No, unfortunately. I didn't want to put him in danger," he said. "Oh, and don't get too emotional or anything. I have my own reasons for doing all this."

If he was under a magical contract, I'm sure he did; there was more to Vance than I'd realized. And he was clearly terrified of the Morashi boss. "You're welcome on my crew any time," I said, slowing as we neared the bath house where Margot was changing. The crunch of footsteps sounded behind us, and I quieted my voice. "See if you can locate an all-key we can borrow, okay? I don't mind doing a lift and replace if we can't afford it."

"We probably can't afford it," he replied.

My lips pinched. He was pulling a Carmen, just spreading negativity.

"I'll see what I can do, boss," he amended.

I started nodding. "That's the right…wait."

He patted my arm on his way toward the men's section of the bath house, where I assumed he'd change clothes and faces to exit as someone completely different. "Your plan, your job, your rules, boss. See you later," he said casually.

I stood in place, releasing a huff before my lips slowly

framed a smile. It was a bit premature, but he was right. As long as we were on the job of saving my sister, I had to be the boss.

CHAPTER 25

HERO'S WELCOME

MISS BARRIOS WORE a loop of keys on her hip when she gathered up my crew alongside a gaggle of other RSI kids to escort us to the parade. "We are here to give our soldiers a hero's welcome," she instructed us.

Carmen was beside herself, abuzz with what could only be excitement and nerves all in one package. "Maybe we'll see my father and uncle march by. They told me what company they were assigned to," she said.

"Maybe," I agreed. I hadn't paid much attention to parades in the past, too eager to wander behind the distracted masses and have my choice of pockets to pick. Uncle Jace always pushed for me to acquire as many clorets as possible. Today would be different, as I told myself I needed to be beside Carmen. These may be the final hours we had before her father came to the institute to take her home. I'd miss her, but I knew this was the best thing that could happen for her.

"Remember to be on your best behavior," Miss Barrios was saying. Her gaze seemed to find me in the group and linger for a moment too long before she turned to lead us into the city.

I cast a nervous glance at her back. Hadn't I earned her trust at this point? Maybe she still understood that I was tempted by the pickpocketing I *could* do today. I wondered if her all-key was on the loop she wore with the other keys… To save my sister, it would be so much easier to borrow hers, or to lift the clorets needed to pay for a few hours with another.

But here I was, surveying the roadway we crowded onto for a candy vendor, ready to stand here and let those opportunities pass me by. "I know you must be excited," Margot said to Carmen as she slid into the space just behind the two of us.

The tall girl flashed a rare smile. "Yeah."

"Family is very important," Fariq added. He scooted in on my other side, and the two of us were soon pressed shoulder to shoulder.

My expression started to fall. Family *was* important, and we were about to say goodbye to one of our crew right before a big job.

"Hey," Carmen murmured. "I, uh, wanted to let you know that I wouldn't mind helping with your sister. Maybe my family will want to stay a little longer to enjoy the celebration." Maybe her thoughts had gone down the same path as mine about what would happen by the end of today.

"Really?" I asked, looking up at her hopefully.

"Yeah, of course," she said.

She waved off my thanks with some of her usual gruffness, but the offer alone lifted my spirits. I ended up calling over a man selling sweets and buying the four of us candy to eat while we waited for the parade to reach us. Well, Davit bought them for us actually, since I paid with the clorets I'd lifted from him.

I figured we were toward the middle of the parade's path, if they started at the city gates and ended at the palace for a homecoming feast. There was an announcer with a magical amplification device somewhere, his voice booming through the whole city. "Kaiamear, welcome home your heroes returning victorious from the Storm Front!"

The city bells rang with a joyous tune, and distant cheering swelled toward us as time passed. I was all the way through a stick of cloud candy and halfway through Fariq's, who offered to share his with only a little piece torn off, when the first group of soldiers turned down the corner of street we were on. Carmen cupped her mouth and whooped, joining the cheering crowd as they marched by.

Here were Kaiamear's missing men, putting their boots down in perfect sync. Most stared ahead rather than acknowledge the crowd at all, though here and there, was a wave or a wink or a blown kiss.

I soon heard screams of excitement following the announcer introducing the gryphon knight corps, beginning with the Third Gryphon Flight. I shaded my eyes and craned my head way up, eager to catch a glimpse of the giant beasts flying overhead. Gryphons always soared overhead too fast during the parades; all I ever saw was the general shape of their bodies and the stoic riders leaning over their necks or holding steady a flag with their flight's colors.

As someone far down the food chain from gryphon riders, I'd never gotten closer to the blessed beasts than moments like this, seeing the sun shining through glossy feathers and across the deadly curve of their beaks. They stretched the lion-like back half of their bodies flat, tufted tails streaming in the breeze.

Carmen grabbed my arm, startling me. "This is it. They should be in this group," she exclaimed over the noise around us.

I nodded and reluctantly lowered my gaze from the gryphon riders and instead focused on the parade passing us by on foot. With the soldiers all wearing the same uniform, it was hopeless for me to spot anyone who could be related to

Carmen, but I tried. Judging by the way she stood frozen, I didn't think she'd seen them either.

"It's a big group. They wouldn't be able to pick you out of this crowd either," I pointed out.

"You're right," she said, her smile hardly dimming. "I'll see them once they're done with their feast!"

I nodded in agreement, my gaze lifting toward the heavens to watch the gryphon riders again, who were finishing their part of the parade a lot quicker than the men on foot. The echo of the announcer's voice was soon introducing the last flight. "And last but not least, our newest flight of wild-born gryphons, led by Commander Nathaniel Walker and his daughter, Squire Sivana Walker!"

My voice lifted to join the rest of the crowd, even though it was lost in the crash of thousands of others. The sun caught the golden plumage of the beast at the front of this group. Just off its wing was a redheaded rider holding the flag of Altare high—it was her! The first female rider, accompanied by chain of gryphons that just kept coming as the moments passed. I could only assume these were the wild-born beasts, as many of them showed off with flips and rolls through the sky rather than flying in strictly regimented lines.

I was grinning broadly even after the sky cleared. For a moment, I wondered what it would like to be on the back of such a mighty animal, an apex predator of the sky. I figured hundreds of girls were thinking the same thing, but I may have been the first one to put the thought back down.

I had Chance. Somehow, we two mice had found each other. That was special, too.

CARMEN WASN'T the only student waiting in RSI's front foyer with all her belongings packed up beside her. Fariq, Margot, and I stood with her and ended up being her moral support. We watched uniformed men come in one at a time and reunite with their children. Happy tears were shed, and some of the smaller kids were literally swept out of the school by their fathers.

Twenty waiting students became twelve, and soon we were in the single digits. Carmen wore a tract in the carpet, pacing back and forth. "He might not be coming," I said out of the corner of my mouth to Fariq when she was at the far end of the foyer.

"Too soon to tell," he replied quietly.

"Carmen, darling," Margot said, beckoning her back over. "When was the last time you heard from your father or uncle?"

"A long time. But..." The tall girl's gaze landed on me, and her distressed expression flickered toward a smile briefly. "That doesn't necessarily mean anything. They've had a lot of traveling to do since my father wrote last."

"That's right," I said. For her, I tried to hide my nerves. If they hadn't written since we last talked about this when the city bells first rang with Altare's victory, she was hanging on to the same hope I'd offered her then.

She began pacing again after the city bells rang the late afternoon hour. I watched her expression rise and then fall hard when another soldier arrived for a different kid and felt my heart sink with hers. "Hey...doesn't your aunt live in the city?" I asked.

"Yeah." Realization hit her, and she glanced down at the plain bracelet she wore to replace the copper one. "They probably went to see her and my cousins first!"

We went to Miss Barrios, who stood by the doors with her quill ready to note who left with their family today, and told her where we were going. "All right. Be back before nightfall," she said, waving to Carmen, who left first. The Tulari secretary glanced toward me briefly, looking like she was going to say something else before thinking better of it with a tight press of her lips.

"Is something wrong?" I asked her.

She shook her head. "Be careful out there. There are sure to be plenty of people day drinking and roaming the streets."

I had a feeling there was something else on her mind and the possibilities of us running into drunkards was somewhere down on her list of concerns. But I knew when to leave an adult be. "Okay," I murmured, slipping out of the school at the back of my group.

We followed Carmen through the busy streets, nearly tripping over revelers who'd settled anywhere there was room. Oddly, I wanted to gawk, as around every corner, there were men and older boys repopulating the city and shifting the balance of genders everywhere back to what it used to be.

I was in more danger of spending the rest of my meager stash of clorets than anything else, as vendors roamed with carts of smoked sausages, fresh fruit juices, and a variety of sweets that had my mouth watering despite my sugary breakfast. On more than one occasion, Fariq held my sleeve like I was half my age and pulled me along before I could get distracted.

He was right to, as we only had a few hours before we had to return to RSI. It took half a bell's worth of walking before we turned down a street lined with houses. With the way space was highly valued this close to the city center, each small home was built nearly on top of the next, side by side and back to back.

Carmen's aunt and cousins had lived so close to RSI this whole time, but I couldn't remember a single time when they'd made this walk to visit her. All she'd said on the subject was that her aunt "couldn't handle her," which had gotten her sent to RSI in the first place. Considering Carmen's fighting nature, I'd believed it.

She stopped before the gravel walkway to a home with a

small garden out front, the soil freshly turned over. Swallowing audibly, she crossed to the door with a few long strides and knocked.

No one answered after several moments. Carmen knocked again while the rest of us exchanged glances behind her. "Maybe they're not in right now," Margot suggested.

A chain rattled against the other side of the door. I wasn't the only one tensing when it scraped against the latch before revealing a stout woman with tear tracks trailing down her cheeks. Her black hair was disheveled around her head, a leather tie hanging half-forgotten with obvious furrows where she must've grabbed handfuls and pulled.

My heart hit the bottom of my ribs with a painful lurch. Carmen's shoulders fell. "Auntie." The single word wavered with the weight of her dashed hopes.

Carmen's aunt sobbed and embraced her.

Margot had brought her lacy fan and unfurled it, hiding all but her shining eyes behind its edge. "Perhaps we should give them some privacy," she suggested quietly.

"No, please," Carmen murmured. "Auntie, these are my… friends, from RSI. Can they come in too?"

She sniffled wetly and nodded, releasing Carmen. "Of course. All of you, be welcome," she sighed, stepping aside. We didn't go far, with a modest living room right off the entranceway. A pair of crying boys leapt to their feet and hugged my friend's legs. They couldn't be more than three and five years old, and further into the house came the sound of another crying with the distinct wail of a baby.

Frazzled, Carmen's aunt hurried into the other room and returned with her third son in hand. She bounced him, trying to shush him to little success. I knew from experience that he was probably picking up on her distress and held my hands out tentatively. Even though I was a stranger, she still handed him over with a breath of relief and brief thanks.

I cuddled him, murmuring in a soothing tone. With my

gang siblings, I was best with the kids a little older, who could talk back and reason for themselves, but I'd done my share caring for new ones too when they needed time to be held and have a chance to peer up at a friendly face. When he calmed himself, I used the folds of the soft blanket wrapped around him to dry his cheeks.

In the meantime, Carmen's composure had broken as she knelt next to her aunt over a set of open luggage. "You just missed the men from their company," the aunt was saying. "They called themselves battle brothers and…" She hiccupped, covering her mouth with a cloth and blotting her cheeks until she could speak again. "They wanted to deliver these things personally."

"I can't believe it," Carmen murmured.

"They said your father died a true hero—" her aunt began.

"Does it matter?" she interrupted with tearful sharpness.

The older woman's shoulders squared defensively. "I guess not," she said with an edge of her own. "Since you're here, you should look through his things for anything you want before you go back to your school."

"Carmen, I think you should hear out what she was going to say about your father," Margot said. She and Fariq sat on the floor nearby with her two older cousins.

For a few long moments, all Carmen did was toss sets of male clothing to the side. There wasn't much else in the luggage, but she was looking for something with single-minded focus until she found a pocket on the inside of the lining and withdrew a battered wooden box with the lid at a broken angle.

Her fingers shook as she lifted the top and withdrew a band of polished black leather. Her thumb brushed a wrin-kled symbol in its center. "Do you know what this is?" she asked her aunt, who shook her head.

"It's all I want. You can keep his things…or sell them. Just let me have this." The emotion had dried off her face already, leaving only a blank expression and fingers curled loosely around the leather band.

"All right," the aunt said.

"A long time ago, an Endolian master gave this to Tosh Montes, customized with the creed of Tosh Zorena. It's passed from son to son since then." Her voice dropped. She fixed it around her forehead, pinning back the short hair hanging just over her brow. "Master to master. But now I have it, and that makes me a master, despite everything."

She turned to her aunt, emotion returning to brim in her eyes. "Did he die defending Altare with honor and purpose?" she asked.

"I would say so. They told me he went out saving dozens of his battle brothers." Her aunt cracked a smile for Carmen, a hint of pride for her in the expression.

She traced the symbols in the band where they rested on her forehead. "Then he died a true master. It's what he would've wanted more than anything," she said, taking a deep breath to keep herself composed. "He's with my mother in paradise, celebrating with the masters who came before him. He wouldn't want us to mourn."

"It's all right," her aunt murmured. "Honor is cold comfort."

Carmen sniffed, brushing away another set of tears forcefully. "What else do I have?" she asked.

"You have me…us." Her aunt gestured to encompass the little boys but caught up the rest of the crew in the circle of her hands too. "If you wanted…we could take you out of RSI. I can use some help around here. You could help me raise the boys."

Carmen bit her lip.

But her aunt wasn't done, more reluctantly adding, "Or you could return to your gym…maybe take your cousins with you when they're old enough to learn."

Temptation crossed my friend's face as she considered it.

Here was her out, what she'd said she wanted when she left RSI. With a glance at Fariq, Margot, and finally me, Carmen shook her head slowly. "There's something I have to do first," she said. "I'll visit you all when I can now that I can. And the gym will be there when I'm ready to go back. This summer, maybe…with friends."

CHAPTER 26

FOXGLOVE

"WE HAVE a day to kill before it's time, right?" Carmen asked me once we returned to RSI.

"Tomorrow, yeah."

"Get changed," she ordered.

She was in a mood, like a thundercloud about to erupt into a violent storm, so I knew she needed a session to practice her art and forget. If I knew Carmen, then I knew she was going to punch her emotions down and compact them deep inside until she was ready to deal with them. *If* she would ever be ready to deal with them.

I changed and met her at the gym with the drum in hand. She had me place it aside, and we met face to face on the mat. "The first thing you need to know about Tosh Zorena are what we call zones," she began.

I blinked at her dumbly as she told me more. "In a fight, you're safest with your opponent a certain distance from you." She took a step back, looking down to gauge. "About this, where you can easily keep them at bay with the threat of a kick."

"What?" I murmured.

"Most dangerous is here." She continued like I hadn't

spoken, getting up in my face. "Where your opponent can punch you or swing a weapon. Okay, hug me."

Still confused, I did so. "Safe or dangerous?" I asked.

"Safe," she answered, grabbing me. The next thing I knew, I was winded and on the ground with her pinning me down. "Most people panic when they end up on their back in a fight, but as you learn more, you'll realize you can still be in control from here."

She released me and lent me a hand up. I clued into what was happening, my eyes widening. "Are you going to teach me your art?"

"Everyone should know how to defend themselves, pipsqueak. I..." A hint of vulnerability flickered over her expression. "I wanted you to be my first trainee. If that's okay?"

I had some understanding of how much this meant to her. She hadn't felt qualified to share as a beginner herself, but since she'd taken up the headband from her father's things, she'd said that made her a master...someone who could teach others. This was a role her family had taken on for generations as mentors passing down Tosh Zorena. It was an honor she'd picked a Mouse like me to be her first trainee.

"Of course. I'd love to learn," I answered.

Carmen's expression regained its sharp edges as she nodded once. "Good, because you're tiny, and your upper body strength needs a lot of work. Let's get started," she said.

Glad to be your friend too, I thought, recognizing her odd style of affection.

I was sore by afternoon the next day, when I bowed out at the end of a morning training session with Carmen. She was keeping herself moving and exhausting herself in the process, but there was something else I needed to do before the big job tomorrow.

"Why are you wearing my necklace?" Sybella asked Nessa while I walked several steps behind them in Hawthorne Hall. I'd taken a quick bath and had started my practice session on them.

Nessa grabbed the chain I'd snuck around her neck and stared at it. "I…sorry?" she said in confusion.

I ducked into the room we shared before they could turn and realize I might be involved in the trick. Margot was still here, while the rest of our roommates were out in the city celebrating, or about to be.

"I found as many types of latches as I could in my things." She gestured an elegant hand to my cot, where a few necklaces or bracelets were laid out. "Do you remember what type the Eye of Acuity had?"

"No," I said, breathing a huff of frustration at myself. I'd been so enchanted by the sparkle of its opal that I hadn't noticed that detail. I could only tell her all about its heavy metal chain, too masculine to be proper evening wear for a lady.

"Well darling, there are only so many ways jewelry latches," she said, standing guard over the few valuable pieces she had left.

I fiddled with the latches and had her stand still as I snuck each on and off her wrist or neck, having her rate whether she'd felt the addition or removal. Musty devils, I was rusty, and the neck was one of the most sensitive spots on a person.

"It would help if I didn't know you were practicing on me," Margot said after a while. She had small bumps up the back of her neck, as she'd had to sweep her curls aside to make it possible for me to sneak a necklace on and off her.

"You're right," I sighed. But if I picked a random victim and they noticed what I was doing, they'd assume I was stealing from them. All the more pressure to do it right.

Margot was in the process of packing up her jewelry when I noticed movement out of the corner of my eye. "Chance," I gasped, nearly heady with relief to see his little self squeezing under the door. I held out my palm for him to scamper onto and kissed the star of white on his head.

"Hello, Chance," Margot said warmly. "I thought he'd gotten lost?"

"Hi hi!" the mouse squeaked, standing up and striking a proud pose with paws upraised. "I follow and spy and do good job."

I glance over at Margot and back to him, making a decision even as I said, "Do they have it?"

"They does, yes yes. They keep in magic pouch and hide under bed."

"That's a relief," I murmured. "And you're okay too."

"I ride lady's clothes. She come here."

"What? Cartier and Rozma came around here?"

Chance bobbed in confirmation and started cleaning his face and whiskers.

"Are you conversing with him?" Margot asked.

"Uh, yeah. Long story," I answered. "Chance, what did they do? Why did they come to RSI?"

He paused with his paws over his ears. "I forget."

I scrubbed down my cheek, frustrated. "You forgot what they were talking about?"

"I sorry," he squeaked, taking a leap off my palm and landing on my pants leg. "Sorry sorry sorry." He chanted the word on his way down and over to Margot to visit with her instead.

Well, I needed to get moving anyway. "Want to come with me into Kaiamear? I wanted to do a little shopping," I said with a sigh.

She brightened immediately. "Of course!"

She pulled out her cosmetics bags and had me join her in the girls' bath, where she sat me on a stool. "You're tanner than me, but I can work with this," she said, having me close my eyes. "We can't promenade without you wearing the proper look!"

"Promenade?" I echoed in surprise.

"I miss taking a nice walk with companions," she answered. Her brushes swept over my face like butterfly wings, spreading powders and pastes. I wasn't sure what she was doing, but I kept my lips clamped so no giggles escaped.

When she had me look, I hardly recognized myself. She'd covered my blemishes, making my face look one even shade, with the hint of a blush on my cheeks and darker shades around my eyelids to make my brown eyes seem less round-eyed Mouse and more…mysterious, for lack of a better word. The girl in the mirror had secrets. She was older and more prepared for everything, including taking a walk through the city.

"Wow. Can you teach me how to do this?" I asked.

Margot looked me over with an approving nod. "Of course!" As she packed up, she shared a few tips about shades before we were ready to go.

I was soon leading her out of the institute and explaining little wonders to her as soon as we were down the road, out of earshot as another pair of girls going shopping amidst the large crowds still celebrating Altare's victory. All the while, I worried over why Cartier and Rozma were scoping out RSI.

"I need to go to a store for Tulari," I said once Margot had reintroduced herself to Chance and shook his paw with the tip of her index finger. She would be a good choice for a little wonder of her own, if we met another.

"For Tulari?" she echoed, raising a manicured brow.

"I need a tool that only a Tulari would make," I said.

"Ah, a magic supply store, perhaps."

"Sure. Let's keep an eye out for one."

"We'll go to an assortment of shops, darling. Kaiamear is

the center of fashion, I'll have you know." She glanced upward and batted her lashes rapidly.

My first thought was *oh no*, because I could tell she'd want to shop until we had to return to RSI. But on the other hand, the only thing I had to do for the plan today was secure an all-key somehow and pen a coded message. Anxiety would take hold if I allowed myself to stand still…so why not spend an afternoon promenading with Margot from shop to shop?

That was exactly what I ended up doing. Between us, we bought nearly nothing; she encouraged me away from the sweets shops and she didn't need any more things. She had already filled her whole storage space back at RSI with all her clothes and stuff.

"When I'm done being trained at RSI, I'm getting my own apartment to hold all the dresses I desire," she muttered.

"All on your own?" I asked. I doubted she'd enjoy that.

"I'll have my jobs at the employment agency to keep me busy with others. Anything they ask me to do invariably involves working with people," she said.

"What kinds of things might you be hired to do?" I asked curiously.

Her gaze was a little faraway as she seemed to imagine it. "Oh, most anything. I could be an instructor in dance, piano, or other skills a girl of fine breeding should know. Or I could be a companion or personal secretary to a lady for a time. It is a chance for me to show my versatility."

I heard the soft *but* in her tone, the hesitance that hitched her voice, and waited for her to finish her thoughts.

"But it is not what I would've envisioned myself doing for the rest of my life," she said primly.

"I'm sorry," I murmured.

She waved the thought away. "After yesterday's tragedy, I've come to realize how fragile life can be. All the more reason to cherish and protect what you have, family and friendship alike. Isn't that right?" She directed the question to

Chance as she tickled his side. He'd stayed nestled in her palm since I'd gotten frustrated with him.

"That's right," I answered anyway. "I'd do anything for my sister...and the family we scratched out for ourselves." I pictured my gang siblings, many beloved young faces that I'd helped raise or support. My guilt for picking RSI over them was still a hot needle between my ribs. They needed to be saved just as much as Jackie, in their own way.

It wasn't much longer before we found a store dedicated to selling supplies for Tulari mages. And its insides were a lot of what I expected, with one half of it being a dusty library. The other half was dedicated to wands and other implements they needed for their magic, like dried herbs and...preserved animal parts suspended in colored liquid. Bile rose in my throat, and I rushed past the shelves with those jars in search of a shopkeeper.

He was behind a wooden counter, with a case beside it displaying expensive Tulari-made goods under an etched pane of glass with an intricately looped double-release spell. "Can I help you?" The shopkeeper looked at me suspiciously over the rim of his spectacles. He was wizened and grayed by age, but a staff rested against the wall behind him, a sign that he was strong in his magic. My eyes narrowed in on his cheek, where it looked like his wizard-blue spell circle rounded the corner of his jaw and disappeared under the wiry sprigs of his beard.

I'd received similar looks across the city today. RSI kids had a certain reputation, and my hands were watched extra closely because of it. "Hello, sir," I said, lacing my fingers in front of me to show that I was no threat. "Do you have any all-keys for rent?"

He seemed less than impressed. "The likes of you wouldn't be able to afford even an hour's fee with an all-key."

A throat cleared nearby. "Excuse me, don't speak to my

help that way," Margot said, honing the highbrow accent in her voice sharp enough to cut. "We have a specific need for such a specialty tool."

For a moment, I wish we'd taken the time to change her into one of her dresses again, as the shopkeeper subjected her to the same scrutiny over the rounds of his lenses.

"Very well," he said, sliding open a drawer behind his counter. He straightened with a crack of his joints, laid out a velvet cloth, then opened the box he'd retrieved and withdrew three keys.

The first was tarnished silver and only two knuckle lengths across. "Eight hundred clorets per hour. It's a five-hundred-cloret fee if you bring your item here to be unlocked by it," he said as he placed it down.

I sucked in a gasp. Vance wasn't kidding about how expensive this would be.

The second one was double in both fees and three times the silver key's size, plated in shining gold and ending in a fancily looped fringe. "Does it do the job twice as well?" I asked doubtfully.

The shopkeeper scoffed. "No, the original owner is deceased. It is an untraceable key. And this one…is mine." He pocketed the third one rather than put it on display. "What will it be, girls?"

I exchanged a glance with Margot. We might be able to afford an hour or two with the less expensive key, but presumably, it belonged to another living mage. I wondered how he'd acquired it to sell its services in that case.

"They will be accepting neither offer. Mister Brooks, are these two bothering you?"

I nearly startled out of my skin when Miss Barrios approached on her cat-silent feet. "Not at all, Sasha," he replied. "Just a bit of fun looking at expensive items, I would guess."

Margot and I exchanged guilty and panicked looks as

Miss Barrios put a hand on either of our shoulders. "Come with me, girls," she said coolly, nodding to the shopkeeper before steering us toward the door.

"I can explain—" I began hesitantly.

"Oh, I'm sure you can," she replied. Her voice was uncharacteristically tight. After releasing us from her hold, she had us follow her to a dressmaker's shop a few doors down, where Margot stroked the air toward the beaded lavender garment they had on display in the window.

"Margot," Miss Barrios said, startling the girl from the covetous look she shot at it her second time by it. "I need a few minutes alone with Heather."

"Of course," she said, turning an apologetic look my way before she drifted toward the accessories hung on the shop's wall.

I flashed her a brief smile before following Miss Barrios. She drifted past a young woman with a nod of greeting and kept going to the curtain of a changing room and gestured me inside. Once the curtain snapped shut behind her, she rounded on me with her hands on her hips. "You want to explain why you haven't asked me to help save your sister? You were going to steal an all-key—a capital crime, by the way—rather than ask for my help," she accused.

My lips were parted to start spinning up a lie. No sound escaped my mouth except for a huff of shock. "This is a warded room. One of many we keep for our business," she continued, pointing to a symbol on the wall over our heads. A subtle etching of crossed keys nearly blended in with the rosy color of the wallpaper. This room was too small, though, especially with two of us crammed in it and no place to sit down. "If there's anything you'd like to tell me, it won't be overheard by any other ears."

I was still knocked dumb, my jaw hanging. "But..."

She didn't help me this time, standing there with an impatient expression until I finished my thought. "But how did you know?" I asked.

"You're one of my Littles. Of course I know what you're into." Her lips quirked, the very image of displeasure as she looked down on me. "I've been waiting for you to ask for help ever since our resident feligryph overheard the beginning of your plan."

Oh, musty devils. I'd forgotten Patches was even there, too wrapped up in the fear of losing Jackie. I'd needed to bring my crew in, so I'd told them everything about me—and Patches must've told Miss Wilkes, and that information was then set in Miss Barrios's hands. I still wilted under her anger, tucking my metaphorical tail between my legs and hunching to be smaller.

"I wasn't going to steal an all-key just now," I mumbled. "I wanted to know what one looked like. That shop was riddled with wards and protective enchantments. Plus that master wizard standing right there with his staff."

"I would gladly lend you mine for free...if you asked," she said.

I shook my head quickly. She didn't understand we were going up against the Morashi, and how would she when I hadn't told her anything? "It's too dangerous. It involves the Tulari gang, Morashi Venom ..." I swallowed the big lump in my throat and slowly stood straighter, meeting her eyes. "I can't trust you with the plan if you turn around and squeal it. It's too delicate to be handled by the peacekeepers."

Her gaze softened first, then her stance loosened. "I don't squeal, Little. I was born a few streets down from where you lived and played by the same rules for the first half of my life."

"You...did?" I asked slowly.

"Mmhmm." She looked around and sighed, leaning her weight on one of the walls. "Wish I'd picked a warded room with chairs. Anyway, yes, and my family hid my mark well.

The Morashi didn't discover me until I was twelve, and by then, my skin was peeling and showing the wizard blue underneath. I was taken, and I met one of the leader's many faces. In trying to convince me to sign a binding contract with her, she taught me one of the fundamentals of what Tulari call *the old ways*, and I used it to escape from her.

"Unfortunately, as a result of me turning down her contract and leaving, she'd had my family killed. I knew I couldn't turn to the peacekeepers, so I became a thief instead. I called myself Foxglove, and—"

"*You're* Foxglove?" I blurted, my eyes rounding to twice their size. "You left flowers behind every time you stole."

Her eyes creased with amusement. "I should've figured you'd know the name. I did leave mementos behind, so sure in my unique magic that I thought I'd never get caught. Of course, I got careless and was taken to RSI after my arrest. I was small, hungry, sticky-fingered, and distrustful—just like a Little I might know."

I was too starstruck to register what she'd said. "I can't believe you're Foxglove. You're a legend!" I gushed.

"Too kind, but it was really the magic. If the study of magic wasn't so suppressed, anyone with a mark could do it," she said.

My brow furrowed up in confusion. "Oh?"

"Let me tell you a secret that Vance and I already know. Magic, when given a purpose, will develop to fulfill that purpose. My abilities permanently changed to make me a better thief. I can bend light and sound. The only reason I know any other, more traditional spells for a wizard is to cover up the fact that I'm different."

That sounded incredible to me. If she hadn't been so cocky when she was my age, she could've become a truly legendary thief…but then she wouldn't be Miss Barrios. And I wouldn't have the chance to learn from her.

"There are many who would suppress the magic of others

out of fear or a desire to control them, but let's not go too far down this tangent. I've spent the rest of my career trying to uncover the real leader of Morashi Venom, and I thought I had her during my stay at the Tulari Academy but..." She shook her head. "Tell me your plan and what you need. I'll bring my all-key. I *want* Madam Morashi to find me; I'm beyond ready for her."

I nodded and, after a shaky start, ended up telling her everything. It was an act of trust I hoped she wouldn't make me live to regret, despite her admission.

She shared that she knew most of it already, as she'd stood hidden in a patch of sunlight when I met with Cartier and Rozma—"What an awful pair, by the way."—and been tempted to reveal herself when Vance and I had discussed all-keys afterward.

I had no other choice but to trust the former Foxglove. She was now a part of my crew.

CHAPTER 27

EXTRA CREDIT

THE PLAN PROCEEDED as scheduled after I rejoined Margot and returned to RSI with her and Miss Barrios. I visited one of the smaller alchemy classrooms with a fist full of plants I'd snatched on the way back.

Once my business there was done, I wrote out a new coded message in my best handwriting and took care to slowly fold and tear the ragged edge to make it neater for the Spymaster. Since I knew I wouldn't be able to sleep anyway, I kept it resting on my chest until the girls around me were asleep and the mellow night bells rang the midnight hour out in the city.

Only then did I send it to the Spymaster's inbox by pressing it to the symbol on my bracelet and whispering, "No locks." It faded into the darkness of night right there in my hand, disappearing like it'd never been there. I assumed it would be at the bottom of the Spymaster's mail come morning, more likely to be read and responded to later in the day. In it, I told him I needed the Crown's help and why and begged him to send aid for my old gang.

I couldn't help but worry the pieces of the heist tomorrow would slide all out of place at the last minute. No matter that the former street legend, Miss Barrios, was now joining us at a meeting point halfway into the heist. She had her own goals too; I could only hope she wouldn't sacrifice the plan to get her hands on Madam Morashi.

When the night bells rang again, I snuck from the room and pulled a vial of liquid from my pocket, securing it on my belt. I'd made winterbog in a glass, picking all the plants that'd smelled like allergies on the way back from our shopping trip. The process of distilling oils was not hard—even I could do it—but the price I paid was a stuffy nose.

There was a peacekeeper in the front hall, an unfamiliar man. I listened to his footsteps from a crack in the door that sealed away Hawthorne Hall at night. When they grew too faint, I peered from the crack to watch him cross into the boys' hall. Then I started counting.

It took him ten minutes to finish his round and post himself by the front foyer. Then it was a battle with my eyelids as I knelt and watched him shift in place for half a bell. I couldn't sleep in bed, but now that I'd timed the guard, I could sleep in this uncomfortable crouch? My body was being unfair tonight.

He eventually moved, first approaching the girls' hall. I shut the door properly with my heart in my throat, hoping the school didn't allow male guards to come down this way at night. His footsteps approached…and then faded. I timed him in my head until I was sure he'd be opening the opposite doors and leaving for his ten-minute patrol of Irving Hall.

I left the door propped with my folded cloak over the latch and went to kneel before the headmaster's office door with my lock picks out. I'd inspected both sides of this threshold closely in the past, but neither had the obvious symbols of magical protection painted or engraved upon them. It was an ordinary door, and after the guard was gone for a minute and fifty seconds, I had it unlocked.

I shut it behind me quietly, shooting a wary glance at the

doused magelight under its shade in the corner of the office. I withdrew the winterbog oil and a broad brush I'd stolen from the art room. The oil wasn't very strong, but left overnight in an enclosed space, I was sure it'd be enough to give Headmaster Radcliffe an allergy attack. I hastily painted the underside of the headmaster's desk and chairs, picking all the places that'd be hard to clean and sniffing miserably all the while from the smell. Seven minutes, twenty-two seconds in, and the job was done.

I had just enough time to lock up and retreat back to Hawthorne Hall. But I still paused at the curio cabinet and the shadowy shape of the crown within it. *Tomorrow, it'll be mine.*

Until then, I made my exit quickly and used my picks to lock the door again. The guard was just coming back to the front hall when the folded material of my cloak slid away and my finger eased the latch closed silently on the other end.

I woke from Carmen's rough jostle of my shoulder. "Let's go, pipsqueak. Today's the day."

I blinked away the sticky film that blurred the world and trudged after her for a bath and a breakfast I didn't really taste. A couple hours of sleep wasn't enough, and the musty winterbog had stuffed my head unpleasantly from my stunt with the oil.

I also knew I had to tell the rest of the crew what'd changed and see what ideas Vance wanted to bring if he did end up joining us in the detention rooms. Today was *the* day, and my whole body ached with stress.

The rest of the school was still celebrating Altare's military victory. We were stopped by multiple teachers along the way to the detention rooms, who shared the same news—that the nightly feast at the palace was open to the public for the next three days. My tired intuition twinged. The absolute perfect time to heist would be the first night, tonight, when everyone would attempt to squeeze into the palace halls.

"The winds blow in our favor," I murmured to Carmen.

"'Bout time something did," she grumbled back.

Chance was back in his place on my shoulder, bathing himself leisurely. "What wind?" he squeaked.

I had an opportunity to reply as I kept walking toward Fariq's favorite place while Carmen split off to go straight to the detention rooms. "Not a literal wind. I'm just saying, I feel a little lucky there's a big feast tonight," I told him.

"Feast? We go to feast, eat lots, yes yes?"

"I wish," I sighed. But my belly didn't grumble bitterly at the idea of overlooking a big, free meal for once.

"Is it because I forgot important thing yesterday?" he asked in a smaller voice.

I almost tripped over my own feet. "What? No." I held my hand out to him, and he climbed into my palm, looking up at me with big, guilty eyes. "It's okay, Chance."

"You not mad?"

I kissed the little star of white fur on his head. "Not at all. I don't think it'll be a big deal. Besides, how could I be mad at such a good mouse?" I cooed.

Chance brightened and licked my fingers affectionately.

"Maybe by the end of the night, I'll be introducing you to my sister," I added, feeling my heart lurch at the thought. It shouldn't be a *maybe*, but my anxiety kept reminding me of the risks ahead of us.

"Finally," he stated. "Only one sister? What about the rest?"

"What do you mean?"

"I have many sisters and brothers. If you ever come to family home, I introduce you to them all."

I was eager to meet them, especially if they were as sweet as Chance. "How many is *many*?"

"Well there's…" He started listing off overlong mouse names rapid-fire, counting on his paws. He kept this going when I transferred him to my shoulder, as I'd reached the innovation lab and knocked when the door was locked. Fariq opened it, gesturing me inside with a big smile.

"All done. Come see." Fariq had custom made a few tools for me, including the extendable grabber I'd wanted when he'd shown me his notes.

I fiddled with each, making sure the grabber and clamps had enough pressure for what I needed them for. Fariq looked on with pride as I nodded and piled them up before me once they passed my quick inspection.

"That makes ten," Chance said, then listed more names.

"These are perfect, Fariq," I said, inspecting my belt for what I could remove to make room for them.

"Ah, also…"

Fariq lifted something he had coiled under the table, offering it to me with a darkening across his bronze cheeks. "I bought this for you."

It was a belt with a bow tied around its buckle. I took it with my mouth popped open in surprise. It was solid leatherwork, a step up from any of the other belts I'd worn in the past. While it was too broad to loop into my uniform pants, it was reversible, with one side tooled with delicate patterns of swirls and the other sporting two smaller belts where I could hook in double the number of satchels and tools and maybe something more solid, like a knife or thigh pack.

I couldn't imagine how much it cost. "This is the nicest thing anyone's given me," I said, feeling my eyes sting. A lack of sleep had to be why I was getting misty over a belt, even one so marvelous and useful as this one. Still, I hugged him just as tight as I would one of my gang siblings. "Thanks, Fariq."

He jolted, startled by the sudden affection, and I let him go before he fully returned it. "You're welcome. I'll help you move everything over?" he suggested. We laid out the new one and the old, battered one I had on, unclipping each satchel and pinning them in place on my new gear. Fariq had an eye for balance, which was good, as the clamps were heavy and awkward even with their weight distributed.

When the new belt was in place, I paced the length of the room to get used to the extra weight resting on my hips. "That makes…ten," Chance squeaked, making me realize he was still listing his siblings and now peering at his paws in confusion.

"Wouldn't it be twenty?" I suggested in a murmur.

"Huh?" Fariq asked, looking up from cleaning around his work bench.

I waved it away like I hadn't said anything. "Oh, yeah, maybe," Chance said thoughtfully. "I have either ten or twenty siblings!"

I giggled. Guess I would need to figure out exactly how many myself someday.

"He has a lot to say," I told Fariq, offering him Chance. "I have a secret to tell you about him soon."

He tried to roll my mouse onto his back, but Chance resisted and squeaked a "no no" with a scolding swipe of his tail. I watched in fascination—I hadn't tried to rub his belly, and he hadn't asked for it. "Try rubbing his head or sides," I suggested.

"Sorry, *misk*," Fariq said, doing just that. Chance settled in his palm with one last indignant twitch of his whiskers.

With his workstation clean, we headed to the detention rooms. I hoped Vance was able to make it, as I had some questions about his magic. Namely, if he'd be able to alter anyone else's face and body like he did to himself. As closely as I'd planned the upcoming job, I hadn't spared much thought as to how he'd be joining us in attempting to beat the recorded time in escaping the detention rooms. Even the elderly minder would be suspicious of peacekeeper Brinsley joining us.

When we got there, I had my answer. Vance stood between Margot and Carmen, wearing the RSI uniform and his real face, Tulari mark and all, the collar of his uniform pulled up to hide the snake tattoo. Very few people in the school would recognize him like this. His brown hair was more of a mess than the last time I saw him like this, and he shifted with discomfort. I wondered if he felt exposed without a fake face overtop his own, worn like armor.

"That's all of us," Margot said primly.

The elderly detention minder checked her notes as I read the current record for solving the detention rooms: four hours, twelve minutes, and forty-six seconds. "You kids are here to set a new record," she said. "You have the whole day or until the rooms are needed for discipline."

With that, she started our time, and we went into the first room. As soon as the latch clicked behind us, Vance turned to me. "Can you pick your way to the room with the flowers?"

"Isn't that cheating?" Fariq asked. They all watched as I pulled out my lock picks and got to work on the first door.

"I was thinking we could do this anyway and solve the puzzles afterward," I said absently. "There's no rule against using what you have on hand. I checked."

By the time I had this first door opened, Vance had withdrawn a couple vials of what looked like water from his pocket, plus his wand and a tiny book that doubled in size when he tapped the rune engraved on its spine. "Exactly. And the last time we were here, I noticed two rooms in particular. This second one…good, it's what I remembered."

Each room was themed, and the second one resembled a healer's office. Vance started rifling through the tools and empty flasks, nodding in satisfaction and setting them out in some particular order. I watched him out of the corner of my eye as I started on the lock to the next room.

"You're going to make us potions?" Carmen guessed.

"Yeah. I'll have to warn you, magical potions are usually made by crafter-class healers," he said as if we knew what that meant.

"And you're not one," the tall girl stated. I could practically feel her scowl from across the room.

"I'm not. Crafter-class Tulari are the ones with the staves because they have too much raw magic to channel through something small like a wand," he explained. "And crafter-class healers make the incredible potions you've probably seen in your circles, Margot."

"How interesting," the noble girl said politely. "But what will you be making, then?"

"Well, the same thing. They just won't last as long," he answered with a shrug. "If you want to get really technical…"

"No," Carmen grumbled.

"Please do," Fariq said. I had the door unlocked at this point but looked over curiously from where I knelt.

Vance was now reclined against the countertop like he owned it. "If you've heard the terminology before, I can make the lesser version of most potions. There are two kinds— greater and lesser. They use the exact same ingredients, but the difference is the creator." He hooked his thumb toward himself. "This book I have outlines all the effects, and once someone gets me to the flowers, I can tell you what I can make from what's on hand."

He shot me a look, and I sighed, heading into the third room. I jiggled the handle of the next door out of old habit and realized it was already unlocked. Brow furrowed, I opened it and peered around the miniature florist's shop the fourth room resembled. Chance stood upright on the knob, chattering playfully. "You open door slow human way. I help!"

He offered his paw in a tiny fist, and I bumped it before taking him onto my palm and stepping out of the way for

Vance. "What a good mouse," I cooed. "All right, everyone. We can take a few minutes to discuss what's next while Vance works."

"Much thanks," he said dryly.

Ignoring him, I started explaining little wonders to everyone but Margot, who'd already heard all of it and was eager to help me demonstrate Chance's intelligence. "He's going to help us set a record," I said.

Carmen didn't seem impressed, even though the two boys were. "It's still just a mouse," she pointed out. "Also, how?"

"I knew there was something about him," Vance murmured. He was consulting the book he'd brought, looking between it and the handful of flowerpots he'd relocated to the second room, where we'd assembled.

"Watch this," I said before cupping my hand and whispering to Chance. He bobbed his head occasionally.

"Wait for lady sleep, take watch, not wake lady, give watch to you. Yes yes?" he repeated. When I nodded and set him down, he scampered away.

Vance shot a look over the side of his book at Carmen. "Looked pretty smart to me," he said.

She rolled her eyes. "Where you been, by the way?"

"Trying not to die, mostly," he replied flippantly.

I wished I had a fan like Margot in that moment, to hide the way I cringed at the vulnerable flash that came and went over her expression before it shaded with anger. "He's been helping my gang siblings," I butted in before she could explode.

"*And* Heather," he added.

"And me. We've got a lot to talk about, actually," I said.

"Let's hear it, boss." Vance caught me off guard again, reminding me that I was leading this job.

Before launching into every angle of the plan, I made sure I understood his magic by having him answer a few questions. He *could* change how we looked too, but the lesser potions he was going to make us would drain away his reserves of magic. He'd need some left over to make his escape from RSI one last time before he allowed Miss Barrios to place another copper bracelet around his wrist.

"She'll probably put a tethering band on me this time, too," he said, trying to joke. We were all a little tense, though, and what that did was remind me of what was at stake tonight.

"About Miss Barrios…" I said, bracing myself for a different kind of explosion. "She's been spying on us. She already knew most of what we were planning."

Margot sighed. "She cornered Heather yesterday. Did she make you tell her everything?"

"Yeah. She was mad we didn't ask for her help."

I began telling them everything, including where Miss Barrios had inserted herself in what was to come. The only thing I kept to myself was her identity as Foxglove. The only one present who might know the street legend's name was Vance, but he was interested to hear what little she'd told me of her magic.

He was in the process of heating a batch of lesser invisibility potions for us. We'd been lucky that there was a sparker and burn plate on hand, as he hadn't packed either. It felt like the school had set all this up for students clever enough to figure it out, down to having the rare coro de mare flowers that were key to this potion.

"So, you're saying she bent her magic's potential to be a better thief," Fariq summarized while Vance kept his hands moving, looking thoughtful. "Which means she can hide in plain sight and walk without sound?"

"Those are two things I have confirmed she can do," I said. Something told me a good spy never showed her whole toolkit, not even to a Little. "She will be using her all-key to release Jackie. She also *wants* to get Morashi Venom's attention."

Vance pressed his lips together and shook his head in quiet disapproval. "Well, that's her funeral, then, isn't it?" he asked.

"She also told me to give the Eye of Acuity to the Spymaster if we're successful tonight," I added.

A few glances were exchanged around the room. I wasn't quite won over about it, but I saw why Miss Barrios insisted. If someone as dangerous as Madam Morashi got her hands on a tool that could watch a specific person or place without detection, it would empower an already incredibly elusive enemy to the Crown.

Fariq asked the questions that'd lingered with me ever since Miss Barrios traded her services and all-key for the Eye's fate. "What about your gang? Won't the Morashi continue hunting them with the excuse of them having the necklace?"

My eyelid twitched with anxiety. "She said she had a plan but needed to talk to the Spymaster directly before anything else."

"I don't know if I like that," Carmen said.

Fariq held up his index finger. "I do for one important reason. We will no longer be breaking the law and giving the necklace to Morashi Venom."

"The spy leadership will know what to do with it," Margot agreed.

Vance scoffed quietly but didn't say anything. That was about my reaction too, but I'd been on the wrong side of the law for so long that I found it hard to think our leadership, tied directly into the same network as the peacekeepers and the Crown, were worthy of such valuable trust. I only hoped they were—thus the message I'd sent to the Spymaster in secret.

A tug on my pants leg had me looking down. Chance put his paws up to signal that he wanted me to lift him onto my hand. "Lady asleep. I take watch. It over there." He pointed with a paw. I had figured it would be too heavy for him to drag far, and it seemed he'd given up getting it under the door. With a little wiggling and tugging on its chain, I slid it the rest of the way to this side and smoothed out the furrow it'd made in the rug.

"*Great* job, Chance," I said, returning to my crew with it in hand. "All right, everyone. Any questions about the plan?"

We spent some time clarifying last-minute questions, mostly from Margot, who kept wringing her hands. Vance tried to comfort her while I answered her questions, and eventually, she sucked in a deep breath and nodded.

"The crown heist is a go," I said, feeling a tingle to declare it like a boss once everyone was set.

We broke our huddle to begin making it look like we'd solved the challenge rooms honestly. Vance put back the flowers he hadn't used and cleaned out the glassware as best as he could before distributing vials of lesser potions to all of us. "I want to come back and finish the challenge for real," he commented.

"Me, too," Fariq said. "Honestly."

Carmen was the one who shoved the last door open with as much force as she could, making a *bang* that woke the elderly minder. As she looked around in disorientation, I stooped and pretended to pick up the stopwatch and handed it to her. "Looks like this fell. Here you go, ma'am," I said, putting it in her palm.

She clicked it to stop the time and squinted at it. "Well, I'll be," she said, looking from its face to the chalkboard. "That's a new record for sure! Congratulations on earning some extra credit."

CHAPTER 28

THE CROWN HEIST

IN REALITY, we spent something closer to five or six hours in the detention rooms, between the explaining, planning, and potion brewing. The detention minder was sure to be confused right after she wrote down our time and walked outside.

I was feeling my lack of sleep as I waited in the girls' bath for Chance to retrieve the couple pinches of desda powder he'd squirreled away for me. Standing in a mirror, I restlessly checked and rechecked my belt. I was weighed down with more tools than ever, and if most of the school wasn't off waiting in line to get into the palace for the feast tonight, I'd be mocked for looking more like a repairwoman than a student.

Chance scampered up to me with the little bag's drawstrings tied around his neck. With how little powder it held, it flapped behind him like a cape. I tucked him away into his satchel, still placed on my hip for safekeeping, and tied the little bag into place next to the four vials of lesser potions Vance had given me.

Then I donned my old slippers…which didn't fit so well anymore. I looked down at my feet, attempting to wiggle my cramped toes. While I was no stranger to ill-fitting shoes, I hadn't realized I'd grown out of this pair so quickly.

Chance poked his head out of his bag. "Why sad?" he asked.

He'd realized it before I did. I *was* upset as I perched on a stool and gingerly peeled the slippers back off my feet. Mere minutes before I committed to this heist, I realized this wasn't me anymore. Instead, I laced my boots back on and stood facing the mirror.

I saw myself as Jackie would tonight. I didn't have the same bony angles anymore, no longer bearing the marks of hunger and wariness in the thinness of my limbs and the starkness of my eyes. I looked...healthy.

I'd chosen myself, RSI, and potential service to the Crown, and on the surface, all Jackie and my gang siblings would see was the physical reward. "I'm not a sneak anymore, Chance," I said, but what I meant was, *I'm not a street kid anymore. I'm not invisible.*

Uncle Jace would not call this version of me a Mouse. I tweaked my stance and the set of my shoulders and hips, forming the most confident look I could muster.

"But...that's okay, I think," I added, smiling down at him.

His pointed little head bobbled after a moment. It seemed like approval. Even though Miss Wilkes said little wonders didn't share emotions like the mightier beasts, I wondered if that was fully true when he'd picked up on a bit of my tangled emotions.

"Anyway, it's time to go." I tied on my cloak as I walked, using its volume to hide my full supply belt. By the time I passed the open doors to the front hall, I exchanged a nod with the peacekeeper on duty and swept my way directly to the front desk.

Miss Barrios sat there with a bored expression. "Still here?" I asked. "Not going to the feast?"

"The headmaster was feeling ill today, I'm afraid. The

allergies have been terrible to him this year. He asked me to keep an eye on the front tonight," she answered, though her gaze slid up and down me and she raised a brow.

"I'm sure he didn't mean for you to skip the festivities." I nodded a couple times.

"Well, Coach Stryker is on extra duty tonight. Perhaps I could get away for an hour or two." She got to her feet and slid her wand into her sleeve. "I'll see you soon, then? We're extending curfew tonight so everyone can enjoy the feast."

"Yes, ma'am," I said, but I couldn't take it anymore. "Did you happen to speak with—"

"Later. Sundown is in less than a bell," she hissed out of the corner of her mouth. "Coach Stryker should be along soon, I sent for her with a spell here." With obvious movements, she withdrew a coin slightly bigger than a cloret and put it face up, where it blinked with blue light. She put on one of her usual bright smiles and swept from the desk and out the front of the school.

I put my thumb on the coin, and the spell stopped blinking. Then I turned and signaled to the peacekeeper, who met me halfway, right in front of the headmaster's office.

"Do you know how bad this uniform smells?" Carmen grumbled. With a bit of makeup and wearing the crested peacekeeper helm, she was indistinguishable from any other sour-faced guard forced into a posting here.

"Boys were wearing it. Of course it smells," I said with sympathy. Brinsley had been overjoyed to have the night off and thought Vance was standing in for him at the moment. "If I'm not out in fifteen minutes, I've probably been caught in that spell I told you about. I'm sure Chance will let you know something's wrong."

"Right. I will stand here and be useless in the meantime," she said, attempting to salute me and banging the side of her hand into the helm's edge.

I giggled and cringed in sympathy at the same time, but

we both fell back into our roles. I didn't even hesitate on my way to the headmaster's door, opening it without trouble and retrieving Chance standing on the knob on the other side. The room still smelled of winterbog, but at least it was fading. Either that, or my nose stuffed up quickly enough that it wasn't much of an issue.

Cracking my knuckles, I set out my tools and turned to the curio cabinet and the spiky shape of the crown within. I didn't speak my concerns aloud, thinking there was a chance the headmaster had put a siren spell on his magelight. But I was taking a gamble that I could bypass the double-release spell completely based off of a few stolen glances at this curio and Fariq's homemade tools.

Vance's contact in Morashi Venom had clearly explained how the double-release spell was designed to counter desda powder. It was a good deterrent in general, being a giant and visible engraving on the glass section of the curio's doors. I took a moment to inspect it fully. Not the spell—I knew and loathed its swirls and loops—but the crossbar of the lock joining the two doors together. And then my eyes skipped to their well-oiled hinges.

I turned to Chance and put my finger to my lips in the universal gesture of silence. He mirrored it back and then fist-bumped me when I held my fist out for one for good luck.

Time to see what would—and wouldn't—activate this double-release spell. What nobles and mages never seemed to consider when they designed home security magic was that there was always more than one way to steal most valuables. If the easiest solution was blocked, a good thief would figure out another way.

I selected the smaller of the two screwdrivers I'd taken with me and started loosening one of the top hinges, keeping an eye out for any flashes of blue magic. Nothing yet. I used the first of the tools Fariq made to catch the top of the door with the pad of an angled clamp, careful not to touch the wood with my fingers.

I secured the door in place and went ahead and added a second clamp to the other door now that I knew this would work. The pads were coated in a type of glue that would bind to the wood while I made short work of the rest of the hinges and held my breath as the doors remained in place with just the pressure of the clamps.

Fariq had wanted to do this without permanently damaging any property, so the glue would come off with an application of a chemical he wanted me to leave behind. I held my breath and prayed he'd done this right as I started to unscrew the clamps at the same pace and the whole front of the curio came unsealed and hung wobbling from those two points of contact.

Success! It held even as it hung at the end of the clamps' reach, with enough space that I could simply reach in and grab the crown. I held my excitement in check and reached for the grabber tool, sure the spell would still activate if one of my hands closed around it. I extended it and maneuvered it to clasp one of its tines, scooting it forward until I got a better grip on it from the underside.

I retracted the grabber and tilted the crown just so. "Yes," I breathed, placing it aside to close the clamps and put the curio doors back in place. The headmaster might not even notice if it weren't for the four pieces of hinge I left on his desk.

I gathered up Chance in one hand and the grabber in the other, opening the door out into the hall cautiously and peering left to right. Carmen gave me a thumbs-up from where she now stood by the front desk. Margot fussed with her dress next to the false peacekeeper. It was the same dark green one as before, but she'd foregone her expensive emerald earrings and probably had on her RSI-issued boots under the bottom hem.

"Do you have the box?" I asked as I approached with the crown still held out from me carefully by the grabber. Home security spells usually didn't have much range, but I didn't want to risk getting accidentally paralyzed.

Margot lifted a box of ebony wood nearly as tall as her torso. "It's a little big, but shouldn't something like Stone's Crown have an important box?" she asked with a wisp of a laugh.

"It's perfect," I said, dropping the crown in carelessly when she held the box open.

"Use some caution!" she gasped.

"Why?" I smirked as I placed the grabber tool back on my belt. "It's fake."

Before I could warn her, Margot reached in and fussed with the crown. "Well, I'll be. It *is* fake," she muttered. She seemed fine, so we were out of the spell's range.

Carmen glanced between us with a furrow appearing between her brows.

"It's light as air," I told her.

"Real jewelry has a certain heft to it," Margot said breezily. "Something like a crown would be designed with extra weight to keep it on a princess's head. You're not concerned this will be a problem, Heather?"

Despite myself, I chuckled. "Not when they'll have to reach into that giant box. All right, that's enough gab. Let's get going."

I reactivated the coin to call Coach Stryker to desk duty, and we all filed out the front. The magic would read us leaving the school late as three students, not as a cloaked shadow, a lady, and a peacekeeper. The sun was well into setting by now, which meant by the time we reached the alleyway, Cartier and Rozma should be waiting to meet us.

Carmen went one way at a fork in the road while Margot and I took the other path. The streets were quiet, as most of the city was elsewhere celebrating. We kept a wary eye on those who remained. Margot stood out and drew the occasional glance from the servants bustling about their evening business and the slumped-over drunkards who rarely left their shadowy alleyways.

"I think I need to take that courage potion early," Margot murmured. She jumped at every scuffle and sound, her cheeks reddening in the darkening night when someone catcalled her.

Nobles didn't get this kind of treatment when they did their promenading in full daylight. "This is completely normal," I assured her. "We're almost there."

In truth, I was just as scared on the inside as she seemed, knowing the plan could come unraveled from here on for several reasons beyond our control. "Just remember to play it straight. You have Stone's Crown, an incredibly valuable piece of jewelry," I said more quietly.

She gulped an audible swallow. "I do," she agreed.

"You want to get the necklace as close to me as possible."

"And what if one of them is *wearing* it?"

I smiled briefly at the thought. "That would be perfect."

"And…" She took a deep breath. "You're sure they will have ruffians with them?"

"Guaranteed. Springfield's gang is notorious for unfair deals and thefts. We planned for this, Margot. We're going to be okay," I said in my most reassuring tone.

"We're going to be okay." She repeated it several more times and quickened her step when she started lagging behind me. I marched toward the shadowy figures of two people ahead of us, their body shapes slanted by the distant glow of a streetlamp, all the while holding my nerve by my fingernails.

They'd cloaked themselves to hide their features, but I'd recognize Cartier's bowlegged stance and Rozma's tall bulk from anywhere. Even though they seemed to be alone, I knew better. The alleyway to the left was completely shrouded in shadow under the cover of night. It was part of why Rozma had demanded we meet after sundown, to take advantage of us.

"'Ello again, Lady Norston." Cartier stepped forward, not bothering to hide the sneer in his tone. "And that little shadow of yours must be Mouse, of course."

"Good evening," Margot replied in her sharp noble voice. "I have Stone's Crown, as previously promised. Let's see the Eye of Acuity."

Rozma loosened her cloak, and I held my breath. There was a pretty big chance they wouldn't bring it...yet she had. She displayed the opal pendant on her chest. "Got it right 'ere," she said.

"Well...aren't you going to take it off?" Margot demanded.

"Sorry, missus, that's not how this is gonna go," Cartier said. "Let's see that crown."

He stepped forward, fingers wiggling with apparent eagerness to hold it. Margot breathed a sigh and opened her fancy box, holding it at a shallow angle to force him to dip down and really reach to pick up its contents.

I slipped around them, inching closer to Rozma.

His knees popped with the motion of him jerking back suddenly. "What the—it's fake!" he shouted indignantly.

He put his fingers to his lips and whistled. The bulk of several men approached from the shadowy alley, and I heard the crunch of more approaching behind us. "They's playing a trick on us, boys. Beat 'em bloody, but leave the kid alive. We got a plan for her," he said.

My eyelid twitched. I couldn't help but remember Vance saying that the boss of the Morashi had *a use for dead children.*

One of his men grunted, and another shouted in surprise. More shadowed shapes joined us, jumping from the roof of a low-slung building to our left and onto Springfield's men. "Not while we're 'ere!" shouted the last voice I expected to be here. Ram, my headstrong gang brother, who charged at and tackled Cartier to the ground.

My mouth hung in surprise. Of course Ram had known about this meeting, but I'd made it clear to Vance that the rest of my gang needed to stay away. "What are you doing?" I exclaimed in disbelief.

After a scuffle, Ram stood and turned my way. "Saving you, lil sis."

I should've expected that he wouldn't follow directions. My plan exploded around me mere moments before I could get my hands on the Eye of Acuity.

Our other gang siblings were still fighting, judging by the thuds and grunts in the dark. I'd been relying on Cartier's whistled signal for another reason, and it came flooding in from our right as Miss Barrios ran our way with her wand raised, a ball of blue light balanced at its tip. I was expecting her alone, if the Spymaster hadn't answered the request in my letter. But he must've, as she led a pack of adult peacekeepers our way.

She stopped short, her eyes widened in surprise as her magic illuminated the all-out brawl.

"You sold us out!" Rozma backed away, her finger pointed straight at me.

"You betrayed me first," I answered in as steady a voice I could muster.

Rozma's nostrils flared, her expression creasing with hate. "Ya squealin' brat. You'll pay for this with blood."

Musty devils, I remembered myself too late. Instead of taking advantage of the distraction, I'd stood here like a gawking bystander. She had a straight path behind her and took it, running away with the Eye of Acuity still around her neck.

CHAPTER 29

ONE LAST STOP

I TENSED to run after her. "Heather, wait!" Miss Barrios exclaimed. She crossed the rest of the way to my side and shoved something into my palm. Our gazes met, and she nodded firmly, closing my fingers around what felt like leather. "Go save your sister. Go!"

I took off after Rozma, but I'd already lost her in the dark. That didn't matter; I knew where she was going. We'd come from the same street, she and I, and were raised to know the most efficient route to several key locations. The Last Stop, Springfield's base of operations, was one such place.

My cloak billowed behind me like a sail as I ran full out, dodging and ducking into alleyways and corridors by blind instinct. The streetlamps were often damaged on this side of the city, and my eyes adjusted to the gloom just in time to encounter a single one lit like a beacon in the night. I nearly ran headlong into the side of one building and almost tripped and tumbled over my feet several more times from the unpredictable placement of several folk passed out from their cups.

I didn't waste precious time slowing to look at what Miss Barrios had given me. My fist was white around its shape, and if it didn't have a leather case, the edges of the key within would've cut into my palm. I hadn't expected her part in the job to be done so quickly, but she was needed to contain the brawl I'd left behind with the peacekeepers the Spymaster had sent with her.

Margot was meant to stay there and explain our cover story to the peacekeepers. Not that it would work now that a dozen or more of my gang siblings would be arrested too.

My eyelid wouldn't stop pulsing, stuck that way. Why hadn't I anticipated Ram acting like a fool to "save me"? If only I'd communicated better to my gang siblings to let them know I'd stuck my hand into Cartier and Rozma's trap on purpose. *They* were supposed to get arrested. Whether they'd had the stones to bring the Eye of Acuity to the meeting didn't matter when we knew where they kept it hidden.

Stupid, stupid, stupid, I thought with each pounding footfall. The one good thing I'd done for myself was change back into my sturdy RSI-issued boots. I reached the tree with its hanging wheel just up the hill from The Last Stop, where I skidded to a halt. My legs throbbed, and I bent, holding my knees and panting hard.

Rozma's big form reached the doors to the club, and she shoved them aside even as I recovered. I glanced toward the tall girl swinging from her perch on the hanging wheel. "Something's wrong," Carmen stated. She was still dressed in Brinsley's peacekeeper uniform.

"Yeah," I puffed out, getting one word out at a time. "Rozma. Necklace. I…need…a…distraction."

Carmen perked up. "*Any* kind of distraction?"

I nodded rapidly. We'd planned for this assuming we'd have Miss Barrios to throw a stiff wind to blow around cards and chips throughout the club and disrupt its operations. But there was one scenario I'd instructed everyone through that I'd just called *the chaos option*. Every good plan had a last resort that was total mayhem, and I was looking at just the girl for the job.

"It's time for chaos," I told her. "In a second."

"Say no more!" She stood and nearly vibrated with impatience.

I turned toward the nearest streetlamp, inspecting the color of the potion vials I whipped off my belt. Two were yellowish brown, for invisibility, one meant for me and the other for Jackie. I also carried the single lesser mending potion Vance had made just in case she was hurt. The final one was a muddy color, also meant for Jackie if I didn't need it—the courage potion.

My fingers shook as I debated with myself. Vance had called this "one minute of invincibility" since it was the hardest of his three brews to define. It could turn a Mouse into a Gryphon.

"Sorry, Jackie," I murmured, loosening a few seals and jogging toward the club. I gestured for Carmen to go ahead of me.

As she shoved the door open, making an obnoxious crash, I knocked back one of the invisibility potions and rushed in before the threshold could slam closed in my invisible face. The change to my limbs and perception was dizzying. I could barely see myself or where I was heading.

"Heeeey. Which one of you guys am I gonna have to arrest tonight?" Carmen half-shouted, half-slurred her words, moving in an exaggeratedly fluid way. I think she was pretending to be drunk.

I took a moment to look around before approaching the back wall, where a bar served a handful of men. A door behind the bar led to a kitchen so The Last Stop could keep folk here longer with food and drink.

The establishment wasn't large, but it did encompass two stories. My glimpse of the second-story balcony had shown that Boss Springfield himself stood there watching Carmen with a lit cigar dangling from his fingers. I would have to do something about Rozma standing next to the boss, whispering in his ear even now.

The invisibility potion only lasted fifteen seconds, unfortunately, but it was enough time to reach the bar and reappear while Carmen made a fool out of a real drunkard by the sounds of things. I didn't look back even when there was a great *crash*.

"Where's my sister?" I demanded in an undertone to the two men seated together at the bar, who were actually Fariq in an ill-fitting trench coat and Vance wearing a face I hadn't seen yet. He might've touched up Fariq's face too, as my friend looked significantly older than his usual self.

Fariq jumped and fumbled his mug, spilling what I assumed was water. "In the kitchen," Vance replied, pointing to the door behind the bar.

With the rest of the establishment hopefully distracted, I didn't hesitate to vault over the bar top and rush into the back. Humidity hit me straight in the face from the dome of a lit oven, and I found a girl at the wash basin, scrubbing pots for all she was worth. She was alone back here.

She noticed me after a second and squealed, dropping the pot with a liquid slosh. "Shh. It's me, Jackie," I whispered, holding a finger to my lips.

Jackie's eyes widened, and she hushed immediately, the animal panic that'd flared the whites of her eyes fading. She was frightfully small, more so than I remembered, just a slip of a thing under a baggy tunic she wore like a dress. Her tangled hair hadn't seen a brush in weeks, I thought. How could grown men see her like this and not think anything of it? Worse yet, expect to be served by a barefoot little girl?

She stumbled over to me, and I took a knee, the two of us hugging fiercely. "Heather, it's really you," she whispered before breaking out into sobs. I sniffed, too overcome by this moment to do anything but hold her through the worst of it.

"I wish I could've come sooner," I said tearfully.

"It's been so bad here." She gulped air, talking all at once. "Boss Springfield turned against us, Heather, declared war all over some necklace. They said you was dead, but the men here thinks you were alive with the necklace and—"

I nodded, shushing her again and brushing my palm down her tangled hair. "We don't have much time."

"They kept me here with magic." She clung to me as I tried to let her go. I tilted my head to see her bare ankle, where an unbroken circle of gray metal was placed. It must've been heavy, as she'd limped her way to me. It reminded me too much of RSI's bracelets.

"I know. We're going to set you free, but I need you to trust me. Do you trust me?" I asked, taking her by the shoulders.

She swiped at her reddened nose. "Uh-huh," she murmured.

I peeled my fingers away from the leather case Miss Barrios had pushed into my hand and upended a small silver key into my palm. Just like the all-keys in the Tulari supply shop, it didn't seem special or magical; it just *was*. Since there didn't seem to be a keyhole on the tethering band she wore, I touched the all-key to its side and held my breath.

Air hissed from within the band, forming words. *"Releasing prisoner."* It was a neutral tone, not male nor female. *"I was unlocked by Tulari Ana Salavieja."*

It clunked to the wooden floor in two pieces. I gave Jackie the mending potion and nudged the disabled tethering band with disgust as she struggled to drink it down. Even though Miss Barrios wanted me to leave the band behind to be discovered, I'd brought my desda powder to destroy it.

But now I worried it could still hurt my sister if I tried anything. It was Morashi-made, an evil piece of magic. "I'm going to give you to my two friends, Fariq and Vance. They are going to get you to safety," I whispered to Jackie, turning away from it. "There's something else I have to do here, and then I'll join you."

She looked up at me with big, watery brown eyes. "Promise you'll be safe?" she asked.

"I promise." I bumped fists with her like old times and then reached into Chance's pouch to present her with the mouse. "Chance here will take care of you too. This is my sister, Jackie," I told him.

"Finally, one sister! Hi hi!" He waved a paw, climbing onto her palms when she reached out with them cupped. She seemed a little dazed from shock or fatigue, but she loved animals as much as I did, and Chance had her charmed immediately. I poked my head out of the kitchen and motioned to Vance and Fariq, who climbed over the bar top and escorted her out the back.

The club was quiet. Though Carmen had knocked over several card tables and laid a few drunkards out cold, her distraction was more like a sacrifice with one of Springfield's men holding a knife to her neck. I had to do something fast.

I popped the loosened seal on one of my last two potions, downing the bitter swallow of courage. Clarity filled my head as I saw what I had to do. I pushed myself into motion, slamming into the man's back and drawing his head to the side with my elbow around his neck. Surprised, he lurched and nicked Carmen's skin before the knife was at a less harmful angle.

"Go!" I shouted.

She laughed and leapt back into motion, kicking the knife from his hand when he went to try and stab me. "No way. Don't you know how long I've wanted a partner to fight with?"

I lost my grip on the man and tumbled to the ground, which was just as well, as Carmen took him down and wrestled briefly until she won the exchange with her thighs becoming a clamp around his neck, squeezing off his airway. He was unconscious in moments.

I looked up at Boss Springfield, who put out his cigar on the railing and motioned to Rozma. She cracked her knuckles and started descending the stairs. "They's mine. Back off," she announced to the couple of others who'd gotten to their feet to defend The Last Stop.

The courage potion only lasted one minute, and in the moments it took Rozma to come fight us, I devised a new, bold plan. "Rip her cloak off her if you can," I muttered to Carmen. She nodded, falling back to a tense ready stance.

"Boss Springfield!" I shouted, drawing the stout man's attention. He was graying like Uncle Jace but built twice as broad, a stoic and unflappable figure even with a portion of his club destroyed below him. I felt his dark, cold gaze upon me and heard the tearing of cloth. Without turning, I gestured over my shoulder toward the two fighting women. "She has the Eye of Acuity! She's had it all along!"

Just as quickly, his frigid attention turned away from me. I scooted out of the way in time as Rozma and Carmen rolled past in a tangled lock of flailing limbs and punching fists. Rozma's cloak lay on the ground in a heap.

Thump. The boss himself descended one heavy step at a time, holding his cane tucked under one meaty arm.

He loomed over us all, over six feet of menace in a suit. "Stop," he said.

Rozma, who'd gotten the upper hand over Carmen, paused immediately with her fist hanging midair. She stood hastily when Carmen tried to take advantage of her distraction with a choke hold.

The Eye of Acuity's gold and opal pendant glittered in the club's low lighting as it swung free on the adult woman's neck, no cloak to hide it.

"Rozma, why are you wearing that?" he asked with deadly calm.

She froze and felt her neck, realizing it was exposed. "This ain't the Eye," she fumbled.

The courage potion had worn off from my veins, reminding my heart to pound hard with a feeling of dread at being this close to Boss Springfield. "She and Cartier played you," I told him.

Rozma clenched her fists and jaw, bruises starting to bloom on her exposed skin. "Quit running your gob. Ain't nobody here to run to your rescue this time, Mouse," she said.

The sound of metal hissing free of its sheath had me shuddering and backing away. "No," Boss Springfield said coldly. "Leave the kid alone. Do you understand what you've *done*?" He had his saber free from the cane he always carried. Folk said he skinned traitors and turncoats with the weapon he now held to Rozma's throat.

"I-I can explain." I'd never heard such a meek tone from the musclebound woman.

Carmen met my gaze, hooking a thumb over her shoulder with a clear question in her expression. I hesitated but nodded back. She tilted her head and watched me for a moment and how I didn't move to leave, setting her feet to stay as well. I was just waiting for the right moment.

"You sold us out to the worst devil out there. Did you think the Morashi would simply forget about the necklace?" he demanded. She didn't move as he worked himself into a frothing rage. "Did you think they would just *leave us be* when the Menagerie was gone? How many kids have we bargained away for more time…just for you to have the Eye all along?"

He glanced over his shoulder at me. "Kid, come here." I'd never disobeyed Boss Springfield the few times we met, so I stood where he pointed.

"Back from the dead, the missing link to this whole story. Mouse." He dipped his chin toward me in acknowledgment. "Tell me exactly what happened Yule—"

BOOM. The front door to the club banged open with an

echoing crash that had to be magic. Everyone's head whipped to the side as in charged a veritable flood of peacekeepers. My eyes widened in shock. This wasn't part of the plan.

"Get on the ground! All of you! You are under arrest!" several of them shouted at once, turning on the remaining patrons and the few gang members Carmen hadn't knocked out.

"I told you, boss, she squealed on us," Rozma was saying. She touched the side of her neck where Springfield's saber wasn't resting. "Wait—the necklace?"

He was looking at where he'd bid me to stand. "Where's the Mouse?" he asked.

I hadn't let myself get caught off guard a second time tonight. I was invisible and several feet away, grabbing Carmen's hand. "C'mon," I muttered, unsure if she could hear me while I was impossible to see. She downed her vial of the same potion and kept a firm grip on me as we stumbled around the peacekeepers and out into the night.

I was glad for Carmen's presence, as a dizzy spell had taken the space behind my eyes the moment I went invisible a second time. I lurched more convincingly than her drunk act as my potion wore off before hers. Carmen practically dragged me toward our rendezvous point, the swing, and my knees gave out a few feet from it.

Jackie sat in the grass close by. "Heather," she gasped. "What happened?"

Another set of hands helped me kneel more comfortably. Vance lifted my top eyelids. "You took the other invisibility potion, didn't you?" he sighed.

"Yes," I croaked. There were about three of him right now, the whole world blurring to one side like a painter had gotten bored and swiped his hand over his creation.

"I told you that one was for Jackie," he muttered, pulling out his wand. He drew green lines midair. It might've just been me, but they trembled there rather than formed a solid spell. "Everyone, just give her some space. She needs to vomit."

With that, he threaded the tip of his wand through the spell and jabbed my throat. The meager contents of my stomach twisted, and I bent over, throwing it all up in a bitter flood. Someone held my hair back as I heaved. My dizziness lifted when it was all gone. I looked up to see Fariq restraining my hair with a concerned expression.

"All better," I said, managing a smile.

"Well, that went...interestingly," Carmen commented from where she stood closest to The Last Stop like she was keeping watch.

I breathed a shaky laugh. "It was perfect. We saved my sister and..." I lifted one of my hands from the ground, shaking bits of grass off the formerly pristine Eye of Acuity. "This too."

"All this over some stupid necklace," she said, starting to grin. "You grabbed it right off her neck."

"I did," I said proudly. The two of us started to laugh like loons, which turned into an infectious bout as the two boys joined in and finally Jackie too as I stood and hugged her again, holding her like I'd wanted to for months.

CHAPTER 30
DEBRIEF

"Anyone know where Miss Barrios lives?" Vance asked as soon as we recovered from whatever mania had brought on that laughing fit.

I shrugged and sighed. We were well past even the extended curfew time at RSI, so there was no chance we'd be able to sneak back in. The plan was to spend the night in the Tulari secretary's apartment. But who knew where she was now? My troubles seemed to return one at a time as I wondered how my gang siblings were doing, plus a helping of concern about Miss Barrios and Margot.

"We could see if she's at the city jail," I suggested.

Carmen tensed. "We've got company," she hissed.

A cloaked man approached from the direction of The Last Stop. "That won't be necessary," said the last person I expected to see tonight. Manny dropped his hood, his long features faint from the distant light of a streetlamp. "You all must be exhausted. Come, there is an inn nearby."

I elbowed Vance before he could say anything. "That's the Spymaster," I said in an undertone.

"So, you're saying I should disappear," he murmured back.

I rolled my eyes and followed Manny's shadow, my arm around my sister's shoulders protectively. I secured the Eye of Acuity to my belt, hiding its shine under the fold of my cloak on my free side. Nobody said a word as we trailed behind the mysterious man we'd all thought to be a janitor until recently.

He secured three rooms at the local inn. One for Fariq and Vance, who had decided not to run. His magic must've run out, as his face was the one he was born with and the Tulari mark on his temple had dulled to a color closer to black than green. The room next to it was for Carmen, Jackie, and me, set up with two cots, while the last was for Manny himself.

He didn't demand the necklace of me, and I ended up passing out with my full kit still tied around my hips. Jackie slept beside me like old times, while Chance curled into a ball between us with a content chatter of his teeth.

I woke thinking the crown heist had been a surreal dream, except there was a heavy chain making an impression into the side of my belly. I blinked awake in the exact same position I'd fallen asleep in, the morning sun well into the sky and bursting into the room past the battered shutters covering the inn window.

Jackie whistled her sleeping breath between her parted lips. I'd heard that sound for countless nights and took comfort in the fact that she was safe. My carpenter mouse perched on her sleeve, cleaning himself with his usual meticulousness.

"Food?" he squeaked when he realized I was awake.

I glanced over my shoulder, where Carmen was still fast asleep on the other cot. "Sure," I whispered, scooping him into my palm and seeing the inn with fresh eyes as I crept out of the room. It was as rundown as the shutters implied, but the smell of something greasy and filling was wafting up from the kitchen, and that was good enough for me.

Vance, Fariq, and the Spymaster all sat eating at the same table with Miss Barrios, who looked completely fine. My heart gave a nervous flutter to see her, as I knew her real name now and that felt a bit like a secret I hadn't earned. Margot was there as well, slowly eating her breakfast with an expression that bordered on vaguely distressed by its taste.

Once I paid two copper clorets for a bowl of porridge and a small plate of dried fruits and nuts to add to it, I sat next to Miss Barrios. Chance hopped onto the table and started chewing on the plate of bits I set aside for him.

"Good morning, Heather," Fariq said cheerfully.

"Morning," I murmured.

Miss Barrios patted my hand. "I know that look. Everything's taken care of," she told me.

"Everything?" I repeated before practically swallowing a spoonful of porridge whole. It wasn't that it was tasty, but my stomach was painfully empty.

She nodded and motioned toward the second floor. "I understand your sister is free and resting off her ordeal. Once she's awake, she has a spot at RSI, just like we promised."

I blew out a relieved breath. That reminded me to draw out her leather all-key case and pass it to her. "I used it," I said. "And it recorded…a name."

Her expression never changing, she pocketed her all-key. "Very good."

"Thank you for your help."

"Such as it was, hmm?" she asked wryly. "This was all you and your team, Heather. I just cleaned up the mess your street family left."

I paused with my spoon halfway to my mouth. "About that…"

"I'll let Manny explain. He wanted to talk to you anyway. Eat," she encouraged.

The Spymaster sat at the head of our table quietly, just observing us and the small tavern-like area where we sat with a few others also eating and waking themselves up. He noticed my attention on him and nodded briefly in acknowledgment. I was still struck by how plainly he dressed when he was in such an important position. Pretending to be a janitor was humbling for a man that must have the King's ear any time he wanted it.

It sank in as I ate. The Spymaster himself wanted to speak to me after the events of yesterday.

"Why scared?" Chance asked.

The grip I had on my spoon was shaking. I reached out and pet him, accepting the piece of dried fruit he put in my palm like an offering. "Chance, can you go back and look after Jackie for me?" I asked him. "She's going to worry when she wakes up and sees that I'm gone."

"No need to be scared for single sister! I protect," he exclaimed. He crammed as much food as he could pack into his cheeks and scampered off.

I had to laugh, some of my tension broken by his earnestness. "It's cool he understands you like that. I want one," Vance commented.

"Well, you're in luck. He has anywhere from ten to twenty siblings," I giggled.

"You'd need a little wonder that's more solid," Fariq said to him.

Now that I was looking at him, I saw that Vance was paler than usual, and his mark was still that shade of sickly green-black. He'd put a bandage on his neck to hide his tattoo. "You okay?" I blurted.

"Hmm? Oh." He touched his fingertips to his temple. "I'll be fine. My magic just needs some time to recover. We are talking in depth about potion safety once we get back to RSI, by the way."

"Someone didn't tell me it was unsafe to drink two invisibility potions," I pointed out.

"That's enough for now," Manny said, interrupting Vance's retort. "Heather, come along."

His chair scraped as he stood, and I rushed to join him,

walking out into the brisk spring morning with my cloak enveloping me. He slowed his steps so we walked side by side. "Well, Miss Mouse. Yesterday was a good day for the Crown," he commented.

I didn't know how to reply to that other than a begrudging "Yes, sir." Up until recently, the Crown had been nothing more than a necessary evil, a huge entity with valuables to spare.

"Not the biggest fan, hmm? That's good."

"Sir?"

He smiled as he steered me down a fork in the road, heading for what looked to be a housing district. We passed by several people, so I knew he wasn't speaking as plainly as he could. "I like it when RSI kids don't come in with blind loyalty. It means you think critically, and at some point, you decided to stay on the path you were set on on Yule night."

I supposed he had a point there. I had seen the benefit to RSI's system and even pulled in my sister to join me.

"I want a debrief, Miss Mouse. Tell me what happened yesterday." It was an order, but he made it sound more like an invitation.

So, I told him. As we strolled into the nicer part of the city and passed some spacious family homes, I began with how I'd taken the fake Stone's Crown from the headmaster's office and stopped when he chortled.

"You unhinged the doors?" he asked past his laughter.

"Yeah?" I looked over at him, confused.

"Gods, why?"

"The double-release spell on them…"

He laughed even harder. "What double-release spell? The decoration on the glass?"

My eyes widened as I realized…if there was no double-release spell, I could've just picked the lock and had the crown in hand within a couple minutes.

He slapped his leg and tried to contain his mirth. "We

don't make beginner challenges that hard! We just want to see how your team responds to a difficult task. And wow, your team went above and beyond. Custom tools, oil that smells like winterbog rot... You must've wanted that extra credit!"

A blush rose to my cheeks. "Uh, yeah. We really needed it," I murmured.

"Off to a great start. What happened then?" he prompted.

I was able to explain directly, as we'd come to a side street where we were the only ones walking. Manny nodded along, seeming unsurprised by everything, including Miss Barrios's real name. "She hasn't gone by that since she was a student. Actually, we set up her last identity with a fake death," he said.

"Wouldn't the general public know her name from the plays she was in?" I asked. She'd loved theater, she said.

"Ah. It's amazing how well you can hide in plain sight," he said, coming to a stop beside the lawn of a wealthy family's house.

"Why are we here?" I hadn't realized it before, but judging from all the empty plots of grass and pretty gardens around us, we'd entered a section where nobility or well-to-do merchants must live.

"There's something I think you should know," he answered. His serious tone and apologetic look had my eyelid twitching. He gestured to the house whose lawn we stood next to. "A man by the name of Jason Vireos lives here. No one knows exactly how he's gotten his money, but they suspect he married an heiress, as he speaks fondly of children yet has none that accompany him. No servants, either, but occasionally, he will seek a buyer for valuable pieces that must come from a personal collection."

I started to relax. He just wanted to tell me about the man who lived here, not strip me of my identity as an RSI kid like I thought.

"The Crown has long suspected him of running some kind

of scheme, but he has been elusive until a recent break-through led us to pinpoint him as the owner of a second home by the sewage grates."

Just like that, I tensed up again. "Jason...Uncle Jace?" I asked in a small voice, taking in the grand home with its empty plot of grass in a new light. It was a sign of wealth to have land just...sitting around, growing nothing but a thick carpet of inedible greenery.

"That's right. We discovered he was keeping a large group of children in what amounted to a hovel and teaching them to trick and steal on his behalf. Did you ever think, when he left you there each night, he returned to a house this large?" His face turned toward mine, his gaze inscrutable.

"No," I murmured. "I thought... He always said... Does Boss Springfield know he lives here?"

"Presumably, yes. He trusted Jason to raise unwanted children into their gang."

My breath came shorter, and I flexed my hands under the fold of my cloak. "But...this house looks untouched. Did Boss Springfield look for the necklace here?"

"He did not," Manny confirmed. "He may have 'declared war' against Jace's Menagerie, but that just meant they were trading your fellow children's lives for time while they scrambled to find the Eye of Acuity. They both must have thought you took it."

Heat rose to my face. If Chance were here, he'd ask why I was so angry. "Are you saying...while Jace told us there was never enough money for food or clothes or soap, he lived in *this* house? When he pressed us to work harder and bring him more money, it went *here*? And he let Springfield murder my gang siblings because they were looking for me?" My voice broke by the end with a flood of furious tears springing to my eyes. No matter what happened every night at the gang's house, Jace was elsewhere, living in comfort.

He watched my emotions flare with a short, approving

nod. "That is what I'm saying, Miss Mouse. I would like to remind you that they were motivated by fear. Any who have met Madam Morashi are absolutely terrified of her, and we're still trying to find out why."

I breathed heavily and looked skyward to prevent myself from crying too much in front of the Spymaster. But what could be more important than the fact that my so-called loving uncle had played me and my gang siblings so hard?

Wait...but what about Thylacine? My elder gang brother who had apparently sent us nothing after promising me he'd pay for the rest of the gang to survive. *Musty devils*. He must've realized he was being taken advantage of. I wasn't the only one who'd had to make a selfish choice for a better life.

"If you proceed on the path you've been walking, you will learn there are never enough agents or time to right every wrong. I decided to tolerate the likes of your former gang. It provided RSI with a trickle of candidates, like yourself."

I sucked in a surprised breath. "But—"

"We cannot fix every problem, Miss Mouse. If you want to work for the peacekeepers, you'll find strong personalities who want to do the right thing and *save* our fair city and everyone in it," he interrupted. "We don't save many orphans, but we do stop wars and make the worst criminals disappear in the dark of night. Do you understand?"

That was a lot he'd just laid on my shoulders. He would've let Jace's Menagerie continue on, focused on more serious matters than a group of petty criminals. By the way he looked at me, he was waiting for that to sink in.

My troubles were my whole world, but there were problems that eclipsed the Menagerie and took up his agents' time. That thought didn't stop the kernel of resentment burning in my chest. "I understand," I answered grudgingly.

He didn't move. "Do you want to be a peacekeeper, Miss Mouse? Do you want recognition for your deeds and the assurance you're on the right side of the law? I will set you free from RSI today if you do."

My eyelid flickered at the thought. With the Eye of Acuity now in my possession, it could be as easy as handing it to him and disappearing back onto the streets. Even though I knew I couldn't go back to my old life, I was well aware that I'd never say yes to his questions anyway.

"I don't want to be a peacekeeper, sir. I still want to be a spy one day," I answered.

His lips twitched, and he nodded in approval. "Very good. Of course, the Eye of Acuity has changed everything. It has blown up the whole gang organization you were once a part of, and now the Crown has moved to dissolve it all. The men you know as Uncle Jace and Boss Springfield have been arrested, and all their known associates are either also awaiting trial or being identified for arrest as we speak. Their assets have been seized, including this house."

From the depths of his pocket, he produced a key. Sunlight glinted off its bronze surface as he extended it to me. I took it and held it out like it was a venomous creature rearing to bite me.

"Let's go inside," he suggested.

I trod over Jace's old lawn with spite, surprised to see multiple people inside the house already, moving around items or placing tags with approximate value on them. "Hello, sir," said one woman. She passed him a still-steaming cup of tea as we sat down at a mahogany-wood table esti- mated to cost at about two thousand clorets.

"I have something else to tell you," he said.

I made a soft sound of relief when the same woman came back around with a cup for me still steeping its way toward tea. "More?" I asked, a little nervous to hear what else he wanted to drop on me.

"Yes. Many good spies learn this about me a little later in their career, but I feel you've earned the right to hear it now.

We just spoke of having a deceased identity. Miss Barrios has one…and so do I." He lifted his cup in a delicate way, sipping the steaming tea in a manner that could be called dignified. When he spoke again, I had an odd sense of déjà vu, like I'd heard his voice framing words in a royal accent before. "I'm the departed brother to King Alonso Cortes. Long ago, I was a spare to the throne, Emmanuel Marin Cortes."

My jaw nearly hit the expensive table we sat at. He sounded *exactly* like King Cortes when he spoke with the royal accent. I'd only heard the King address Kaiamear at large on important days or for speeches, but there was no mistaking it.

"You let yourself get mistaken as a janitor?" I asked, flushing with embarrassment. "And tutor kids in arithmetic?"

He smiled and dropped the accent as he said, "Of course. You'd be amazed what you can hide in plain sight. Dress me in expensive clothing and jewels, and I will be Emmanuel, a prince. Give me a mop and overalls, and instead, I am Manny, a friendly janitor. I am much happier as Manny."

"Yes, sir," I murmured, then realized myself. "Your Highness?"

"Prince Emmanuel is dead," he reminded me. "Though don't tell my brother that. He will be looking for me in the crowd at his latest event, so I must be off soon to give him that encouraging nod he needs."

I practically burned with curiosity. He took one glance at my expression and chuckled. "I'll answer any question you have," he said.

"Did you fake your death to become a spy?" I blurted.

His eyes creased with amusement. "Ah, no, Miss Mouse. I was a lieutenant to the Spymaster at the time when I decided it would be easier to disappear from the public's eye. Plus, it gave me the chance to pursue the relationship I desired with my now-husband rather than be forced into a political match.

Before you ask, his identity is one secret you will never uncover."

"It's not the headmaster?" I asked.

He laughed just like he had about the curio cabinet. "No. Arthur is one of my lieutenants and a fabulous gentleman spy, but he is married to someone else."

"Does the rest of your family know?" It'd been hard enough for me to let Jackie and my gang siblings think I was dead for a couple months.

"My nephews and niece do, yes. Princess Odalis had dreams of following in my footsteps before destiny told her her talents were needed elsewhere," he said. "And my brother, of course, knows. He resented being left at court alone, but at the time I 'died,' he was a year into an arranged marriage that'd become a love match. He has not needed me much until times of late."

"You gave up so much…" I didn't understand, even for love, why he would sacrifice the titles, power, and money that came with being a prince.

His expression softened. "And you are young yet. It wasn't all for my husband. There is a sickness, let's call it, that takes root any place people settle. Corruption, crime, poverty, homelessness, hunger…all things you would *think*, as a prince, I could've done something about."

I nodded on cue when he paused for a moment.

"But I couldn't. In many cases, I made things worse by trying to fix them, until I reduced myself to the same level as everyone else. I began fixing the problems in Kaiamear with a pair of shears rather than a hammer, and a lot more got done. I've been able to cut away the worst of the rot plaguing the city one snip at a time. Case in point." He circled his wrist to encompass the house we were in.

"What happens to all of this now?" I asked.

"Well, that brings us back to you, Miss Mouse, and the other young people victimized by being a part of Springfield's gang," he answered. "But we can get back to this in a moment. Perhaps you've been wondering why your sister was spared from death at the hands of Madam Morashi."

"They thought I had the Eye of Acuity," I said.

He took a leisurely sip of tea like this was a pleasant post-breakfast chat. "He and Springfield believed you would turn up to exchange the necklace for her freedom. To outsiders, she was bait for Jason, who is said to have a great deal of affection for her, but in their schemes, she was only there to get you to surface along with the Eye. And as fate would have it..."

"They were right," I murmured. I finally pulled the Eye of Acuity from my belt and placed it on the table between us. An ember of resentment in my chest turned into a raging fire when I thought of how Jace had treated Jackie. I'd never thought he liked me special, not like he loved Jackie, yet look what he did to her.

My next breath hurt my throat like I'd swallowed shards of glass. "Jace does not deserve the clorets from selling the Eye of Acuity. He does not deserve *anything* after what he's done," I said fiercely.

Manny watched me with that calculating look. "I would still like to hear what you would do with the belongings around us, if you had the choice."

He gave me some time to think as he sipped his tea and tilted the opal pendant of the necklace to catch the light. It was a stunning piece of jewelry, even if I wanted to throw it in the nearest furnace to keep it from Madam Morashi forever.

When I had an answer for him that would benefit the kids I considered family, Manny threaded his fingers together and listened. I wanted it all gone, sold or donated. If Jason Vireos somehow escaped from prison, I wanted there to be nowhere for him to go except for the musty old hovel where he housed his orphan thieves. See how long he would survive in the life he'd made us live.

"And I think the clorets should go to the former Menagerie kids," I finished.

"I agree, Miss Mouse," he said after a moment. "RSI will need the extra funds to support all the new students about to enroll."

I held my breath, barely daring to hope he meant what I thought he did.

"But there's one more thing that needs a new home." He slid the Eye of Acuity back across the table. "I want you to keep this safe. Don't let it leave RSI."

"Sir?" I asked, taken aback. He had some kind of talent, still keeping me in a state of surprise.

"It would be stolen again if it were placed back in its rightful place at the Gladbeck estate, but I believe returning it was central to your agreement to become a spy candidate in the first place. That means you should keep it safe for now," he commented.

I lifted the pendant, dazzled for a moment by its multicolored gleam. I undid the clasp with a quick twist of my fingers and fastened it around my neck, letting it settle with the heavy weight of responsibility. "I won't disappoint you, sir," I promised. "The Morashi will never get this necklace."

"See to it. Oh, one more thing."

Musty devils. He was going to "one more thing" me to death. My anxiety could hardly handle it.

From his pocket, he produced a copper cloret, passing it to me by shaking my hand. The vague shapes of a mouse and a stalk of heather were engraved on its face. "This is your symbol, yes? Your teachers say it's doodled on half your assignments, rather than your name. Go add it to the Wall of Achievement for what you've accomplished."

He pulled out a small box and slid it across the table next. "And this...well, consider it a gift for impressing me."

I took it when he gestured for me to open it. Inside was a ring of dark gray metal. "Give it a spin," he encouraged.

With an uncertain glance up at him, I picked it up from its cloth holder and realized the center part did spin. It was made of little V shapes that became a blur as it spun separately from the band…and the inside started to glow with orange light. "Whoa," I breathed, holding it closer to my face and spinning it faster. The band grew warm to the touch as the light intensified to the yellow of a sustained flame.

"Much more efficient than matches," the Spymaster said.

"This is really for me?" I asked.

"Really. Be careful with it, Miss Mouse. It won't glow if you ruin it with a splash of desda powder."

Nodding, I slipped it on my first finger, flicking it back and forth with my thumb. It was sure to fascinate me for hours, but first, I burst out, "Thank you!" It was also the first piece of jewelry I could call *mine* and the kind of gift tailor-made to fill a need I might have in the future.

"You've earned it. Keep up the good work with your team," he said.

I basked for a moment in his approval. Gleaming in my palm next to the ring was a token, sure, but one my crew and I had earned mere months into our stay at RSI. There would be more. That, I could guarantee.

CHAPTER 31

FIVE & CHANCE

The end of the week was the final day of celebration, and I finally got to attend with my friends and…well, I used to call them my gang family, but our gang was gone. That made them my brothers and sisters by choice, which delighted Chance as I explained my reasoning to him and Jackie, who nodded in quiet approval.

"You *do* have big family like me, yes yes!" the mouse exclaimed.

"I do. And if they're all okay with it, I'll introduce you," I told him. He held up hairpins one at a time as I arranged Jackie's newly shorted hair into the fanciest style I could manage in the girls' bath. The barbers hadn't been able to salvage much of her tangled mane, but it was a little longer than Carmen's, capable of making one complete curl.

Sybella had lent me her curlers for the task. There was something in her expression every time she noticed Jackie, a look of understanding that left me choked up. Jackie was not what she used to be. She jumped at loud noises and shied away from men and boys she didn't know. There were shadows in her eyes and a twitchiness to her fingers that was unlike her.

But she would be all right, I told myself. She wore the RSI uniform now, one of the smallest sizes they had, and had access to more food than she could fit every morning and night. She was clean and safe, and I would go to the ends of the continent to keep her that way.

"Heather?" she asked quietly.

"Yes, sweetling?"

"I'm ten."

Anyone else would take that quiet statement to mean that she wanted a birthday celebration or a gift. Some kind of acknowledgment that she'd made it one whole decade in this life. I glanced meaningfully at Chance, who scampered away. We'd discussed what her title would be…one of the last ones I was going to give to a member of our former gang.

"I've been thinking about your title for a long time. And I need a helper to explain it," I told her. While we waited, I pinned the last of her curls into place with a satisfied nod.

It didn't take long before Patches leapt onto the counter in front of her reflection. "Oh!" Delight broke through Jackie's melancholy as she reached for the fluffy cat. "Look how pretty you are. And plump!"

Patches's fur brushed out in delight, and she paced back and forth for Jackie's pets. "This is Patches. I think she represents you," I explained. While I'd told her about carpenter mice and the special connection I had with Chance, what I was about to show her was new.

"You think I'm a cat?" she asked, her expression starting to fall with doubt. "But we already have Wildcat…"

"Why don't you take her with us?" I suggested, motioning toward the door. We weren't far from the library, and Jackie babied Patches all the way to a more private place in a library nook, where I took off the feligryph's collar to show her Patches's true form.

Jackie gasped and held her hands back from Patches as she grew larger and spread her wings to display them. "She's a feligryph," I explained, waiting for Jackie to chance another pet and realize Patches was just as friendly and cuddly like this. "Sweet, but fierce and unexpected."

"You think I'm fierce and unexpected?" she asked doubtfully.

"I think you will be one day, if you want to be," I said, starting to second-guess this decision from her reaction. But Patches must've sensed it, as she nuzzled under my sister's chin and purred thunderously, encouraging her to cuddle her. "Very few people know about feligryphs, so we could call you Gryph, maybe."

Slowly, Jackie's doubt faded, replaced by a glimmer of something else in her eyes. A spark of resolve, perhaps. It was as welcome as the sun on a chilly day, her slow smile a ray of hope. "Thanks, Heather. I love it."

Miss Barrios herded all her Littles to the palace together. Nearly two dozen of my siblings had been of age to join RSI and come under her direction as a mentor. Some of them, like Ram and Dexis, were too old to do more than spend a year or two at the school and graduate to become informants for the Crown, if they figured out what kind of school they were at. Everyone wore copper bands for now.

The younger kids, like Jackie and Bear, were true spy candidates who'd excel with time and patience. Miss Barrios had warned me not to get my hopes up on keeping everyone around, though. The Spymaster intended to root out those who were unsuited to spy work and send them off to the brightest future possible, where they wouldn't stretch RSI's resources once the clorets from selling Jace's assets ran out.

As for the babes and toddlers of Jace's Menagerie, they'd been placed in the Crown's orphanage to await loving families. In the same conversation, Miss Barrios had also assured me that there were many couples around Kaiamear who could provide them a better home than we could, and I believed it. She'd unknowingly become one of us the moment I told Jackie she was once Foxglove.

"Can I call you Fox?" she asked the woman now as we found places in the crowd with folk from all walks of life around Kaiamear. Jackie fixed the Tulari secretary with her sweetest look, her amber-toned eyes and hopeful smile enough to melt even the most stoic adult's heart.

"If you'd like, sweetheart," Miss Barrios said. I hoped she was ready to be a Big Sister to a whole pack of misfits who titled themselves after animals.

"You can call me Gryph," she replied proudly. "If you want."

"Okay, Miss Gryph," she said, smiling a little wider when Jackie flushed happily at hearing her title in such a way for the first time.

Someone nudged me. It was Carmen, offering over a stick of cloud candy, which I accepted with an eager grin. "When do you think we'll get more solid food?" she asked.

"Guess when they decide to start gabbing," I replied, gesturing upward at a distant balcony that overlooked us all. We were packed nearly shoulder to shoulder, waiting for the king to address us directly. It was a rare moment in history, and I was sure we'd study his upcoming speech in detail in Rhetoric and Persuasion class.

I, for one, was thrilled to finally be able to participate in the celebration of Altare's victory without an ounce of guilt, my family safe and getting along with my crew.

The fact that the five of us were guaranteed to pass our classes *and* remain a crew into next year by finishing all three extra credit challenges certainly lightened our moods. We might also be receiving a bracelet upgrade soon and having our class schedules shifted. Spymaster Manny had promoted us to being an Intermediate team, I'd learned when I spotted our newly agreed upon team name on the middle board.

We were Five & Chance, accidentally named when I had said, "Five…" and waited for inspiration to strike about the right animal to encompass the members of my crew.

"And me!" Chance had squeaked.

"And Chance," I'd said agreeably. Fariq and Vance had liked it, the latter of whom was behind me, back in the RSI uniform with his usual fake face in place. His bracelet was copper… This was his last outing for a long while.

A sudden hush went over the crowd. I looked up to see the distant shape of an elegantly dressed man raising his arms for silence. I wished we were closer so I could compare his features to Manny's and confirm for myself that I worked for a "dead" prince. As his voice washed over the crowd, I heard the likeness in their royal inflections.

"People of Altare, lend me your ears. We entered a difficult time together after a coalition of Rathi struck a mighty blow to blacken the eye of our great nation, but I am delighted to say that we have recovered our dignity by returning victorious."

The crowd roared, still enthusiastic despite a week of celebrations.

The King waited a moment for us to settle before speaking into the magic voice-amplifying device he held. "The brave men and women of our military were victorious despite great odds. Each of the vicious, monstrous eldrafn our enemy wielded against us fell. Their god-blessed berserkers engaged an army that couldn't be bested by sheer strength. We must give thanks to the soldiers who stepped away from their families to fight for their nation and to the gryphon riders who kept the skies safe.

"We give thanks to our newest Hero of Altare, who not only singlehandedly killed the largest eldrafn Altare has ever seen, but also challenged and changed long-held beliefs by yours truly. Give a warm welcome to newly knighted Dame Sivana Walker."

She'd been made a Hero of Altare? I screamed along with the kids around me as a second figure stepped up beside King Cortes, smaller and feminine.

A few moments later, a third head crested the railing of the balcony, the bold, bird-shaped face of her gryphon, the blind Arimus. I think I called out louder to see him beside her. There was the beast that'd chosen her and made her the first female gryphon rider.

The king seemed to fumble for a moment. "And her gryphon, Arimus," he announced. "A proud representative of his race, who was key to Sivana's every success. All of her heroic deeds wouldn't be possible without him, and they did it all while navigating the unique challenges of his blindness."

As the king listed their accomplishments, Miss Barrios leaned over to whisper, "You know, we'll never get acknowledged like this for our work. We don't do anything so glorious as ensuring a war victory and slaying monsters."

I nodded in agreement. But how I would shrink standing up there instead of Dame Sivana Walker while most of Kaiamear cheered for her. To be the center of attention with so many people looking at her…

"But," Miss Barrios added, "there are victories big and small, and heroes who rise to the occasion, no matter how brief. Remember that."

I missed the moment that had the crowd gasping as I looked over at my crew.

Fariq, a boy with a heart of gold, who could design any kind of tool and was approaching fluency in two languages.

Carmen, our fighter, who came alive when she could put her skills to the test. She would come into her own as a spy. I was sure of it.

Vance, incredibly talented with magic I still barely understood, who could pretend to be someone else with the ease of changing clothes.

Margot, a gem of a noble-born girl who'd taken to spy life with the ease of someone who'd been looking for purpose her whole life.

And then there was me, our thief, somehow the crew's leader despite my Mouse nature. We were those smaller-time heroes today, with my family safe and close by. I couldn't be prouder to be a spy candidate.

HEATHER **and her crew's story continues in Royal Spy Institute 2: Five & Chance!**

INTERESTED IN MORE? Join my newsletter as one way to get access to a bonus scene from this book! Sign up on my website.

STAY up to date with Royal Spy Institute and the Altare world by joining my Facebook group: People of Altare! In this community, we'll talk about fantasy book releases, share fun posts, and have the occasional giveaway.

PLEASE REMEMBER TO REVIEW! Reviews help other readers find stories they may love. Consider leaving a review for Royal Spy Institute 1: The Crown Heist on Amazon and other websites.

ALSO IN THE ALTARE WORLD

GRYPHON RIDER ACADEMY

Are you ready for a high-flying adventure on gryphon-back? Join Sivana as she becomes the first female cadet at the highly competitive Gryphon Rider Academy after the blind gryphon Arimus chooses her as his new rider.

Dragon Riders of Pern meets Song of the Lioness in this YA fantasy series in which a pair of underdogs rewrite what's possible in a formerly all-boys military academy.

- See Gryphon Rider Academy on Amazon -

ABOUT THE AUTHOR

Elise Hennessy is an author of young adult fantasy full of adventure and found family. She holds a master's degree in journalism and enjoys crafting unique stories. When Elise is not busy writing, she's trying to reduce her prodigious TBR list. She lives in Texas with her family and is owned by two cats.

Find out more about her books at: www.elisehennessy.com

www.ingramcontent.com/pod-product-compliance
Lightning Source LLC
Chambersburg PA
CBHW021244190726
48289CB00005B/1477